W9-BVL-913

TOADS
AND
DIAMONDS

TOADS AND DIAMONDS

HEATHER TOMLINSON

HENRY HOLT AND COMPANY

NEW YORK

Henry Holt and Company, LLC
Publishers since 1866
175 Fifth Avenue
New York, New York 10010
www.HenryHoltKids.com

Henry Holt® is a registered trademark of Henry Holt and Company, LLC.
Copyright © 2010 by Heather Tomlinson
Distributed in Canada by H. B. Fenn and Company Ltd.

Library of Congress Cataloging-in-Publication Data
Tomlinson, Heather.
Toads and diamonds / Heather Tomlinson.—1st ed.
p.   cm.
Summary: A retelling of the Perrault fairy tale set in pre-colonial India, in
which two stepsisters receive gifts from a goddess and each walks her own
path to find her gift's purpose, discovering romance along the way.
ISBN 978-0-8050-8968-4
[1. Fairy tales.   2. Stepsisters—Fiction.   3. Blessing and
cursing—Fiction.   4. India—History—Fiction.]   I. Title.
PZ8.T536To 2010
[Fic]—dc22   2009023448

First Edition—2010
Book designed by April Ward
Printed in February 2010 in the United States of America by
R.R. Donnelley & Sons Company, Harrisonburg, Virginia

1   3   5   7   9   10   8   6   4   2

For Bethany

TOADS
AND
DIAMONDS

CHAPTER ONE

Diribani

DIRIBANI ran toward the stepwell. Squinting against the glare, she splashed through the road's deep ruts, pink skirts slapping her calves, her long black braid thumping her shoulders. One hand steadied the empty clay jar on her head. Mud sucked at her bare feet, but the rest of her was dry for a change. Overnight, the goddess Bhagiya had driven her tiger chariot across the heavens, chasing away her sister Naghali's rain snakes. Diribani didn't mind the mud when the fresh-washed sun beamed down on her.

Each panting breath brought rich new smells: wet earth, growing plants, a hint of curried lentils from a farmer's hut. Diribani's empty stomach growled at that, but her stepsister, Tana, couldn't cook their midday meal until Diribani returned with the water. Although their courtyard well served for washing and cleaning, its water had a sour taste. And Diribani had forgotten to fill the drinking jar at the sacred well this morning. Again.

Her stepmother had reminded her that a young woman of

fifteen, old enough to be trusted with two gold dowry bangles, shouldn't waste time drawing animal pictures in the sand to entertain the neighbor children. Since Ma Hiral wasn't present to scold her for baring her legs like a sweeper, Diribani hiked her dress wrap above her knees and ran faster.

She hopped over small puddles and waded through others with a heron's long stride. Lucky spotted frogs leaped away on either side. Then a stirring in the soupy mud alerted her to an upside-down turtle, struggling to right itself.

"How'd that happen, little sister?" With one bare foot, Diribani flipped the turtle over. She waited to make sure it wasn't injured. Slowly, the turtle got under way, its four stubby legs swimming as much as walking.

"Laaaaa-zy girl," a high voice trilled.

"Who's there?" Diribani spun around, almost dropping the pot. "Show yourself." Behind her, the road was clear to Gurath's town walls and Lotus Gate. Ahead, a small boy led a cow.

"Lazy." The taunting voice came closer. "Lazy girl, girl, girl."

Yellow flashed in a clump of reeds. Diribani held tight to the clay jar—their last one, for she'd broken the others—and bent at the waist to peer into the weedy tangle. A piltreet's bright-black eye stared at her. White wings flipped; the golden throat-patch quivered. "Lazy, lazy."

"Peace to you, too, piltreet-ji," Diribani said. "I trust you spent a pleasant holiday abroad? It was very wet here."

The piltreet whistled. "Lazy."

"What, is Governor Alwar paying *birds* to tattle on honest Gurath folk?" Diribani cocked her head. "His livery does become you, sir."

The piltreet flew to another reed. It bent under his weight, swaying over a ditch full of cloudy brown water. Diribani's fingers itched to capture the picture he made, this cheeky creature and his dancing reflection. Once, before she'd had to sell her paints, she could have mixed the exact shades of his yellow and white feathers, the rice shoots pulsing green in the flooded field behind him, the blue sky overhead.

However insulting, the piltreet's song expressed the joy everyone felt when the rains ended. No more sitting inside, watching drips eat away their mud-brick walls. No more fighting the black mold that furred every surface, no more grieving past losses and fretting about the future. Especially for her family. Together, Diribani and Tana had gone over their plan again and again. Ma Hiral wasn't convinced, but they couldn't wait any longer for her approval. The time had come to act.

During the cool, dry season after the rains, the port town of Gurath would swell with travelers arriving by ship and caravan, eager to trade for fine cloth and spices, metalwork and gems. As the skies cleared, market tents would unfold like flowers between the guild halls and the customs house. Vendors would set out all manner of delicious food. Diribani licked her lips, thinking of sliced pinkfruit, fried dough sprinkled with cardamom and ginger sugar, spicy fritters dipped in tamarind sauce. Then a loud voice banished all thought of the treats they could no longer afford.

"Look, Chihra, someone left the barn door open."

Diribani straightened to find her way blocked by a group of servant girls from the overseers' quarter. Like her, they carried water jars on their heads; mud daubed their bare feet. But instead of short blouses and draped wraps in bright colors, the traditional dress worn by women who worshiped the twelve, these girls wore Believer garb. The emperor's stern religion prescribed the flared white coats and close-fitting cotton trousers to cover a woman's flesh from throat to ankle, be she princess or laundry maid. Diribani felt sorry for the girls encased in such plain fabric, adorned only by the yellow ribbons fluttering from their long sleeves.

She recognized the two in front and offered the customary greeting, though they were unlikely to return it. Converts to the invaders' faith acted as if they themselves had melded the Hundred Kingdoms into an empire. "Peace to you, Chihra, Gulrang."

The round-faced girl, Chihra, surprised her by nodding. The other one, a tall, lean young woman a year older than Diribani, folded her arms over her chest. Her water jar remained perfectly balanced on her head. "Did the cow speak?" she drawled. "Move aside, hay-breath."

"Come on, Gulrang." The shorter girl tugged on her friend's sleeve. "No more trouble, my lady said."

"Not at all," Gulrang sneered. Intent on Diribani, she didn't notice the white mare and rider behind her, or the horse's interest in her water jug. "I wouldn't trouble myself to spit on the dirt-eating— Help!" When horse lips smacked near her ear, Gulrang shrieked, lost her balance, and stumbled into a puddle. Both hands flew up to catch the full jar before it toppled off her head. Water sloshed out to splatter her white coat.

The mare shook her mane in alarm as the previously convenient water jug ducked out of reach.

"Peace to you, Trader Kalyan." Diribani tried to keep her amusement from showing in her face. She reached her free hand to the mare. "And Jasmine."

"Peace, Mina Diribani," the young man said pleasantly, as if he hadn't guided his mount into Diribani's tormentors on purpose. "Ladies."

Chihra shot Gulrang an alarmed look. Without spilling a drop from her water jar, she dipped her knees. "Please excuse us, sir. We were just taking our leave."

"Then I'll wish you all a good day." His smile brought an answering simper to Chihra's round face. The other girls giggled behind their hands as they followed her.

Not Gulrang. Her back to the horse and rider, she glared at Diribani. "Until tomorrow," she said.

To an outsider, it might not have sounded alarming. Diribani understood she would face a reckoning the next time they met, but it was worth it to see haughty Gulrang outfaced by a horse.

The servant girl flounced after her companions, back straight and bony hips swaying under the flared white coat. The extra flourish in her walk was for Kalyan's benefit, Diribani was sure. The young trader and his mare were marketplace favorites. Occupied with his father's errands, Kalyan would still make time to let a child stroke Jasmine's soft nose, give a stranger directions, or exchange remarks about the weather with the porters at the customs house. Their two families might have been rivals in the gem-trading business, but Diribani's father had often held up Trader Nikhat's children as models of good behavior.

Jasmine whuffled over Diribani's palm. Glancing down, she realized her dress wrap was still hiked above her calves. Kalyan's older sister, Hima, would never be caught so in public. "Your family is well?" she asked, holding Kalyan's gaze as she surreptitiously let down her skirts. "Your mother and sisters?"

"All fine, praise the twelve," he said, then grinned. "Frantic, of course, since Prince Zahid's ship just landed after a voyage abroad."

"His Highness must be anxious to return to the palace in Fanjandibad if he's willing to push a caravan through these conditions." Diribani waved at the road's deep ruts and standing water.

"I suppose so. Father said the governor's people didn't expect him for another week. Mother's beside herself."

"The royal ladies will be visiting your house before they set off?"

"We hope so. You know how it is: Dress up and wait." Kalyan tugged on his embroidered sash. He wore court fashion, Diribani noticed, though not, of course, in Believer white. His coat was a charcoal gray over close-fitting trousers, his sash worked in metallic thread, silver and gold, in a geometric design. "They'll probably ask us to bring jewels to them at the fort. But my mother wants the house, the inventory, and all of us polished and ready, just in case."

"Oh, they're likely to call on you," Diribani assured him. "My father used to tell us that Trader Nikhat had the best selection besides . . ." She faltered. *Besides us* was no longer true. Or, at least, not until Tana's work bore fruit. "In all Tenth Province," she finished.

"We do have some fine stones this season," Kalyan said, as if he hadn't noticed the awkward pause. His expression grew serious. "May I offer our family's condolences, Diribani? Your father's passing leaves a great hole in Gurath. We were all so sorry to hear the news."

"Thank you, Kalyan." Diribani patted the mare's neck, combing the silky mane with her fingers. Tears pricked her eyes, but she wouldn't cry in the road. "I don't know what I would have done without Ma Hiral and Tana."

"Er . . ." The young man coughed. "Speaking of Mina Tana, did she happen to mention—"

"My sister's in excellent health," Diribani interrupted. She touched Kalyan's hand in warning as two older women passed them.

He continued in trader-talk, tapping her wrist. *Transaction completed?*

Diribani glanced around. The women lingered within earshot, but their backs were safely turned.

Unknown value. More study required, she signaled back, and withdrew her hand. "Ma Hiral is improving," she said aloud, in case the women were listening. Of course they were! Nikhat's son conversing with Javerikh's daughter? What a delicious tidbit of gossip, even if their speculation completely missed the mark. Diribani liked the friendly young trader, but her sister, Tana, would have made ten trips to the well for the sake of this brief conversation, and then treasured Kalyan's every word as she would a precious stone.

"Please convey my greetings," he said.

"I will," Diribani replied. As if her face showed some of what she was thinking, Kalyan looked at her with a question in his dark eyes. At the same moment, Jasmine took exception to a pair of long-horned water buffalo. The trader saluted Diribani. He gave his restive horse her head and rode toward Lotus Gate.

"Lazy girl," the piltreet commented.

"Be quiet, you." Diribani hurried in the opposite direction. Water. Ma Hiral and Tana were waiting, and it was her fault.

But the world was so beautiful after the rains! Even hunger couldn't dim Diribani's pleasure in the sun's warmth on her shoulders, the vibrant colors all around. Cultivated fields alternated with junglelike thickets, alive with birds. It occurred to Diribani that poor girls had more freedom than rich girls. In her old life, she would never have been permitted to go to the sacred well without a chaperone. Beyond the family compound, a servant would have accompanied her, even if she just wanted to visit the corner vendor for a savory pickle. Diribani's mouth watered.

Poor girls have the freedom to go hungry. She could hear Tana saying it, tart as one of those very pickles. Dear Tana, whose face grew thinner with every passing day because she never took her fair share of rice, pressing it on her mother or Diribani. Though not related to Diribani by blood, Ma Hiral and Tana were more truly her family than her father's grasping cousins. And Ma Hiral had been so ill, disappearing into a fog of grief upon her husband's death. It had been up to Diribani and Tana to plan their futures. Their plan *must* work. Diribani was ready to pledge her two gold bangles on a successful outcome.

Tana wasn't beautiful, but she was so unselfish, and worked so hard, she should have a husband who appreciated her. If Kalyan didn't return her feelings, there were other rising young traders in Gurath. Rustam, Manekh, or maybe Bhim . . . With the slightest improvement in their fortune, Tana could take her pick of suitors.

Suddenly, after one incautious step, the greasy mud slid under Diribani's foot. Both hands flew to the clay jar as she staggered, then fell to her knees. She landed with a splash in a puddle, just missing a long green ribbon. Diribani had never seen fabric so brilliant, as if it had been woven from threads of enameled metal. It would look lovely in Tana's black hair.

Before she could reach for it, the ribbon coiled upon itself. Diribani stared, her knees cold in the mud, her hands locked on the clay pot. Too late, she recognized the naga's muscular body and triangular head. A grass viper's fangs contained a potent poison. If it bit her, she'd be dead before her numb lips kissed the earth.

The serpent inspected Diribani, from sweat-beaded forehead to mud-spattered pink wrap.

Poor girls might walk alone on the road, barefoot, with skirts hiked to their knees. But, rich or poor, no girl could afford to ignore the goddess Naghali's snake messengers. Wisdom, good fortune, or death—which fate would this one bestow upon her?

CHAPTER TWO

Tana

"FOOLISH, foolish girl!" Ma Hiral banged an empty iron pot into its storage niche. Plaster flaked off the wall and sprinkled the stone floor with ocher-colored dust. "I forbid this mad scheme, do you hear? Forbid it!"

Kneeling by the banked kitchen fire, Tana turned the two thin gold bracelets around her wrist. "Mother, please understand. We don't have a choice."

Her mother shook a wooden spoon at her. "And when the white-coat soldiers break down our gate and throw you in Alwar's prison for trading without a guild stamp or permit? When they strip Diribani of her dowry bangles and kick us both into the gutter? What then?"

Tana heard the fear that underlaid the shrill words. "Don't worry." Gently, she took the spoon and put it away, next to the empty jars that had once held hot mustard oil, gram flour, and spices. "I'm not working on my own authority. Trader Nikhat will sign the report for the Jewelers Guild. When he sells the stones, he'll pay the taxes. Nobody's going to prison."

Ma Hiral changed tack. "You're only sixteen! You'd no business calling on a rival merchant without my permission."

Tana swallowed the answers that rose hot to her lips. Both she and Diribani were old enough to face the unpleasant truth. Their family might once have competed with Trader Nikhat's, but those days had ended two seasons ago, when bandits attacked her stepfather's caravan, killed Ba Javerikh, and stole all his capital. Crazed with grief, his widow had retreated to her bed. Only lately had she expressed an interest in household matters, and then mostly to complain about the lack of good tea, fresh flowers, and sandalwood soap. If Tana or her stepsister had waited for her mother's permission to do anything, they would have starved.

Ma Hiral spoke louder, as if Tana hadn't heard her previous remark. "Decent girls don't tarnish their reputations by allowing men inside our gate at night, bringing who knows what kind of trouble with them."

"Men?" Tana looked up from the rice jar. "You mean Kalyan?"

"That showy white horse of his! The neighbors will be talking."

Tana shook her head. "Everyone in Gurath knows that Kalyan runs his family's errands all over town." Her nails scraped the bottom of the big clay jar as she scooped out two small handfuls of rice. Glad for an excuse to keep her face turned away from her mother, she spread the grains in a tray. "Why shouldn't he bring a message from his sister to Diribani? He only stayed long enough to drop off the box, not much for people to gossip about."

"They'll blame our poor hospitality."

And they'd be right, though Tana knew her mother wouldn't appreciate her saying so. The previous evening, there had been a bit of fresh water left, but no tea leaves to brew with it. How humiliating that she couldn't even offer Kalyan the courtesy of a welcome-cup. He'd pretended that another commission demanded his attention. So late? Tana doubted it. That was just Kalyan being kind. Given her family's reduced circumstances, she had to settle for his pity, though once she had dared to hope for more.

Tana shoved rice grains from side to side. Bought from the cheapest vendor, the rice was flecked with bits of straw and grit she needed to pick out by hand.

Her mother sniffed. "If you'd been more welcoming, perhaps he would have stayed longer."

"I was polite," Tana said, stung by the unjust accusation. "It was a business call, not a social visit."

"When a personable young man comes to the house, you could make an effort to please. Why can't you act more like Diribani? A sweet word for everyone, and always so composed."

Tana made a face at the rice. Actually, she *had* taken special care with her appearance, hoping that, for discretion's sake, Trader Nikhat might send his son instead of a servant. But, like a scolding piltreet, her mother repeated the same reproaches over and over. Why didn't Tana take better care of her hair and skin? Did she want rough hands like a dairy maid? And she wasn't eating enough! No man would want a girl skinny as a stick and surly as a flea-bitten mongoose.

Tana knew that even if she wore twelve heavy gold bangles instead of two thin ones, combed her hair a thousand times a day, and spoke with a moonbird's voice, men wouldn't look twice at her when Diribani was present. But she couldn't dwell on that when more urgent problems consumed her waking hours. At last Tana had found a solution that might carry them through the next little while. Her stepsister agreed, but did Tana's own mother support her? No. Ma Hiral only voiced fresh objections.

"What if Kalyan doesn't approve of your meddling? What if he tells the authorities?"

"Mother." Tana spread a cloth over the rice to keep off the flies. "Kalyan wouldn't cause trouble for our family or his."

"Men." Ma Hiral threw the free end of her gray dress wrap over her face and rocked back and forth. "Who knows what they'll do? Even dear Javerikh, twelve gods bless him, abandoned his family to this world of illusion. How will we live?"

"I'm doing my best, and so is Diribani," Tana muttered, but she said it after she had left the kitchen.

Fortunately, her mother hadn't yet thought of the one problem that had made Tana hesitate to approach Trader Nikhat. She and her mother had no claim on this house, except while Diribani remained unmarried. Whenever Ba Javerikh's cousin, the next inheritor, visited the house, his shrewish wife poked her nose into every room, as if measuring the bare stone floors for the carpets she'd lay down once she became its mistress. Which she would, the day Diribani crossed her bridegroom's threshold. If her stepsister's relatives discovered Tana's secret dealings, they might evict her and Ma Hiral from the family property. Then they'd ship Diribani off to the first man the marriage broker suggested and have the place to themselves.

Diribani had reassured Tana, saying that her father's cousin wouldn't find out. Besides, Diribani insisted, she wasn't in a hurry to wed. She wouldn't consider any proposal that left Tana and Ma Hiral without a home.

Still, Tana worried. As pretty as Diribani was, some man would snap her right up. No, as she'd told her mother, they didn't have a choice. They'd already sold Ma Hiral's dowry bangles. They needed money, and of the three of them, Tana was most qualified to earn it.

Tana blew out a long breath as she walked to the courtyard and closed the cane shutters. She could hear children playing in the street outside and women talking over a garden gate. Tana didn't expect callers, but the neighbors' mud-brick walls stretched two stories above their modest compound. The last thing she needed was some bored auntie spying through a window.

In the main room, narrow bars of sunlight pierced the shutters and striped the floor. Tana had swept the stone pavers earlier that morning. If only Diribani were as diligent with her chores; she had yet to return from the sacred well with water to boil the rice. Tana pulled the door cloth across the opening, stood in the brightest part of the room, and frowned. With the shutters closed, it was too dim. She found a clay lamp and shook it, listening to the faint sloshing of oil within the bowl. Should she burn the last of their fuel, or open a shutter and risk being seen? Tana bit her lip. Better to be safe, she decided. Lighting a twig from the banked kitchen coals, she touched it to the lamp wick.

The flame burned, small but steady. Carrying the bowl in both hands, Tana set the lamp on a stand. She spread a piece of black cotton fabric on the floor under the lamplight. With another glance at the closed shutters, Tana fetched the jeweler's scale from its shelf. An iron poker served to pry up one of the floor's square paving stones. Underneath was a small iron box. She removed the box from its hiding place and brushed off a few crumbs of dirt. Oiled hinges opened to reveal layers of cotton wadding, and a thin roll of yellow cloth tied with silk ribbons.

Tana put down the box and knelt beside it. She smoothed her red dress wrap across her lap, as much to dry her sweaty palms as to straighten out wrinkles. As she picked apart the first knot, her fingers trembled. Perhaps her mother was right, and Tana's foolish pride would destroy her family. Who was she, to claim her judgment exceeded that of men who'd apprenticed with the Jewelers Guild? If the authorities found out, or if Tana had mistaken her abilities . . .

Let the stones speak to you.

Her head jerked in fright, but the room was empty. Tana's racing pulse slowed when she realized she had heard the voice of memory. Her stepfather had once given her that advice. She remembered the encouragement in Ba Javerikh's voice, felt the weight of his attention whenever he watched her work, ready to correct or praise. He had believed in her. She wouldn't fail him, or the widow and daughter he'd left destitute.

She unrolled the lumpy cloth packet. Like frozen raindrops, sapphires trickled onto the black fabric.

Then a flicker of movement caught Tana's eye. She hunched over the gemstones. Had she forgotten to cover a window? Left the gate open? Or perhaps little Indu had climbed over the wall again. The pest! If the inquisitive neighbor boy saw Tana with a double handful of sapphires, the whole town would know before sunset, and Ma Hiral's worst fears might come true.

From the shadows under the household shrine, a long, narrow

shape rippled across the stone floor toward her. Alternating patches of tan and gold glimmered in the light. Tana eased back on her heels. It was only the house naga, looking for a warm spot to bask in after Tana had closed the room's shutters. She pressed her palms together. "Peace to you, naga-ji."

The snake's head swayed near her ankle. Tana felt the brush of cool, dry scales against her bare feet. Ratters usually ignored the people whose homes they cleared of vermin. Its favor was an encouraging sign. Perhaps the snake's patron, the goddess Naghali, didn't mind Tana's working in secret.

"Be careful, friend," she said softly. "When the rains ended, Governor Alwar doubled the reward for snake skins."

Unconcerned, the snake coiled back on itself and then moved on, sliding under the door cloth and into the courtyard.

Tana removed the last sapphires from the wadding. The quilted lines of stitching had come loose, allowing the stones to slide from one section to another. Ba Javerikh had taught her better; she would repair the roll before returning it. Anticipation stirred within her as she spread the gems across the black cloth. Small jewels, she noted, of medium to poor quality. She sorted them into rows by weight, shape, and color, engrossed in the familiar task. The stones did speak to her, in a fashion she couldn't explain to her mother or Diribani.

Gems didn't have souls like living creatures, to be reborn from one body to another, but Ba Javerikh had taught her how they, too, passed through various stages of existence. In infancy, they were shaped by the same forces that raised mountains and sundered oceans. Leaving the womb of earth, they were brought to light by wind, water, and men's persistent digging. A jewel achieved its full virtue after being cut and polished to reveal the fire within. When Tana held a rough gem, she could sense how best to express its character.

These had been poorly cut. Tana pursed her lips as she turned each one in her palm, listening with her fingers. Diamonds, the brightest, most powerful stones, had the loudest voices. Sapphires spoke in more muted tones, but these were clearly unhappy. Tana found herself insulted on their behalf. Even small, flawed stones deserved to sparkle. She would recommend a better cutter to Trader Nikhat. Her stepfather's old rival wouldn't be sorry he had entrusted Tana with the inventory. And if she gave a helpful report on this assortment, perhaps he'd send more valuable items in the future.

At the bottom of the iron box, Tana found a blank clothbound ledger, bamboo pen, and small clay pot of ink. One silent tear, then another, dropped to the black fabric at this thoughtfulness. Trader Nikhat or his wife, Ma Bansari, must have seen Tana and Diribani before the market stalls were packed away, hawking whatever they could spare in order to tide them through the rains.

Immediately after the tragedy, when Ma Hiral had been in no condition to help them, the girls had rented a stand and sold the goods themselves: blank ledgers like this one, Ba Javerikh's books and carpets, the best dishes and silver serving pieces, all their formal dress wraps, pretty blouses, and embroidered shawls. Diribani's beauty had ensured a constant stream of customers; Tana's bargaining had brought excellent prices.

Out of compassion, the townsfolk hadn't haggled too fiercely. In Gurath's merchant community, everyone knew that one failed expedition could end a family's comfortable existence overnight. Diribani had given up her paints and drawing paper, Tana her dreams of expanding the family's gemstone business. Trader Nikhat must have guessed she would need the most basic supplies to compose her report.

Now she uncapped the ink and sniffed, angry with herself for dwelling on what couldn't be changed. They'd saved their dowry bangles, hadn't they? In the worst case, the gold bracelets would enable Tana to hold her head high when she visited the marriage broker's garlanded tent. Diribani should have them all, of course. Beauty and good breeding were important, but everyone knew that a girl's dowry mattered. Even if Tana had no prospects, Diribani deserved a good husband, young and handsome and kind. Perhaps he wouldn't mind if her stepmother and unwed sister joined his household as well. Tana would work so hard, her new family wouldn't see them as a burden.

Meanwhile, if this job earned even a tiny commission from Trader Nikhat, Tana wouldn't have to sell her mother's one remaining treasure, an engraved silver pitcher, so they could eat. Assuming Diribani brought back the water for cooking before the day faded into night. What was keeping her?

Tana's stomach cramped. She ignored it. She'd gone hungry before, and would again, no doubt. The sooner she returned these sapphires to Trader Nikhat with an accurate report of weight, classification, and value, the sooner they might buy some garlic or onions to season their plain rice.

After dipping the pen into the ink jar, Tana drew a grid on the first page of the ledger. She labeled each square with the symbol embroidered on the carrying case's corresponding panel. The first sapphire could be cut to eliminate a flaw on one facet. She turned it over. Yes, a fraction off this side would improve the jewel's symmetry without dropping the weight below a half-rati. With quick strokes of the pen, Tana wrote down her recommendation. "Will that suit, my lovely?" she said under her breath.

The stone twinkled in response. Tana set it down and picked up the next. Absorbed in her work, she didn't notice her mother watching from the doorway, worry etched on her features.

CHAPTER THREE

Diribani

"P-PEACE to you, naga-ji," Diribani stammered.

The viper's triangular jaws opened. The forked tongue flicked in and out, as if the goddess's messenger could taste a girl's character from the air around her. Trapped in the clammy folds of her dress wrap, Diribani lowered her eyes to stare at the mud.

How would the naga judge her? If fifteen years was the allotted span for Diribani to enjoy a human girl's body, had she spent the time wisely? Unlike Believers, who feared a hell and prayed for a paradise that their one jealous god reserved for humans only, the followers of the twelve understood that the earth encompassed both. For all creatures, each lifetime's actions determined their condition in the next.

What had Diribani learned—or failed to learn—that might doom her to return as a lower being? She knew that laughing at Gulrang hadn't been very compassionate, but was it enough to make the gods send her back as a rat, say, or a scorpion?

Her arms ached, and a muscle burned in her thigh. Diribani didn't dare shift position. Her nose itched. Mud dried in scales on her skin. Quiet as a temple statue, she waited. The green snake considered her, the tip of its tail vibrating.

Diribani worked so hard to keep still that she almost missed the moment when the snake uncoiled. Moving with abrupt decision, it swept past her, across the road to the field beyond.

So. Death was not her fate today. If the goddess was kind, perhaps wisdom or good fortune would mark Diribani's future. Now that she had one.

Diribani shuddered and pulled herself out of the mud. Her legs trembled. She put down the clay jar and stretched her arms to the sky until the gold bangles danced on her wrist. Relief bubbled up inside her, hot and sweet as strong tea. What a story she had to tell! She was almost tempted to run straight home. Duty dragged the pot back onto her head and started her feet toward the well. The naga might regret sparing Diribani if she acted like the lazy girl the piltreet had called her.

Within a grove of mango and pinkfruit trees, the well's entrance pavilion beckoned. On either side of the biggest stone archway, two oil lamps burned in their niches, adding their small flames to the day's brightness. Diribani ducked between the carved pillars. Dim light soothed her eyes; cool air refreshed her skin. Diribani washed her feet and legs in a large clay basin. She poured the dirty water into the waste channel and refilled the basin with clear water for the next visitor. After straightening her blouse and twitching her skirts into order, she paid her respects to the goddess's shrine with extra gratitude. Then she carried the jar along the covered walkway to the stepwell proper.

Mostly open to the sky, the sides of the large tank were faced with stone blocks and divided by many flights of steps. The stairs descended deep into the ground, separating the wide expanse of the well into areas for bathing and washing. Strung along the edge of the stepwell like pearls on a necklace, pavilions offered shelter from both rain and sun. During the dry season, the water level inside the tank might drop eight or nine or twenty levels, but it was always accessible from the flights of steps.

The recent rains had filled the well to the brim. Water lapped the top stairs and spilled into canals that irrigated the fruit trees surrounding the tank. Unusually, the only other visitor was a goatherd, driving his animals up the livestock ramp at the far end of the stepwell. That didn't make it quiet; monkeys quarreled, and birds whistled in the trees.

Diribani stopped in the shade of a pavilion and set her clay jar next to a pillar. She splashed a handful of cool water on her neck, dabbling her fingers at two fish in the pool. One darted away, a sliver of gold and green. The other didn't.

Curious, she reached down to touch it again. The unmoving fish had been chiseled from one of the submerged stone steps. Diribani smiled at the mason's whimsy. She had enjoyed discovering such carvings around the well before, fish and shrimp, lucky frogs and Sister Naghali's snakes.

As the water stilled, the reflections of the pillars shimmered around her hand, inviting her into a shadowy world. Looking into the water, Diribani felt like a cloud spirit surveying the earth below, or perhaps a sea nymph waving from the waves at her celestial sister. Light played across the surface of the pool, blurring the boundary between the submerged depths and the limitless sky. Diribani flicked the water again. Diamond-bright drops splashed, their ripples dissolving into the stepwell's vast peace. A distant parrot squawked, then quieted.

In the drowsy calm, hope surfaced like the little darting fish. Tana's transaction with Trader Nikhat should succeed. *A diamond in the rough*, Diribani's father had called Tana. *Hiral, my fiery ruby; Diribani, my unmatched pearl*. She blinked away tears at the memory. How happy she had been when her father's remarriage had blessed her with a mother and sister both. Without them, how could she have endured his loss? Together, they would survive it. And if Tana could work on a regular if secret basis, perhaps their fortunes were less dismal than Ma Hiral predicted.

Diribani dipped her jar into the pool. Full, its weight stretched her tired arms. Girls like Chihra and Gulrang, who'd been fetching water since childhood, could squat, hoist a pot onto their heads, and stand without spilling a drop. This task was new to Diribani. When her father was alive, servants had fetched their water. She had gotten stronger with practice, although she still needed to hold a full jar with both hands. Grunting with the effort required to lift it above her shoulders, she settled the water jar onto the cloth ring that kept it steady on her head.

Tana would be the first to remind her that poor girls earned their every meal or they didn't eat. Diribani's lips twisted in a wry smile. Perhaps she wasn't as skilled as her stepsister, but she could strive to work as hard.

Leaving the pavilion's shade, Diribani almost tripped over a pile of rags. She stopped with a squeak of surprise when the strips of cloth parted, revealing two wrinkled hands and a disease-ravaged face. Inside the torn garments, a woman hunched on the stone walkway. Praying? Asleep? A traveler weakened by her struggle through the road's thick mud? Diribani didn't recognize her.

"Give me a drink, Mina?" The words were slurred, the voice cracked with age.

"Certainly, Ma-ji." Diribani lowered her jar and stepped forward to pour water over the outstretched claws.

The stranger slurped the water, dribbling it over Diribani's feet. Diribani pretended not to notice. The poor thing couldn't help her infirmity. Bony, sore-pocked legs stuck out from her ragged garment. She must be as weak as a baby bird if she couldn't manage the few paces to the pavilion's shelter.

"More water, Ma-ji?" Diribani asked.

"No, no." A deep cough shook the thin body.

Diribani hugged the jar to her chest and winced in sympathy. "May I help you to the pavilion?"

"Thank you, Mina." Spittle flecked the cracked lips.

Before Diribani could put down the jar to assist, claw hands closed over Diribani's elbows, and the old woman pulled herself upright. Either the coughing or the abrupt upward movement must have cleared an obstruction from her throat. Strangely, the crone's voice emerged as sweet as a flute's. "Such kindness merits a gift. What is your soul's desire, my daughter?"

"Pardon, Ma-ji?" Diribani said, confused by the woman's transformation from beggar to benefactor. She would have stepped back, but the woman held her arms in a firm grip. As they stood face to face, with only the width of the water jar between them, Diribani met the stranger's eyes.

A deep green color, they reflected Diribani's gaze into eternity, two pools as liquid and profound as the well where they stood. Awe closed Diribani's throat. This was no ordinary old woman; her question demanded the absolute truth. *Beauty* was the answer that rose to Diribani's lips, but she had no breath to shape the word.

"Ah," the stranger said, as if she could read stunned silence as easily as speech. Her voice started on a low note and swelled into unbearable richness, a temple bell echoing in the well. "Your sweet nature, kind heart, and hopeful spirit are worthy of reward."

Like nectar, the rich voice filled Diribani with an emotion too intense to contain. The clay jar slipped from her arms and smashed into pieces on the ground. A shard sliced her ankle, but that slight pain wasn't what caused Diribani to clap her hands over her face and sob as if her heart, too, had been shattered.

Joy brought the tears: a rush of gladness greater than any she had ever experienced. Washing over her in an irresistible wave, the goddess's regard bathed Diribani in a beauty like sunrise. Or music.

Or the strong, sure line of a green snake, writing a girl's fate in the sand.

CHAPTER FOUR

Tana

THE courtyard gate slammed. Tana stamped her heel on the loose stone to level the floor over the box's hiding place. She was putting the jeweler's scale on its shelf when Diribani pushed aside the door cloth and stumbled into the house.

"What's wrong?" Tana caught Diribani's arm, guiding her to sit on the floor. The free end of Diribani's pink dress wrap hid her face, but the mud splattering her skirts and the long hair tangled around her heaving shoulders conveyed distress as clearly as words. Tana had rarely seen her gazelle-graceful sister in such a state. And . . . "You're bleeding!"

Ma Hiral scuttled in from the kitchen. "Bandits?" she quavered.

"She'll be fine," Tana reassured her mother. She knelt and wiped Diribani's ankle clean with the black cloth she still held. "Just a shallow cut, more mud than blood, see?"

"Where's the water jar?" Ma Hiral asked.

The bloodstained fabric crumpled in Tana's hand. "Did they bother you again, those flesh-eater girls?"

"Language, Tana!" her mother snapped.

"Sorry, Ma. White-coats, I meant." Tana dabbed the cloth at Diribani's other leg and found only mud, not blood. If someone had pushed Diribani or taken her jar, it was partly Tana's fault for not accompanying her to the well. At midday this early in the season, the road must have been deserted. Nobody would accost a Gurath girl when others were watching, but if someone caught her alone . . . And the servants from the overseers' quarter were so touchy, quick to take offense when none was offered. Tana tried again. "Was there an accident?"

"You broke the jar!" Ma Hiral wailed.

"No, Ma. You don't understand." From behind the veiling fold of Diribani's dress wrap, two tiny pebbles and a red peony fell to the floor.

"Bountiful goddess!" Ma Hiral sank to her knees. She plucked the stones from the floor and brought them to her eyes, then creaked to her feet and took them to the window. She opened the shutter a crack, staring intently into her palm.

Tana looked from the peony to her sister's shaking shoulders. She slid the dress wrap's free end away from Diribani's face. Tears glittered in the doe-brown eyes. But instead of the terror or embarrassment—or bruises—Tana had feared, her sister's face shone with joy, lovely as a rainbow under a waterfall. Tana's heart opened in answering delight before clenching, hard. "You met a man."

Diribani gulped a sob and nodded. Then, at Tana's expression, she shook her head. She touched her fingers to her lips.

"Daughter." Ma Hiral gestured with a closed fist. Tana got up to see what her mother wanted. "Look here." Ma Hiral grabbed Tana's elbow and thrust the stones into her hand.

Bigger than mustard seeds, smaller than dried peas, the light-colored stones clicked against each other. One caught a shaft of light between the shutter canes and lit with an unmistakable fire.

Diamonds.

Tana knew them by touch; a close examination confirmed it. Modest-sized but without flaw, they would need minimal faceting and polishing to sparkle with brilliance. Tana turned to her step-sister. She did her best to keep the question from sounding like an accusation. "Who is he?"

"It doesn't matter who he is!" Ma Hiral crowed before Diribani could answer. "He gave her two diamonds, Tana! They'll feed us until the wedding, allow us to make the proper offerings to the twelve, and host the ceremony. Gods be praised, our dear girl has found herself a prince among men."

"Men?" Diribani's laugh turned into a hiccup. She wiped her eyes with the back of her hand. "No, this isn't about a man. Sister Naghali sent a messenger, and then she herself blessed me." With the words, two speckled lilies and a giant topaz dropped from Diribani's lips.

Tana saw it happen. She watched the flowers and jewel spring from her stepsister's mouth and fall to the floor, and still she couldn't believe it.

Diribani, too, gasped. Her eyes widened, and she clapped one hand over her mouth. The other reached for the lilies. She picked them up and sniffed. In silent amazement, she handed a lily to Tana. Tana returned the two rough diamonds to her equally dumbstruck mother and took the blossom between her fingers.

It felt like a lily. It smelled like a lily. A smear of orange pollen coated her fingertips when she touched its heart. Tana dropped the flower in Diribani's lap. Her knees buckled, and she sat next to her sister. The two of them leaned against each other, though Tana wasn't sure who was comforting whom. Ma Hiral crouched beside them. She touched a peony's fringed petals with a tentative brush of her fingers.

"Tell us," Tana whispered.

"I hardly— It's not possible!" Marigolds shone gold in the dim light, their peppery smell teasing Tana's nose. Diribani's hands opened and closed as the words rushed out. "Gulrang was rude, but Kalyan came and she left. He asked about his father's commission. Then the viper didn't bite me, and I almost stepped on an old beggar woman at the well. Ah!" Diribani reared back like a shying horse as several pink roses fluttered to the ground, followed by a showy bloodstone.

"From the beginning," Ma Hiral commanded.

Tana felt stupid, as if Brother Utsav, the crow god, had turned the world upside down when she wasn't looking. Diribani spoke flowers and jewels. If Tana went outside, would she step on the sky and see the earth above her? Would water feel dry, or sand wet against her fingers? "Yes, unless—does it hurt you to talk?"

"No," Diribani said. "It's just so strange. This"—she swallowed before continuing—"this is how it happened."

The story cascaded from her lips along with an occasional sob and a scattering of flowers and jewels. By the time she finished, red-gold ashoka blossoms, lotuses, more lilies, and branches of jasmine massed in a scented heap on her lap. Rough diamonds, amethysts, sapphires, rubies, and emeralds lay sprinkled over the stone floor, plentiful as colored gravel. Diribani twisted her hands together. "Why did she pick me? What must I do? What does it all mean?"

"We are saved, praise Naghali-ji." Ma Hiral stood slowly and crossed the floor to the household altar. She placed the first two diamonds in a dish that held a few dried petals instead of the flowers, fruit, or incense they had offered the gods in more prosperous times. The older woman knelt and touched her forehead to the floor, praying under her breath. Diribani followed her stepmother's example, heaping the dish with flowers and jewels.

Tana couldn't move. Her limbs were too heavy; her mind was untethered, a butterfly flitting between blossoms. Oddly, Tana could hardly decide what she felt. She didn't think the cold, heavy weight inside her was envy.

Naghali-ji had sent her snake messenger to judge Diribani's soul, and found it worthy. Tana doubted she could have been as brave. With her life in the balance, Tana would probably have begged for mercy she didn't deserve. But Diribani was beautiful inside and out.

Hadn't she welcomed Tana and her mother, five years earlier, instead of being angry at losing a share of her busy father's attention when he married the widowed Hiral? Diribani had never shown, by word or deed, that she resented her stepsister's growing skill with gems, or Ba Javerikh's praise. When his death had changed their circumstances so dreadfully, Diribani hadn't even claimed a greater share of grief. Without a murmur of complaint, she had sold her costly dresses and paints, and accepted the lowly task of fetching water. Tana had heard about Gulrang and others teasing Diribani at the sacred well. The jealous girls mocked her for clumsiness when they could find no other fault, but Diribani refused to answer taunt with taunt.

If anything, Tana was pleased that Sister Naghali had shown her favor to such a truly good person. Rather than envy, Tana thought, despair was the emotion that crushed her chest like an iron weight. Had Tana been so tested, the goddess would have seen her sins, her secret fears, her failings. It would no doubt take Tana many lifetimes to learn the generosity of spirit Diribani naturally possessed.

Like the majority of the empire's common folk—outside of the Believers at the royal palaces, governor's fort, and overseers' quarter—Tana prayed to the twelve at the temple grove on feast days. She left offerings at their household shrine and tried to conduct herself with honor.

But with proof, clear proof, of Naghali-ji's existence piled on the floor around her, Tana realized that she had gone through the motions of religious practice without any real devotion. She hadn't imagined that a miracle would happen to her family. When she thought of gods and goddesses, she had considered them rather like the emperor and his courtiers at Lomkha: distant, glorious beings she would never encounter.

The understanding that a person might actually glimpse one of the twelve in her ordinary life, while engaged in her chores, took Tana's breath away. Longing filled her, pushing against the despair. How could she earn the privilege of experiencing the awe that Diribani's face reflected? At the very least, Tana resolved, she would be more patient with her mother's peevishness, more accepting of adversity, more steadfast in faith. A goddess had shown herself to Diribani. Tana vowed never to forget that such a miracle could happen.

A stinging slap tested her determination to be good. "Ma!" she cried, rubbing her arm. "That hurt."

"Get up, get up, lazy girl. What are you waiting for?" Her mother thrust the silver pitcher into Tana's hand and pulled her upright. "You must go to the well at once."

"Why?" Tana said, shocked into bluntness. "Naghali-ji won't show herself to *me*."

"Maybe not, but we still need water," her mother pointed out. "If the beggar woman asks for a drink, you can serve her properly. A silver pitcher that has been passed down from mother to daughter across six generations shows more respect than a clay pot, don't you think? And, practically speaking, silver won't break like clay if you happen to drop it."

Tana turned to Diribani. Her stepsister shrugged and smiled before jumping up to tuck a pink rose behind Tana's ear. "I hope you see her, too," she whispered.

More petals brushed Tana's bare arm. She smelled honeysuckle.

Ma Hiral shooed Tana through the door and across the courtyard. "Hurry, child. The holy ones don't wait about for us to show an interest." With this parting piece of advice, Tana's mother shoved her through the gate and closed it behind her.

Tana's bare feet squelched in the muddy road. With a reflexive gesture, she tucked the silver pitcher under her arm and draped the free end of her red dress wrap over her blouse like a shawl to hide the glint of metal. Her mother had gone mad. Did Ma Hiral want the tax collectors to think that her family were so rich they fetched their drinking water in heirloom silver vessels?

As the rose's scent reached her nose, Tana bit back a snorting laugh. If Diribani's gift lasted until sunset, they could probably afford to do just that.

CHAPTER FIVE

Diribani

"At last the rains have come,
swift-stooping as falcons,
fragrant as the lotus,
dancing on the water."

Diribani sang and twirled. Ma Hiral had told her to sit inside, but she couldn't obey. Exhilaration bubbled through her body. Her feet wanted to dance, her arms to fly upward in praise. Joy flooded her; if she didn't express it, she'd burst.

Her bare feet thumped the courtyard's sun-baked ground as she shook dust from their bedding and saluted the twelve sacred directions: Grandfather Chelok, Grandmother Khochari, Brother Akshath, Sister Naghali, and the rest. How bored the Believers' one god must be, alone in his heaven. No wonder it made him jealous of his followers' worship.

The twelve were far more approachable, like family. Even

so, Naghali-ji's appearance was as marvelous as a tale from the Golden Age, when gods and goddesses often walked among men. And her gift! Diribani didn't know how the vapor of her breath was transmuted into flowers and gems. Perhaps her duty was not to understand how it worked, but to honor the giver. So, without benefit of a temple grove's drummers, she sang and danced her gratitude.

At her words, flowers and jewels winked into being to adorn the bare courtyard. Every so often, Diribani tasted the edge of a petal or felt a gemstone slide cool over her chin. Otherwise, the goddess's bounty might as well have fallen from the cloudless sky as from her unworthy lips. Why had she been singled out? She had no idea; she would have to allow the goddess's hidden meaning to uncoil like a naga awakening from its slumber.

Oh, and Tana! Would she, too, meet Naghali-ji? Diribani hoped so. The experience was too large for one soul to encompass. If it was shared, perhaps they could make sense of it. She brandished the coverlet like a banner, and sang.

> *"Tonight, beloved,*
> *I light the lamp*
> *to guide my moonbird home."*

"Stop!" Ma Hiral ran into the courtyard. "Be quiet!" She seized Diribani's arm and dragged her stepdaughter inside, heedless of the cloth trailing on the ground behind her.

"But, Ma"—Diribani gathered the coverlet—"I just shook this out."

"Stay here," Ma Hiral snapped, her face stern.

"Yes, Ma." Diribani was worried by the deep lines that bracketed Ma Hiral's mouth. Shoulders tense, the older woman darted into the courtyard and swept the flowers and jewels onto another blanket. All the while, she flicked glances over her shoulder at the neighbors' windows and rooftops. After bundling the corners over one another, she pitched the blanket into the house. Then Diribani's stepmother quartered the courtyard, crouching to pat the packed dirt so she didn't miss any of the precious stones.

When Diribani would have helped, Ma Hiral shook an admonitory finger. Even standing on the threshold to shake the blanket earned Diribani a scolding look. She stepped back into the shadowed room. Unsettled by her stepmother's mood, Diribani sat on the floor and sorted the rough gems into piles: diamond, ruby, topaz, carnelian, sapphire, emerald, amethyst, jade, bloodstone, turquoise.

No pearls or coral, she noticed. Perhaps sea jewels weren't Naghali-ji's to bestow? The thought that even a goddess must respect her sister's domain both amused Diribani and made her think of her own sister. Tana would weigh and grade these stones properly when she returned. Though Diribani's father had taught her the basic principles, Tana's skill far surpassed her own. Most of these jewels were small, less than a rati, but some of the diamonds were so large and fine, Diribani could hardly imagine how much they might fetch.

She swept a considering glance around the room, empty except for two small tables, the lamp stand, and a couple of faded cushions. Unlike the opulent new mansions in the overseers' quarter, where each white-coat strove to outdo the others in their one god's name, the homes of Gurath's traditional elite, the merchants and bankers, tended to simplicity. Piety and prudence both suggested it was better not to excite the twelve gods' displeasure, the neighbors' envy, or the tax collector's interest with a rich outward show. Still,

Diribani thought, it wouldn't cost very much to refresh plaster and paint, or replace the carpets they had sold. Stone floors could chill bare feet, come the cool season.

With a small portion of the fortune heaped around her, they could hire servants to wait on Ma Hiral. They would have money for new paints and paper, scented hair oils, books, fresh fruit, and good tea, not the cheap grade Diribani had been embarrassed to pour for guests. Until that also became too expensive, and her friends had stopped visiting, to spare her the shame of having nothing to offer.

Her friends!

Alight with purpose, Diribani picked through the rough gems again. When Ma Hiral came inside, Diribani had set aside several of the larger stones. "This emerald will suit Geetika, don't you think? And sapphires for Parul." She pointed out the gems for her step-mother to admire.

Ma Hiral settled on the floor beside Diribani. "Generosity is an admirable quality, but you must take care," she warned.

"Take care?" Diribani laughed. "Why, yes, we will take care of everyone!" She spread her hands wide to catch an amethyst, a green beryl, an orchid, a diamond. Dropping the gems in Ma Hiral's lap, Diribani leaned over to kiss the lined cheek. "We'll feed the poor and tend the sick." She danced across the room to lay the orchid in the offering dish. "We'll offer double Alwar's horrible bounty on snakes. Alive, not dead, so we can set them free in the forest. And we can enlarge the animal hospital at the temple grove. Then the priests can accept elephants too old to work, cows that don't give milk, even the white-coats' broken hunting dogs and cheetahs and falcons. Why should the poor creatures be blamed for the barbaric use they're put to?"

Ideas tumbled over one another in Diribani's head, each more splendid than the last. "Gurath needs a library, Father was always saying, and we should have a better guesthouse for foreign merchants. And a theater. And painters!" She clasped her hands. "Oh, Ma Hiral, we could build a workshop, like the one in Fanjandibad, and maybe the painters would teach me, and—"

"Painters!" Ma Hiral shook her head. Exasperation roughened her voice. "Listen, Diribani. No one must know that you've been so favored."

"What?" Diribani turned. "You can't mean to keep me in the house until . . ." Her voice trailed off as she took in the seriousness of her stepmother's expression.

"Not forever." Ma Hiral's voice softened. "Just until this gift passes."

"Passes? You make it sound like a fever," Diribani said. "It's not leprosy or the plague." Small chunks of lapis lazuli spattered like hail on the floor, bruising the petals of three pure white roses. The joy she had held inside since the encounter at the well was congealing, cold wax in her veins. Stiff legs walked her to the shuttered window. She longed for a glimpse of the sun, a breath of air. "Shall I sit behind a screen like the Believers' wives, voiceless and invisible in my own home?"

"Do be sensible," Ma Hiral said. "When it's over, we say that one of dear Javerikh's investments paid off unexpectedly. As long as we pay the guild fees and taxes, the authorities won't ask difficult questions."

"But it's a miracle!" Diribani braced herself against the window frame. She wanted to claw aside the shutter and shout her news to the rooftops. "I can't pretend it never happened!"

"Who's asking you to? Once you've finished speaking jewels, you can tell whoever you like." Ma Hiral clicked her tongue. "You're no longer a child; don't pout like one. If your gift is discovered, Governor Alwar will have a hard time deciding whether his prison can hide you from the emperor's spies long enough to squeeze more diamonds out of you, or whether his religion requires that he burn you as a witch."

"Burn as a witch? Naghali-ji wouldn't permit that." Diribani's voice broke. Her hand closed around an ashoka blossom until red juice stained her fingers. "Would she?"

Ma Hiral sighed. She crossed the room to stand beside Diribani. Two doves landed in the courtyard and pecked at the dirt. A green spark startled one bird into a sideways hop. Ma Hiral dashed outside. She flapped her skirts to scare off the doves, then retrieved the overlooked emerald. Inside, she polished it on a fold of her dress wrap.

"Ten ratis, or I'm the princess of Fanjandibad," she said grimly, and handed it to Diribani. "In this degraded age, who knows what the holy ones will do?" she continued, as if there had been no interruption. "The governor orders Naghali-ji's sacred messengers to be killed like vermin. White-coats slap us in the street with one hand while their other steals the last coin our poor purses hold, and yet the twelve are silent."

"But we don't have to dress like Believers, or worship in their prayer halls," Diribani protested. "The white-coats leave our temple groves alone."

"Not by Alwar's choice," her stepmother said. "Fortunately, Emperor Minaz is more open-minded. Or more patient. After all, it took his ancestors many years to bring the Hundred Kingdoms under their fist. As long as the emperor controls our earthly fates, he is content to let his foreign truth touch our souls in its own time."

"Then wouldn't the emperor say that our religious matters were none of Alwar's business?" Defiantly, Diribani tossed the emerald and caught it, tossed and caught it again. "His god doesn't rule Naghali-ji, and she gave me—"

"When the goddess blesses you with good fortune, it doesn't mean you throw her wisdom out the window. Think, silly girl." Ma Hiral snatched the descending emerald from the air before it landed in Diribani's palm a third time. "To a man as corrupt as Alwar, greed *is* a religion. I'd wager this emerald that his treasury sees more of him than any prayer hall. Please, I am begging you on my knees, do not speak and give that snake-killer cause to destroy our family."

Diribani set her chin. "I still don't believe the goddess wants me to hide in my room, hoarding her riches like a miser."

"Mother Gaari, give me patience. What sins did I commit in my previous lives, to be saddled with two such headstrong girls?" Ma Hiral flung up her hands. "I'm only suggesting you use common sense. Is that so difficult?"

As her stepmother stomped away, muttering dire predictions under her breath, Diribani leaned against the window frame. Insides churning, she stared through the shutter slats at the empty court-yard. She didn't like fighting with her stepmother, but she could not agree with her wrongheaded ideas. Of course, they hadn't eaten today. Hunger and miracles were bound to stir the most ordered lives into turbulence. Practical Tana would know what to do; she always did.

Why was she taking so long at the well?

CHAPTER SIX

Tana

TANA waited for her turn at the foot basin, behind a group of laborers who'd come to fill their drinking jugs at the step-well before a long afternoon in the fields. Their laughter and teasing didn't touch the cyclone of Tana's swirling thoughts. Thanks to Diribani's jewels, their family would soon eat better than plain rice and the occasional curried lentils. No longer dependent on Diribani's cousins for shelter, they could buy their own house, where her mother could spend the rest of her days in luxury. And when the marriage broker learned the size of Diribani's dowry, princes would be competing for her sister's hand! But how would Tana explain their family's sudden wealth to the tax collector?

She shifted the silver pitcher on her hip. First things first: selling the gems. Tana couldn't wait to study the stones in better light. She'd get the best prices if she had them cut and then traded them herself. That assumed the Jewelers Guild would agree that Ba Javerikh's tutoring counted as an apprenticeship. And that a white-coat official would issue Tana a merchant's permit in her own name. The only women she knew who traded independently were widows who had maintained their dead husbands' permits. If Tana couldn't get her own permit or renew Ba Javerikh's, where could she turn? She'd be competing directly with Trader Nikhat; it wouldn't be fair to ask for his help this time. Trader Bhim was a nice enough fellow. He dealt mostly in pearls, and didn't seem like the type to demand an outrageous commission for the service. She could ask him.

"Eyo, Mina," the boy behind Tana said. "Your turn."

"What?" Tana looked up. "Oh, pardon me." She rinsed the mud off her feet and refilled the basin, then hurried across the entry pavilion. The shrine's stone carving stopped her short.

Eyes closed, the dancing goddess lifted her arms in blessing. *Diribani had spoken with her.* Tana gulped. Then, as every girl did from the day she was old enough to reach the statue, Tana traced the serpent twined around the dancer's waist. Generations of reverent hands had polished the stone to satin, the whole length of its draped coils. This image of the goddess and her snake, deadly cousin to the common house naga, was known to bring good fortune to petitioners. Tana wasn't sure whether the well had been dug to honor the ancient image, or whether the statue had been brought from a temple grove to bless the well. In any case, the shrine served as a reminder that the water here flowed freely to all souls: overseer and commoner, man and beast.

In the light of the oil lamps that lined the niche, the snake's jet eyes glittered. Tana felt they were fixed on her. Was the goddess displeased that Tana had brought her worldly concerns about permits and taxes to this sacred place, knowing what she now knew? Had the promise she'd made, to be mindful, not lasted the short distance from Gurath?

Naghali's carved mouth smiled its eternal smile; her snake's stone eyes weighed Tana. She squirmed under the flat regard. Surely it would find her lacking. With all the flowers and jewels at home, she hadn't thought to bring one to offer at the goddess's feet. The jewels and flowers weren't hers to give, she argued with herself. They belonged to Diribani.

The snake seemed to dismiss her excuses: *You didn't think to ask. What kind of devotion is that?* The silent question hung in the air.

Bitter as vinegar, Tana's failure stung her tongue. She folded her hands around the pitcher, acknowledging her fault. Then she remembered that she did, after all, have one flower she could call her own: the pink rose Diribani had tucked into her hair.

Warmed by Tana's skin, the blossom had opened. As she held it out, the rose's petals cupped the lamplight, and a sweet scent spilled into the air, offering fragrance like a blessing.

An arm jangling with gold bangles jostled Tana's, knocking the pink rose to the ground. "Oh, excuse me, Mina-ji."

Tana could have shouted with frustration. Instead, she bit her tongue, hard. She stooped to pick up the rose and set it on the altar in the corner, away from the stick of burning incense that the other young woman had placed there. "Peace, Hima-ji," she said through clenched teeth.

"Tana? So quickly, my prayer answered! Come along and join us." Trader Nikhat's eldest daughter transferred a covered basket to her other hand and linked arms with Tana. As they made their way along the busy corridor, the older girl flipped the free end of her dress wrap over her shoulder so it concealed their fingers. *Transaction completed?* she tapped out briskly on Tana's wrist.

Tana had to think; the business with Trader Nikhat's sapphires seemed so long ago. But she still had the packet, she realized. It was safe in the iron box, under a floor covered with more worthy gems. Smart Hima, to conduct this discussion in trader-talk. Everyone came to the well; you never knew who might be listening behind a pillar. Tana replied the same way. *Yes.*

Hima's smile lit up her plain features. "A party of royal ladies landed in Gurath yesterday, did you hear?"

"No." Tana held the silver pitcher against her other side. She was trying to find her mental balance, jerked from the sad contemplation of her sins to the more interesting topic of business. Hima could be a powerful ally. She had inherited Trader Nikhat's brains, her brother, Kalyan, had gotten all Ma Bansari's charm, and the two younger sisters split her good looks between them. "Prince Zahid's ship arrived early?"

"A whole week," Hima confirmed. "Can you imagine, we spent all *night* readying the inventory." As she said "night," she squeezed Tana's arm and raised her eyebrows in question.

Tana nodded. She'd listen for the soft scratching at their gate tonight. A trusted servant would be sent to collect the pouch of sapphires and Tana's report. Or Kalyan might come himself. She could hope, couldn't she?

"The governor's wife will entertain the royal ladies at the fort while Alwar and the prince are hunting today, so Mother decreed we spend the afternoon beautifying ourselves." Hima giggled. "Might as well put gold leaf on a heifer's ears and call it a gazelle,

I told her. When the trays of jewels come out, the customers don't care about me."

"You look very elegant," Tana assured her. Hima's dark hair was freshly washed, her blunt fingers were manicured, and the nails were painted a coral color. To match her gold bangles, metallic embroidery banded her short blouse and peach-colored dress wrap.

"It's sweet of you to say so," Hima demurred, but she sounded pleased by the compliment. "This way. Mother's in a bathing pool." At her signal, a servant admitted them past the folding privacy screens. Several women lounged in and around the pool, while maids scrubbed their skin or washed their hair. Herbs burned in a brass bowl. The pungent smoke drifted out from under the pavilion's raised roof and into the open air. Hima raised her voice to carry over the chatter. "Here's your sandalwood paste, Mother, and, look, I found Tana outside."

"Peace to you, Ma Bansari," Tana said.

"Peace, Tana." Wrapped in a linen bath sheet, Hima's mother lifted her head from the massage pad and smiled at Tana. Her maid paused for the greeting, then resumed rubbing the woman's bare brown shoulders. The scent of almond oil mixed with the herbs.

One of the younger girls jumped up, sleek as a porpoise, and shook back her wet hair. "Is Diribani with you?"

"No, Mina-ji. She was here earlier," Tana said. "I just came for water; I can't stay."

"Surely you can spare a few moments to visit?" Ma Bansari said. "Hima's maid will tend to you."

Before Tana could protest, gentle hands had stripped her of the silver pitcher and her shabby clothing. Like an errant ewe, she was herded into the pool. Cool water touched her skin, refreshing as mint. The maid scrubbed her back and washed her hair while Tana sat on the steps and let the other women's voices flow around her ears. Hunger and worry and the day's strangeness made a barrier she couldn't climb to make polite conversation. She couldn't tell Diribani's story. It was too unbelievable, until they could see the flowers and jewels for themselves.

Graciously, Hima and her mother didn't comment on her silence. They seemed to expect only that Tana enjoy the maid's expert care.

Lost in a cloud of comfort, Tana waved her farewells when the party left. She put on her old red dress wrap and thanked Hima's maid, who had filled the silver pitcher with fresh water. Silent-footed, the remaining servants packed up the folding screens, the ladies' cosmetics, wet bath sheets, and massage pads, leftover twigs, and herb-burning tray, and departed.

No beggar women in sight. Disappointment mixed with a sneaking sense of relief that Tana had avoided Naghali-ji's judgment on her soul. Diribani's gift would protect their family from ruin; humility was the safest course for a less worthy stepsister.

Aware once more of gnawing hunger, Tana picked up the pitcher. "Home, I suppose," she said aloud. She had thought herself alone in the pavilion until a low voice answered.

"Will you drink?"

"What?" Tana gaped as a tall woman stepped from the shadow of a pillar. Of middle years, she was taller than most men, with handsome dark features and midnight hair knotted at the neck. Next to this impressive personage, Tana felt more insignificant than usual, even if her hair was clean and smelled like sandalwood. She clutched the silver pitcher to her chest. "Why are you asking me?" she squeaked.

The woman sat on the edge of a raised basin. "Will you drink?" she repeated, and dipped her hand in the water.

"No, my lady," Tana protested. A collar of carved jade beads decorated the moss-green silk robe. The stranger's black skin was flawless, her bearing regal. She must be one of the princesses traveling with Prince Zahid, although Tana had thought him her own age and still unmarried. An aunt, perhaps, or an elder sister.

Tana struggled to meet the penetrating gaze. Was it a language problem, and did the woman want a drink herself? She spoke slowly and clearly. "Where are the maids attending you, my lady? I'd serve you"—she hefted the pitcher—"but, for all it's so pretty, this pitcher drips. It would streak that gorgeous silk, and they'd cut off my hand. If Prince Zahid didn't have me killed anyway, for presuming to look at you." Didn't the prince's relatives usually go veiled in public? Unless it was only men who weren't supposed to see their faces, and commoner girls didn't matter.

"Plainspoken, aren't you?" The woman's voice was slow and smooth. Tana's language slipped from the woman's tongue in languid syllables, as if it had been invented for her to speak. "Such candor deserves a gift. What is your soul's desire, my daughter?"

It was too much. The question struck Tana as absurd, and once she started laughing, she couldn't stop. She had to put down the pitcher and lean against a pillar or she would have toppled, fully dressed, back into the bathing pool. The sobbing breaths made her ribs ache. "My desire?" she choked out. "I'm nobody. Why would a foreign princess care about my soul's desire?" Besides, it didn't matter what she wanted. Diribani's jewels would pay for the greatest wish of Tana's heart: to protect her family.

The stranger smiled, displaying sharp white teeth. She gestured at Tana. "Come."

As helpless as a leashed dog, Tana obeyed the command. The woman laid her hand on Tana's hair. "I see a capable nature," the mellifluous voice said. The words seemed to come from the depths of the earth, where rock flowed like water. A strong thumb pressed Tana's forehead between the eyebrows. "A warrior spirit and loyal heart, worthy of reward."

The words reverberated throughout the pavilion. Waves of sound engulfed Tana, thrumming from her head to her feet. Her skull felt assaulted by the noise. Like a swimmer battered by surf, she tumbled over and over inside her own body. Noise overwhelmed her; she would drown in it.

And then it stopped. Tana opened her eyes and blinked in the dimness, surprised to find herself still standing, her hands pressed over her ears. Her head rang. The stranger had vanished.

The holy ones don't wait about for us to show an interest, Ma Hiral had said. Slowly, Tana's knees buckled. She crouched, drumming her hands against her skull, hard slaps meant to hurt. Belated awareness sickened her. The goddess had invited Tana to drink, and she had—oh, so stupid, so thoughtless—she had refused! And not even politely. She had said insulting things, called Naghali-ji a foreigner and a liar, implied the goddess didn't care about her followers. What kind of punishment did such blasphemy deserve?

The noise had shaken all Tana's lies from their places of concealment and exposed her soul as a poor, shriveled thing. Born plain of feature, unlikely to inspire a man's desire, but ambitious for worldly gain—Tana could never be content with her fate. Deep down, she had wanted what Diribani had: compassion, beauty, a divine regard blessing her, too. The goddess had known it. Thus was jealousy added to the toll of Tana's sins.

Like diamond-tipped drills, regrets pierced her heart. She had failed the test by refusing the goddess's request. She had wasted this life, sought her reckoning too soon, and now it would end. Diribani would be so disappointed, and Tana's mother ... Would Ma Hiral even be surprised that her headstrong daughter had insulted Naghali-ji? Maybe one of the twelve would have pity and send her back as an ox, to walk in endless circles, driving an oil press or sugarcane crusher. At least then she'd be useful to someone and no danger to herself.

Dully, Tana picked up the pitcher. Her mother and Diribani were waiting for the drinking water. She could only hope the goddess's mercy extended to keeping the viper from smiting Tana until after she had said good-bye to her family.

CHAPTER SEVEN

Diribani

TRUMPET notes floated in the air. *Ta-ra-rah, ta-ra-ra-lay.* Like a twig poked into a termite nest, the noise stirred Gurath's merchant quarter into a frenzy. Diribani heard it from her seat on the floor, where she braided flowers into garlands and waited for Tana to return. Up and down the street, shutters banged. Voices called; pushcarts creaked and rattled over packed dirt. She moved closer to the door and tugged at the curtain until she could peek out. She didn't expect anything interesting to happen in the empty courtyard, but it made her feel closer to the activity outside.

"Eyo, Mina Diribani, Mina Tana!" The neighbor boy climbed out of his second-floor window. Agile as a lizard, he hung briefly by his hands, then dropped from the sill to run along their shared wall. "Do you hear the trumpets? Come see, come see!"

Motioning Diribani to keep out of view, her stepmother ventured into the courtyard. "What is it, Indu?"

"Prince Zahid and Governor Alwar, back from the hunt. They're coming this way." Indu sighted along an imaginary barrel. "Maybe the prince shot a tiger!"

Ma Hiral made the sign to avert careless words. "By Sister Bhagiya's chariot, let us hope not! Eating animal flesh is indecent enough, but to kill a sacred beast for pride only? Those white-coats will have much to answer for in their next lives."

"But what if the tiger was a man-eater?" Indu straddled the wall facing the street. Mud-brick smudges joined the assortment of stripes and smears that masked the original color of his drawstring pants. His bare feet kicked the bricks. "Wouldn't Bhagiya-ji agree that shooting a man-eater before it killed more people was a worthy deed?"

Ma Hiral snorted. "That's a question for the priests at the temple grove, not for this ignorant woman."

"I'd like to see a tiger. Even a dead one," Indu said, so plaintively that Diribani chuckled.

"Grandson!" Fanning herself with the end of her blue dress wrap, a gray-haired woman leaned out the window through which Indu had exited. "Where'd that boy— Oh, peace, Hiral-ji." Then, more sternly, "Indu, your mother told you to go upstairs. Did you not hear her?"

Indu folded his hands. "Nama-ji, she said she didn't want to see my face within two floors of the milk fudge, and that I should meditate on the sin of gluttony until Sister Payoja granted her prayers and blessed me with some manners."

"Then why do I find you outside bothering this lady with your squirrel chatter?"

Diribani watched as the boy turned big brown eyes on her stepmother. Ma Hiral came to his rescue, as Diribani had known she would.

"No bother," she said. "In fact, the boy offered to describe the prince's party for us. Better he watches safely off the street, eh?"

"I'll tell you everything!" Indu promised. He shaded his eyes with his hand. "War elephants at Lotus Gate! Two lines of them, with shiny armor. The men on their backs carry spears."

"Brother Akshath shield us!" his grandmother exclaimed, but Diribani noticed that she had rested a hip on the windowsill and settled in to listen. "On no account are you to leave that spot, except to return to this room. Is that clear, grandson?"

"Yes, Nama-ji." Indu wriggled with excitement. "There are squads of soldiers, the governor's and the prince's both, by the flags. Next are the horsemen, the hunting cheetahs and their minders, pack camels, ranks of riflemen, and more soldiers on foot."

Sitting inside, the garlands forgotten in her lap, Diribani listened as Indu described the procession winding through their neighborhood. She heard the sounds: the tramp of feet, the musical notes of horns and the louder trumpeting of elephants, people cheering, and pushcart vendors shouting their wares.

Dealers in luxury goods like jewels and fine fabrics received customers at the market tents or were invited to call on their patrons with a selection of merchandise. A festive occasion like the return of a royal hunting party would attract a different class of vendor, selling treats or colorful trinkets to the crowd gathered to enjoy the free spectacle. On any other afternoon, Diribani would have been eager to see it for herself. Her stepmother's concern had affected her more than she wanted to admit. It seemed . . . fitting to wait for Tana. Her sister would help Diribani steer a course between Ma Hiral's warnings and the certainty Diribani felt in her heart that Naghali-ji meant her largesse to be shared.

And then, mixed with the trumpets and the shouts of "charms for luck" and "fine ripe melons," came the sound of a woman screaming.

The wild shrieks brought Diribani to her feet, fists clenched around a finished garland. Not Tana, please the goddess!

"What happened?" Ma Hiral cried, as if she, too, was remembering that her daughter had not yet returned.

"I can't see." Teetering on the balls of his feet, Indu leaned out over the street.

"Grandson!" his grandmother called.

"Oh. Don't worry. It's only a white-coat, not one of our girls, arguing with a soldier." Indu dropped down to sit on his haunches. "I hope it's Gulrang," he said. "She kicked a lucky frog I was chasing at the well yesterday, when I almost had it! Maybe the soldier will give her a bloody nose."

"Indu," the two older women chorused in scolding voices, but the look they exchanged held relief.

Diribani didn't share their feeling. The cries continued, sharper and more frantic. Even if it was a white-coat who needed help—especially Gulrang—this seemed a clear test of faith. Thanks to the goddess, Diribani had the means to bribe any man short of Emperor Minaz himself into letting go of an unwilling girl. Did she have the courage to brave the crowd for a person who might despise her?

What if it had been Tana? Or, if their situations were reversed, would Tana sit idle while another girl suffered?

The instant Diribani's mind posed the question, her body answered it. Fingers grabbed a handful of rubies to go with the garland she still held; feet carried her at a run out the door, across the courtyard, and through the gate. Like their house naga after a rat,

Diribani tracked the scent of fear through the crowded streets. She ducked around pushcarts and between clumps of townsfolk, not caring that Ma Hiral chased her.

With quiet determination, Diribani elbowed her way through a wall of white-coats. Servant-quality coats made of inferior fabric, these were patched and stained and trimmed with colored ribbons. Young women screamed insults, tears of rage streaking their faces. A group of boys had locked arms to keep the girls away from the squad marching past. In the middle of the soldiers, a spitting, howling Gulrang was being passed from hand to hand. Each man in turn smacked a kiss on her lips or took a punch in the face, depending on whether the servant girl had managed to jerk her wrists free. The whole company, even those men she hit, treated her distress as a great jest. Each time her flailing fists connected with flesh, they roared with laughter.

Diribani ducked under a white sleeve and ran to the soldier with the most gold trim on his coat. She sketched a bow and walked beside him, offering the garland to show her goodwill. When he reached out, she dropped the uncut rubies into his palm. Then she gestured at Gulrang and folded her hands respectfully, begging with her eyes that he end the shameful treatment and return the girl to her friends.

Instead, the man stepped on the garland and scattered the gemstones onto the ground. A heavy hand slapped Diribani's cheek. "Cow," he said loudly. "Flowers and rocks don't buy the emperor's men."

Diribani stifled a cry of pain. Face throbbing, she backed into the crowd. The onlookers were packed so tightly that she couldn't escape. She could only watch as the ranks of soldiers passed. Their interest felt like beetles crawling over her skin.

Townsfolk who hadn't protested the white-coat girl's treatment by another Believer muttered angrily at the disrespect shown Diribani. Commoners weren't allowed to carry weapons, but dung pats had been known to stain white coats. In the wake of the procession's elephants, horses, and camels, steaming lumps of fresh ammunition littered the road.

Gulrang had stopped fighting. Arms and legs and neck limp, she let herself be passed from man to man. Closed eyes didn't contain the tears that trickled from under her lids.

The last soldier in that row might have tired of the game, or noticed how the mood of the crowd had changed. He shoved the weeping Gulrang at Diribani. "Take her. If she covered her face like a decent woman, she wouldn't be mistaken for a slut."

Diribani kept her mouth closed, though she wanted to answer. How like a white-coat, to blame a woman for his bad behavior.

"Sh, shh." Ma Hiral had found them. One arm held Diribani; the other wrapped around Gulrang's waist and supported her like another daughter.

A soldier in a subsequent row, more observant or just more curious than his fellows, picked up one of the rubies his leader had rejected. His eyes widened. After a sharp sideways glance at Diribani, the man closed his fingers around the prize and marched on, eyes straight ahead.

Many other people had also witnessed the exchange between Diribani and Gold-trim. More than a few knew who she was, and who her father had been. "Javerikh's daughter," one man said to another. "You remember, the gem dealer." Her name was whispered from ear to ear. A hush followed the whispers. The last few rows of soldiers hastened their steps to get through the crowd of too-quiet people. Though Tenth Province was far from the restless border, the quality of silence in the merchant quarter had become charged with danger, like the pause between the flash of Grandfather Chelok's lightning lance and the bone-rattling roar of thunder. A large gap opened between the marching men and the oxcarts that followed, laden with spoils of the hunt.

An indigo-stained dyer was the first to run into the empty stretch of street. His blue hands scrabbled in mud packed hard by marching feet. A brawny laborer followed him, and then a white-coat servant girl. Her cry of discovery, quickly muffled, drew other people. Vendors abandoned their pushcarts; porters dropped crates and bales. Beggar children squirmed into the fray, skinny elbows and knees jabbing for position.

The approaching oxcart drivers cracked their whips in warning, but the townsfolk refused to yield the way. None wanted to lose the chance of finding whatever the jeweler's daughter had offered the soldier. Rumors crackled like flame up and down the street. More people came, pushing and shoving, even if they didn't know exactly what they were seeking. As the street filled with struggling bodies, the prince's procession ground to a halt.

Her cheek aching, Diribani held tightly to her stepmother and Gulrang. The three of them were almost trampled before they found shelter between the handles of a pushcart full of yellow melons. The ripe scent filled Diribani's head as she watched the crowd's mood change from hope to something darker.

In the middle of the street, a fat man accused another of stepping on his hand, and was kicked in the knee for his trouble. His two friends, both white-coats, jumped on the kicker, and all three disappeared under a pile of cursing, shouting men.

By the time the first of the overseers had worked his way from behind the oxcarts to find out what was blocking the procession, the prince's company of soldiers had returned. They waded into the crowd, knocking quarrelers apart with the flats of their swords. Howls of anger turned to cries of pain. The governor's man whistled for reinforcements.

Pinched between two groups of armed men, the townsfolk were herded out of the street and up against the building walls. Like swimmers emerging from deep water, they shook their heads, adjusted torn clothing, complained to their neighbors about the authorities' rough treatment. The drivers' whips cracked again. The oxcarts began to roll.

Diribani shuddered with relief. Next to her, she heard Gulrang's hard, fast breathing.

"We are going home this instant," Ma Hiral said.

Diribani nodded agreement. She draped the free end of her dress wrap over her face to hide the bruise forming. Her skin felt stretched and hot, her insides hollow. Crabwise, she edged out from between the pushcart's handles and helped Ma Hiral to do the same.

"That's her, in the pink dress," a voice shouted. "That's the one you want, the troublemaker who started the riot."

Before the voice finished speaking, Gulrang had ducked under the cart. On hands and knees, the servant girl crawled out of sight. With people pressing all around them, Diribani and Ma Hiral were trapped against the cart's wooden sides. Diribani glanced over her shoulder, but the melons were piled too high for them to climb over the cart and escape.

"This girl?" The closest overseer fingered his coat's yellow ties. Doubtfully, he eyed Diribani down the length of his long nose.

"She's a respectable merchant's daughter," Ma Hiral shrilled. "Who accuses her?"

"I do." Gold-trim pushed forward, his face flushed with anger. Clumps of mud—and worse, judging from the smell of fresh dung that accompanied him—spotted his coat. Diribani jerked her head back, but she couldn't evade the hand that pushed her makeshift veil aside. "See?" Roughly, the soldier grabbed her chin and turned her head so the governor's man could view her battered face. "Marked the slut myself."

"And I cry justice for it," Ma Hiral quavered, while Diribani bit her tongue so she wouldn't be tempted to answer the soldier's insult. "For shame, striking a girl for the crime of offering flowers."

"You hit her for that?" The governor's man didn't sound happy.

Ma Hiral pressed her advantage. "Her father called on the fort many a time; ask Governor Alwar or his lady wife. There wasn't a more respected merchant in Gurath than Trader Javerikh."

"Javerikh the gem dealer? That Javerikh?" The overseer sounded even less enthusiastic about pursuing the matter. "Listen, fellow," he told Gold-trim, "whatever insult you think was offered, the girl will be wearing that bruise for days. How about we fine her family the cost of laundering your coat, and you drop your claim against her."

"Her father's a jeweler?" Diribani's accuser said. "Well, well. So, Mina, what were those little rocks, then?"

The man's oily politeness frightened Diribani more than his bluster had. Like a flock of crows, all Ma Hiral's warnings had descended on her shoulders to peck at her ears. She steeled herself to lower her eyes modestly and keep her mouth shut.

"Rocks?" the overseer said. "What's he talking about?"

"I'm sure I don't know, sir," Ma Hiral said.

The soldier grunted. "Doesn't the little cow speak?"

"Careful, man!" the local white-coat warned. "This is Gurath, not Fanjandibad."

"Indeed," a new voice said. Not loudly, but with an unmistakable edge of command.

After an instant of shocked surprise, the people surrounding the pushcart drew back. As one, townsfolk dropped to their knees. A space opened around the disputants so that two men on horseback could approach.

One glance told Diribani that the worst had happened. She, too, knelt in the dirt, tugging Ma Hiral with her. She had seen Governor Alwar once before, at a distance. Up close, the cruel line of his mouth seemed even more pronounced.

His companion was much younger, a man close to Diribani's age, and different in every possible way from Gurath's governor. Lean where the older man was stocky, his expression as curious as Alwar's was disdainful, he wore dusty riding clothes in contrast to the governor's immaculate white coat and trousers. No question that this was Prince Zahid. Tousled black hair curled out from under a steel helmet chased with gold. The horse he rode, a dark bay with prancing hooves, was finer even than Jasmine. A cavalry officer's shield, mace, and bow hung from a saddle worked with gold thread. Jewels ornamented the horse's headstall, crowned by a ruby the size of an apricot.

It occurred to Diribani that Tana would have noticed the ruby first. She peeked out from under her lashes, studying the hawklike features of the one man who could save her from Governor Alwar.

"Easy, Dilawar, my brave one." The prince patted his horse's neck. "Captain Tashrif. Twenty-four hours in Gurath, and we're slaying the local ladies already?"

"Sire." Gold-trim bowed deeply, his face a mask. "She incited these people to riot."

"How's that?" the governor said sharply. One hand touched the hilt of the long sword that hung from his saddle.

"Your Excellency. Your Highness." Ma Hiral prostrated herself on the ground. "It's all a wretched mistake. We're respectable folk. I am a widow and this girl is the support of my old age. Please don't punish her."

"No one shall be judged without a fair hearing," the prince reassured the older woman. "Speak, maiden, in the emperor's name. How do you respond to Captain Tashrif's accusation?"

At the familiar formula, approval rumbled through the crowd. Expectant faces turned toward them as people made themselves comfortable. The emperor's justice could be dispensed anywhere, from his Hall of Public Audience in Lomkha to the deck of a ship at sea. Today, apparently, it pleased his younger son and representative to hear petitioners in the middle of the street.

As before, when Diribani had heard Gulrang screaming, not knowing who it was but certain of the task demanded of her, her body responded before her mind caught up with its intent. She laced her hands open in her lap and raised her chin so the prince could see her face clearly. When she met his inquiring gaze, a thrill chased along her spine. Her back straightened.

"My name is Diribani, sire," she said, tasting marigolds and jasmine with the words. "I only wanted to persuade the captain to let another girl go free from his men's rough treatment. I throw myself on Your Highness's mercy for the trouble that followed."

"Word of God!" the prince exclaimed softly. The crowd's excited buzzing drowned the governor's astonished curse.

Diribani scooped up the flowers and jewels she had just spoken. The prince urged his horse closer and leaned from the saddle to accept them. Thin, strong fingers plucked the offering from her hands, leaving her briefly dizzy, as if he had relieved her of a greater burden.

She shook her head, denying the fanciful thought. Hunger or fear was a more likely cause for the strange moment of light-headedness. This day was nothing like any other she had known.

Ma Hiral's wailing was lost in the cries of wonder that filtered through the crowd as those in front told their neighbors what had happened. Steel rang, soldiers drawing swords from sheaths. The prince motioned his men to keep their places, and the governor followed suit.

Reluctantly, Diribani thought, glancing over in time to see an avaricious light gleam in the governor's eyes. A great calm descended, stilling her wild thoughts. She must be prepared to meet the destiny Naghali-ji had assigned her. Wisdom. Good fortune. Death.

"What foul sorcery is this?" Alwar demanded, though he licked his lips when the prince handed him Diribani's offering. The governor dropped the flowers into the street. The gemstones he rolled in his fleshy hand.

"No sorcery, sire." Diribani continued to address the emperor's son. Ma Hiral had been right about the governor; Prince Zahid was the man she needed to convince. "The goddess Naghali-ji blessed me earlier, at the well."

The crowd murmured again, some touching their foreheads to

the ground in reverence. A few white-coats muttered "witch," but not loudly, outnumbered as they were by worshipers of the twelve.

"Did she?" The prince's eyes lingered on Diribani's features, as if he found them as pleasing as she found his. He had kept back a branch of jasmine. He sniffed it thoughtfully before tucking the spray of flowers into his horse's headstall.

"The girl's a menace to public safety, Your Highness," Governor Alwar interjected. "We'd be putting down riots whenever she showed her face in the street." His fist closed around the jewels. "I'll take charge of securing her, lest she break the emperor's peace again in this wanton fashion."

"Please, no, Your Highness," Ma Hiral sobbed. "Don't let him take her!"

"Your mother?" Zahid asked Diribani.

After she had spoken with a goddess, how could a mere prince awe her? Diribani breathed deeply. "My stepmother, sire. Ma Hiral has treated me like her own daughter."

The royal eyebrows lifted in appraisal of the lotuses and lilies, diamonds and emeralds that sprinkled Diribani's pink lap. "Are there more of you at home?" the prince asked. "Other daughters blessed by this Gurath divinity?"

"No, sire," Diribani said, but then she hesitated. "At least," she added, needing to be absolutely truthful with him, "Tana hasn't come home yet, so we don't know—"

"Yes, Your Highness," hissed a familiar voice beside her. "The goddess has touched me also."

CHAPTER EIGHT

Tana

SNAKE!" Governor Alwar wheezed. "Kill it."

A tan-and-gold shape slithered in front of the prince's horse, which neighed and pawed the air. "Steady, Dilawar." Zahid turned the bay in a tight circle. "It's only a ratter, no danger to you." He spoke more to reassure the people nearby, Tana thought, than his horse, which had already responded to Zahid's calm hands on the reins.

A white-coat who wasn't afraid of snakes? Tana's opinion of the young man climbed. She knelt between her mother and Diribani. Setting down her full pitcher, she touched the back of her fingers gently to her sister's bruised cheek. Diribani's face was full of amazement and curiosity, but no fear. Tana tucked the memory of her sister's expression away in her heart. She knew she would cherish it in days to come. Assuming, of course, she lived past sunset. At the moment, it didn't seem likely.

"Tana." Her mother clutched her arm. "My child, what has happened?"

She had no answer her mother would want to hear, so she kept silent.

The snake had disappeared between the buildings. The bay horse snorted, eyeing Tana with equine distrust. She would not have blamed Dilawar's rider for looking at her the same way.

Again, the prince surprised her. He surveyed Tana with the same impartial expression he had shown Diribani before she spoke flowers. Though Tana didn't sense the same heat his eyes had held for her beautiful sister, his voice was courteous. "Will you tell us your story, Mina?"

Tana wondered how many miracles an emperor's son witnessed on a daily basis. Perhaps they were common at court? Thank the twelve, it seemed that reason, not fear, governed Prince Zahid. Not like Alwar—the governor's face had turned as white as cheese when the ratter appeared.

Tana gathered herself to answer. "My name is Tana, sire," she said. She felt a teasing sensation, as if grains of puffed rice were popping a breath away from her lips. "I also met Naghali-ji at the sacred well outside of town." As she spoke, one, two, three tiny spotted frogs winked into life and leaped away from her. A large toad followed more sedately.

One of the frogs landed on Diribani's wrist. It posed there, skin brilliant, like an enameled charm, before springing off. Diribani laughed. "Oh, Tana!"

"Lucky frogs!" Intent on the unexpected prize, a ragged child pounced. He missed. Turning to Tana, the boy cupped grimy hands to make a begging bowl. "Please, Mina-ji, say one for me."

"Over here, Mina Tana! May I have one?"

An overseer's child tugged on his nurse's coat. "Lucky frog! Mine!"

The prince chuckled. His amusement and the children's enthusiasm were nothing like the reaction Tana had expected. She couldn't cry—she was too parched with dread for that—but she found she could smile. She shook her head. "The creatures appear as the goddess wills, not I," she explained. Again she sensed the not-quite-feeling as her words took shape, like a flying spark that turns to ash when you try to catch it between your fingers. Too quickly for the eye to register, *something* crossed the distance between emptiness and life.

The goddess's will, Tana supposed, sending her messengers to earth. This one was a blind snake. Small and pink-skinned like an earthworm, defenseless against the hot afternoon sun, it nudged her leg, seeking the safety of its burrow.

"Ch-ch-ch." Waving a broad leaf, the melon vendor leaned around Tana. He coaxed the snake onto the leaf and rolled it into a protective tube. "What?" he said to the people drawing back. "Blind snakes eat ants. Can't have too many of these little fellows in a melon patch, I tell you, bounty or no bounty."

Only the white-coats reacted the way Tana had feared since she discovered what Naghali-ji had done to her.

A vein pulsed in the governor's thick neck. "Kill the witch and every one of her foul brood!" he croaked. "The dirt-eaters' cursed snakes won't pollute Tenth Province!"

Soldiers advanced, swords raised high, but the prince stopped them with a curt gesture. "My father would be most displeased to hear that civil authorities had interfered with a local religious matter. We absolutely forbid that either of these two young women be harmed."

"As you will, Your Highness." The governor accepted the

rebuke with a show of outward humility. His horse tossed its head, as if a hand had jerked its reins.

Prince Zahid spoke gravely to Ma Hiral. "It seems you and Gurath have been twice blessed in Mina Tana and Mina Diribani."

Diribani's hand found Tana's and squeezed in reassurance. Tana couldn't understand it. The prince's respect sounded sincere. But he was a Believer! A flesh-eater! Hadn't she seen the oxcarts filled with hunting trophies, the corpses of antelope and lion, pheasant and duck and deer? According to Alwar's proclamations, their religion despised snakes. How could Prince Zahid be so accepting of *both* Naghali-ji's miracles?

The prince glanced at the stone-faced official beside him. "However, His Excellency has identified a problem," he continued. "People live uneasily with wonders in their midst. I'm afraid, dear ladies, that you cannot remain in Gurath."

Dismayed, Diribani and Tana stared at each other, then protested in unison.

"But, sire—"

"Please, Your Highness—"

A pink peony and two rough diamonds pelted a snake's bright-green head. The grass viper hissed.

Along with everyone else, Tana held very still, watching the poisonous snake. The grass viper coiled upon itself, tail twitching in warning.

It had not occurred to Tana that the goddess's gift might include the venomous nagas. She touched her lips, but felt no burning or other sign that this one's poison had touched her. Tana was painfully aware that the crowded street offered too many targets for an agitated viper. A sea of frightened faces surrounded her. Her mother's

face held despair; the governor's, loathing; the prince's, a wary alertness. Only Diribani seemed confident that Tana would deal with the danger she had brought into their midst.

Hardly daring to breathe, Tana reached for the silver pitcher. She lifted it behind her back and turned it upside down, trying not to think about the high price she had paid for the water draining onto the ground. The snake turned slowly as it looked for a way out. When the creature faced away from her, Tana brought the pitcher swiftly down. Her fingers shook as she tamped the silver rim into the dirt, trapping the snake inside.

"Rather a mixed blessing," Prince Zahid observed.

Afraid to reply and let loose a cobra or a krait, Tana folded her hands over the trapped viper. She couldn't contain her worry as easily. Where would she and Diribani go if the prince cast them from their home? The breath whistled out of her throat, but to her relief, nothing left her lips but air. She had to utter words, it seemed, in order to bring forth frogs and toads and serpents.

"An unusual situation, but my duty is clear." The prince studied the kneeling girls. A glint of humor flashed in his eyes, though his voice remained serious. "Our esteemed governor prefers that Mina Diribani not disturb the serenity of Tenth Province, so she shall accompany our party to Eighteenth Province. As a guest of the crown, she may reside at the ladies' court in Fanjandibad in all honor and comfort."

"Fanjandibad!" Diribani clasped her hands together, her expression brightening.

Tana, too, dared to relax. She remembered that Ba Javerikh had spoken of the painters' workshop there. If anything could reconcile Diribani to leaving her home, the prospect of studying with master artists would tempt her far more than life in a palace. After the near-riot Tana had witnessed, she had to agree with the prince. In Gurath, Diribani might not be safe from her neighbors, let alone Tenth Province's governor.

A muscle moved in Governor Alwar's jaw. Because the royal command had prevented him from killing the snake girl, or from keeping the girl who spoke diamonds? When he eyed the bejeweled ground around Diribani, ignoring the snake trapped under the silver pitcher, Tana had her answer. Greed ruled the man. Alwar must be furious that he had made too much of Diribani's power to cause unrest. His hasty reaction had given the prince an excuse to carry off a walking jewel mine. "The emperor's justice is renowned" was all he said aloud.

The prince's next words confirmed Tana's respect for both his intelligence and his character. "Fanjandibad does not covet Gurath's blessing," he said. "The largest share of Mina Diribani's jewels shall be returned to glorify Tenth Province, under His Excellency's able administration. Minus a sum for the construction of a habitation for her sister, by this sacred well. Some distance from town, is it?" At Tana's nod, he continued. "Mina Tana shall make her abode there, where any poisonous snakes may be released in the wild lands without endangering the emperor's subjects in Gurath."

"An admirable solution, Your Highness," Governor Alwar said, immediately restored to good humor.

Although she understood the prince's reasoning, Tana didn't quite share the governor's satisfaction at the result. Oh, she understood why she couldn't go to Fanjandibad. The royal ladies would love Diribani, but they'd hardly want a snake girl in their court. It was Tana's misfortune that her relocation also dashed the future she had dared to imagine earlier. If she couldn't set foot in the marketplace, how could she provide for her family through the trade she knew best? The royal command had spared her life, but, for everyone's safety, Tana would have to spend it in the countryside. She had no illusion about what Alwar's soldiers would do if they caught her in town once Zahid and his entourage had gone. Without taking her life, the local white-coats could make it very unpleasant. At least the farmers should be pleased, she thought with some bitterness. If left alone, the nagas would hunt rodents and pests in their fields. Or, if people preferred to collect Alwar's bounty (which the prince hadn't mentioned stopping), they could trap her snakes and turn them in. . . .

Her snakes?

Tana caught herself. *Naghali-ji*'s snakes. Tana's punishment, and Tana's penance, was that she never speak again without fearing what might follow.

"Ma Hiral." The prince was speaking again. "My sister, Ruqayya, and her ladies at the fort will outfit Mina Diribani for the journey. Will you also accompany us to Fanjandibad?"

Tana's mother twisted her hands together, turning from Diribani to Tana. Diribani looked uncertain as she realized she might be parted from her entire family. Tana tried to disguise her own dismay with encouraging gestures. Diribani *must* go, and of course Ma Hiral would love to visit a palace. It didn't matter how lonely Tana would be, all by herself at the well. How long would it be, anyway, before one of the snakes bit her and she died in agony? If her mother left with Diribani, at least Tana would have the consolation of knowing they were both safe.

Ma Hiral's concerned expression smoothed out. "Long journeys are hard on old bones," she said. "If it would not displease Your

Highness for this lowly one to remain at home, I will entrust Diribani most gladly to the royal family's care."

"Then we are finished here," the prince said. "Captain Tashrif, your charge against Mina Diribani is dismissed. Gather your men."

"Sire."

Tana embraced Diribani. She could not cry; she could only squeeze her sister's waist and press her face into the pink-draped shoulder.

"Oh, Tana." Diribani sniffed. "Your hair smells like sandalwood!" She held Tana's elbows and blinked at her with tear-misted eyes. "You'll write, won't you?" She caught a yellow rose and two rubies almost absently and handed them to her stepmother. "These gifts will pass. Don't I sound like Ma Hiral? We won't be apart forever. I'll visit when the prince comes next to Gurath. You'll return, won't you, sire?" she asked the prince.

He held her gaze. "Yes, Mina Diribani."

Looking from the prince's grave face to Diribani's affectionate one gave Tana the same sensation she felt when speaking snakes: that something vital had passed just beyond her reach.

A white-coat helped Diribani into the sedan chair that had appeared for her. The prince urged his horse away; the chair-bearers followed. Diribani twisted in the chair to wave and blow kisses punctuated with ashoka blossoms. "Good-bye, dear Tana," she called. "Good-bye, Ma Hiral. The twelve keep you!"

Tana and her mother returned Diribani's waves and blessings until the chair turned a corner and she was lost to them.

"Move along, move along." The governor's men dispersed the crowd. Alwar had stayed to supervise the collection of every last jewel dropped during the proceedings. He ignored Tana and Ma

Hiral, as did his men. Like all the people resuming their afternoon activities, they gave the upended silver pitcher a wide berth. The melon vendor saluted Tana and took up his pushcart. Slowly, the street resumed its usual bustle, eddying around the two women and the trapped snake.

"Mina Tana."

The whisper distracted Tana from thinking about how much she would miss her sister. Indu squatted beside her, his eyes round with excitement. "I saw, from the wall. A snake came out of your mouth! I brought my naga basket and stick to take him out to the jungle, if you want. But, first, could you say a ratter for me? Our old one died, and we've got mice in the pantry."

Before Tana could answer, the boy's grandmother hurried up to them. "Don't pester Mina Tana," she said.

"But, Nama-ji"—Indu turned soulful brown eyes in her direction—"you said you'd had enough of picking little black turds out of the lentils!"

Tana couldn't help it. She snorted with laughter. Even her mother coughed behind her hand. At least with Indu, Tana didn't have to worry about what creature might accompany her words. He'd befriend any animal that slid, crawled, hopped, or flew. She spread her empty hands wide. "It's not my choice, Indu. Pray to Sister Naghali, not to me."

Heavy and cool, a tan-and-gold snake dropped into her outstretched hands. The way she'd been taught as a child, Tana closed her fingers behind the ratter's head and supported its muscular length with her other hand. The goddess must have a sense of humor. Or a mortal woman's weakness for Indu's charm.

"A champion naga!" Indu thumped his forked stick on the

ground. "Thanks, Mina Tana. Oh-Naghali-ji-we-are-ever-grateful-for-your-blessings," he added when his grandmother poked him in the ribs.

"Why don't you hand me that ratter?" the older woman suggested. "Hiral-ji and I will get him settled with a clean new home and some fresh water. And perhaps a cup of tea for these dusty throats, eh? If Mina Tana agrees, you may help with her other snake."

Ma Hiral frowned. "You'd let the child handle a grass viper?"

"His father made sure Indu got some training from the priests at the temple grove." Their white-haired neighbor took the house naga from Tana. "He'll be careful, and keep a safe distance. Won't you, grandson?"

"Oh, yes," Indu said.

"If you're sure." Still shaking her head, Tana's mother left with Indu's grandmother.

Tana watched closely as the boy readied his forked stick. In a series of practiced motions, he lifted the silver pitcher, trapped the snake's triangular head between the stick's two arms, and manipulated the hissing creature into his basket. "There." He tied the basket's lid with a string and hoisted it on the stick. "He'll be happier out of the street, I'll bet."

Tana smiled her thanks. Then she picked up the empty mud-rimmed pitcher and walked after Indu, toward Lotus Gate. Once again, they needed drinking water, and she was the only one left to fetch it from the well.

CHAPTER NINE

Diribani

A stout door and walls muffled the discussion taking place outside the carpet storeroom, but Diribani heard enough to know they were talking about her. The deeper voice sounded familiar. Hastily, she set a final stitch, knotted the pink thread, and tucked the needle back into the basket where she'd found it. She stood and shook out the creases in the long strip of fabric. Pleating the dress wrap around her waist, she threw the free end over her shoulder so it fell properly over her blouse. The thread's color wasn't a perfect match, but it was the best she'd found in the basket of sewing tools. And she'd rather wear a mended dress wrap than one that split along the ripped place and fell off her body.

She felt insignificant enough already, after spending a long night alone in the small room. Did her imprisonment show what the prince's promises were worth? As the hours wore on, she couldn't help wondering whether she had misplaced her trust.

With so much else to consider, sleep had eluded her. She had thought about making a pouch to carry the jewels. But, unlike the governor, she didn't wish to hoard Naghali-ji's bounty. Instead, she had decided to wait for the goddess to make her purpose clear. Meanwhile, she wove the flowers into a garland and draped it around her neck. Remembering how Tana was always sweeping and dusting, Diribani had tucked jewels into the sewing basket and rugs. Wouldn't the next maid who aired them get a surprise!

"That was *yesterday*," Prince Zahid was saying. "You mean she's been there all night? And this morning?"

"Absent other instructions," a woman's voice answered. "Surely you didn't intend me to house a criminal with the gentle-born ladies?"

"A criminal? Who told you that?" His indignation eased Diribani's worst fears.

"The governor's servants spouted some wild tales. A magician, we heard. She threw jewels or frogs or something, and started a riot. And"—more austerely—"they said you held court in the street. Was that wise, Zahid? Strictly speaking, Tenth Province reports to the crown in Lomkha, not Fanjandibad. Our elder brother will no doubt add this episode to his grievances against you."

"Let him. Besides, when you meet the girl, you'll understand why I couldn't leave her."

"There's always a reason," Diribani thought she heard, but the woman's words were covered by the scrape of knuckles against the door.

She stood as proudly as she could in a tiny closet stacked with carpets. Diribani hoped the smell of jasmine disguised her sweat.

The room was very warm, and a servant had only let her out to visit the latrine, not to bathe or eat. "Enter," she said. A lotus fell to the ground.

The door opened. Bright light streamed into her prison, haloing the two white-coated figures in the corridor.

"A thousand apologies, Mina Diribani," the prince said. "I fear my sister and I have given you a poor impression of our hospitality. It won't happen again."

Diribani pressed her hands together. "Good morning, Your Highness. My lady." Petals tickled her lips. When she read the chagrin written on the prince's face, Diribani's remaining uncertainty dispersed like fog. The promised trip to Fanjandibad hadn't just been a trick to get her off the street without fuss. If the most spiteful thing the governor's staff dared do was make her spend the night in a storeroom, she needn't worry. The prince had said it again: She was going with them. What was an uncomfortable few hours against the royal promise?

The woman clapped slim, dark hands. "Most impressive." She stooped and picked up several bell-shaped flowers with pink-and-white-striped petals. "Where did you get the tulips? I've only seen them in the mountains north of Lomkha."

"I wouldn't know, my lady," Diribani said. "That flower is new to me."

"God in heaven." The princess took a step back as small chunks of tigereye and lapis struck the rolled carpets.

"Their goddess doesn't abide by the usual rules." Mischief played around Zahid's mouth. "It's not a conjurer's trick, Ruqayya—it's a miracle."

The young woman's expression tightened with mistrust. As

Diribani's eyes adjusted to the light, she decided that the two of them weren't much older than she and Tana. Princess Ruqayya had the same aquiline nose and high cheekbones as her brother, but a more delicate chin. Like his, her dark hair curled over her temples; fine dark wisps escaped from the braided loops at her neck. She wore a flared coat of white brocade over tight-fitting trousers, a rope of pearls that hung to her knees, and wide jeweled cuffs on either wrist. A white scarf draped her shoulders; embroidered slippers graced high-arched feet.

"A miracle?" Ruqayya repeated. "What heresy is this, Zahid?"

"No heresy, to allow other faiths their mysteries." The prince's expression reminded Diribani of little Indu, the neighbor boy. He'd always been able to cajole older women—and younger ones, too—into seeing his point of view.

Ruqayya seemed less susceptible. "Don't quote Father at me," she snapped. "Even tolerance can be carried too far." When her brother just smiled at her, she put her fists on her hips. "Very well. I agree that you couldn't leave her in Alwar's hands. Or dear Brother Jauhar's. So she comes with us to Fanjandibad. What do they eat, Gurath saints?"

"I'm neither saint nor witch, my lady. Neither is my sister, Tana." Diribani's tone matched the princess's for sharpness. Ruqayya frowned; the prince looked amused. "I beg your pardon," Diribani continued more gently, over the peppery scent of marigolds. "I don't know much about your religion. But in our tradition, the gods grant miracles for their delight and our instruction. Naghali-ji gave me these jewels and flowers; Tana speaks lucky frogs and snakes. We don't yet know why. Utsav the crow god once blessed a king with donkey's ears, the better to hear his subjects' weeping."

"Snakes and donkey ears? Then I suppose I should be grateful for a tulip girl." The princess shot a look at her brother. "The other one stays in Gurath?"

"Tana will live by the sacred well," Diribani informed her. "His Highness suggested it."

"Good," the princess said.

"So you're ready to go?" Zahid asked Ruqayya, as if resuming the thread of an unfinished conversation.

"Yes. The First Camp wagons left early; they should be ready for our arrival." As if she couldn't help herself, Ruqayya scooped up a handful of the rough gems and flowers at Diribani's feet. She shook her head. "Five ratis, this diamond. Word of God."

"Of the goddess, my lady," Diribani said demurely.

The prince coughed.

Ruqayya's gaze fixed at a point above Diribani's head. "Guards," she mused aloud. "Two at least. They'll have to be women, and a maid. A locking box, a ledger, two clerks . . ."

"When she doesn't laugh at your jokes, you sometimes have to repeat them," the prince confided to Diribani. He grinned at his sister. Busy reassigning her staff, she didn't seem to notice. Diribani did, and her heart softened. How often, she wondered, did the prince let people see this playful aspect? In the street the day before, dispensing the emperor's justice, he had seemed far more serious.

"I heard it. Not funny." Ruqayya crooked her finger at Diribani. "Come along, flower girl. You can't ride in that pink thing."

"Er, ride, my lady?" Diribani followed the princess down the corridor. The prince fell in beside her, matching her steps easily. "Ride a horse?"

"It's not against your religion, is it?" Ruqayya said. "Our horses are treated very well, I assure you."

"No, it's just that I never learned."

The princess swept forward, shoulders back and spine straight. "Then we'll find you a place with the older ladies in an elephant howdah." She consulted her mental list, reminding Diribani of Tana. Neither was beautiful, but intelligence and humor animated their features and made mere prettiness dull. "You'll want a wash, and food?"

"Yes, thank you, my lady." Both were thoughtful of others, too. Practical, swift to action—how Tana would laugh if Diribani told her sister how much she had in common with a princess.

Ruqayya paused to wrap the white scarf around her hair and face until only her eyes showed. Privately, Diribani thought that if the princess didn't want to be recognized she should have tucked the pearl necklace into her coat. Or walked more slowly, less like the goddess Baghiya driving her tiger chariot across the sky.

The corridor led to a much grander one, with carved wooden doors opening at intervals on either side. Diribani recognized the garden courtyard at the end of it. The filigree gate beyond led to the fort's ladies' quarter. After the invading army had captured Gurath, the white-coats had walled off this part of the fort, bricking up all the exits but one. Now, according to Believer custom, the only men allowed past that gate were the governor and his sons.

The more public part of the fort was busy with servants, secretaries, and other officials. Folding tables had been set up in the garden, and a number of local merchants invited to display their goods for the visiting ladies. Diribani searched for Trader Nikhat's family, but didn't see Hima or Ma Bansari among the vendors. Fountains splashed musically; the air smelled of flowers and ferns.

Unlike his sister, the prince had no veil to hide his expression. His stern look was back. Between the two of them, Diribani felt small and shabby in her mended dress wrap. Then she glanced over her shoulder at the striped flowers—tulips—dotting the corridor they had left. The usual rules, indeed. She lifted her chin.

"My lady." A veiled woman bowed to Ruqayya. "Lady Yisha's compliments, and might she inquire about the order of travel this afternoon?"

"Sire." A soldier snapped to attention at the prince's elbow.

As her companions were drawn into conversation, Diribani composed herself to wait without fidgeting. She listened to the fountains and admired the tall vases and artistic plantings. She wondered whether the fort baths were as grand as rumored, and what it might be like to travel by elephant-back. Her father had always hired oxcarts. He'd never taken her as far as the northern capital of Lomkha in Third Province, or Fanjandibad's border stronghold in the southeast, but Diribani had attended several of Horse Month's livestock fairs in the years when they'd been held within a day's journey of Gurath. And she had traveled up the river San to many of the small towns that studded its banks. Delicious mangoes that one artisan village had, where the gem-cutters lived. What was its name? Piplia? Triplia? Something like that. The memory of the succulent orange fruit made her mouth water. Now that she wasn't so concerned about being left to Governor Alwar's dubious mercy, her hunger was becoming more insistent.

A line had formed of women waiting to talk to the princess. Ruqayya dealt with them quickly. A word—flick! A nod—flick!

They bowed and retreated. Diribani realized that princesses must learn the knack of it early; there would always be people wanting their attention. Like that man in the corner, hands clenched at his side, eyeing them intently. His lean features were vaguely familiar, hard dark eyes and a thin neck like a stork's poking out of his white coat. But, as with the mango village, his name dangled just out of Diribani's reach.

"We'll leave you here, Zahid," the princess said. "Come, flower girl."

"Yes, my lady." A carnation brushed her lips as Diribani turned, aware that Ruqayya had caught her gaping about like a country maid visiting the market for the first time.

"Her name's Diribani," the prince reminded his sister.

"Yes, yes." Flick, flick. "Oh, and I have a commission for Steward Ghiyas, after he's sorted out the baggage."

"Very well." With a salute, the prince left them.

Diribani swallowed a sigh. Zahid must be very busy. She should be grateful he had remembered to search her out. Of course his sister would take charge of her; Believers had rules that kept women sequestered. But already Diribani missed the prince's company, especially the undercurrent of humor in his manner. Ruqayya seemed kind, in her way, but . . . brisk. The princess was like a master weaver. Her competent hands kept the threads of court activity meshing smoothly, the little lives running over and under one another. Running . . . Diribani turned her head.

The thin man was running toward them. Ignoring the gravel paths, he jumped over a shrub and kicked a pot of roses out of his way. The earthenware cracked, spilling dirt and roots on the ground.

Ruqayya followed the direction of Diribani's gaze, and then events unfolded with stunning speed. A shrill whistle cut through the murmur of fountains and conversation. The two guards at the ladies'-quarter gate started down the stairs, drawing swords as they came. Ruqayya shoved Diribani hard, pushing her to her knees behind a fountain. With lethal grace, the princess spun on one foot. Her hand whipped a dagger from the sheath hidden beneath her flared coat.

Gravel bit Diribani's knees through the thin pink fabric of her dress wrap. Steel flashed in the running man's hand; emotion distorted his features. But he wasn't aiming his blade at Ruqayya, who seemed to expect it. He ran around the other side of the fountain, toward Diribani.

She raised her hands—prayer or protest, she couldn't have said. The unnatural situation caught her completely off balance.

He came close enough for her to smell the reek of palm liquor on his breath and see the straw dotting his white coat. Just before he reached her, the man screamed in agony. Slowly, he crumpled to the ground.

Diribani recoiled in horror. Ruqayya's dagger had flown to his throat, and another's sword pierced her attacker's chest. Diribani would be seeing that wicked glint and the blood—oh, Mother Gaari, so much blood—in her nightmares. She huddled against the fountain. Water dripped cold into her hair. As if from a great distance, she heard more screaming, and, closer, a peculiar rattling sound.

That noise stopped first. Later, she would realize that she had heard the life departing from a man who had wanted to kill her. But why?

CHAPTER TEN

Tana

INDU!" Ma Hiral shrieked out the window. "Bring your basket."

Tana didn't dare speak. When the neighbor boy came running, snake basket and forked stick in hand, she pointed mutely at the black-and-white-striped snake coiled in the corner of the room.

"It's a krait?" Tana's mother quavered.

Indu inspected it from a safe distance. "No, wolf snake," he decided. "Harmless, even though they copy a krait's coloring to fool hunters. Wolf snakes are half as long, and the white bands are clearest at the head. Be careful, if you're not sure which kind you've got," he lectured Tana, capturing the snake and dropping it into his basket. "The priests say kraits' venom is much stronger than a cobra's. One bite will kill you dead."

"Wolf snake, krait—take it away," Tana's mother begged, and Indu obliged.

Tana folded the last dress wrap and put it into the sack with the rest. She looked around for any items she might have forgotten to pack.

Clang!

"That woman could have the decency to wait one day for us to remove our things before she breaks down the door." Ma Hiral straightened from Tana's bedding, which she was tying into a roll.

Tana shrugged. The room held nothing but sunlight and dust. If Ba Javerikh's cousins were so eager to take possession, they could sweep the floor.

Clang, clang! The gate bell pealed again.

"Hanging on the bell won't move these old bones any faster," Ma Hiral grumbled.

Tana slung the bedding over her shoulder and picked up the bag containing her few possessions. Odd, when she had so little, to know that, thanks to the gems Diribani had left behind, Tana and her mother were probably richer than anyone on their street. When Trader Nikhat had come the previous night for his sapphires and Tana's report, he'd agreed to keep the jewels safe for them. Tana had explained that she and her mother had become homeless, at least temporarily. Upon Diribani's departure from Gurath with the prince's caravan, her father's cousin would lose no time claiming the property.

Indu had already helped carry Ma Hiral's possessions, including the silver pitcher, next door. Tana's mother would stay with his family until the promised house had been built by the stepwell. A temple priestess had helped arrange it, when she visited at first light to hear Tana's account. She had also collected the jewels from the offering dish and invited Tana to stay in the guest quarters at the temple grove south of Horse Gate, outside the city wall.

Tana had accepted with relief. As long as Ma Hiral was comfortable, Tana had no reason to fight with Diribani's relatives about the house. She couldn't linger in Gurath, not after the prince had ordered her to leave.

Her mother murmured a parting prayer before the household shrine. Silently, Tana followed suit. *Naghali-ji, give me the strength to bear your gift with honor.* She'd done the same upon first waking, when she discovered she was still speaking frogs and snakes. Diribani's jewels and flowers continued as well, she assumed. Given the distance opening wide between them, the reminder of their shared experience comforted her.

Clang! Clang! Clang!

"We're coming," Ma Hiral called across the courtyard. She opened the gate and recoiled as a dusty white-coated figure fell at her feet. "You! Haven't you caused enough heartbreak? Get out at once!"

"Please, hear me," the girl panted.

"Gulrang?" In her astonishment, Tana spoke. A toad plopped in the dirt. With an affronted-sounding croak, it took refuge in the shade of the well cover.

Gulrang covered her mouth with her fist, as if toads were poisonous.

"Get out, I say!" When Tana's mother reached for their visitor's coat, with the apparent intention of throwing her into the street, Tana put out a hand to stop her. Tears blotched Gulrang's face. Bits of hay stuck to her crumpled clothing, as if she'd slept in a barn and then run all the way from the overseers' quarter to yank on their gate bell.

"Who is it, Hiral-ji?" At the neighboring house, Indu's grandmother appeared at an upper window. "That one! Shall I have my son-in-law get rid of her?"

Tana frowned and shook her head. "No, thank you, Nama-ji," Ma Hiral said.

"It wasn't my fault," Gulrang said behind her hands.

"Speak up, girl." Indu's grandmother rested her hip against the window frame. "What's happened to bring you here in such a state?"

"My lady dismissed me yesterday evening," Gulrang said.

Ma Hiral sniffed. "And you expect sympathy from us? After Diribani risked herself for your unworthy hide?"

"I know." Gulrang bowed her head. Like a tent frame collapsing, the tall girl seemed to fold in on herself, her limbs a bundle of sticks. "My parents are weavers in a small village upriver, so I went to stay with my brother, a groom at the governor's stables. He was so angry. He and his friends had been drinking palm liquor. All night, they were drinking. And he said, he said—" She broke off, shuddering.

The older woman leaned out of the window. "Are you going to tell us or not? These ladies aren't interested in hearing a girl complain about the curry she dished up for herself!"

"My brother blamed Mina Diribani for my disgrace," Gulrang wailed. "He said she was a witch, a cursed witch. He said no true Believer would let her live."

The two older women gasped.

"Did he hurt her?" The bedding slid from Tana's shoulder to the ground. Her insides felt frozen. She was surprised that the two pale-yellow frogs leaping from her lips didn't shatter like ice chips when they hit the ground.

"I tried to stop him. I told him, over and over, that I'd been stupid, and then unlucky—it had nothing to do with her. But this morning he tied me up—his own sister—and left me in an empty stall. He had a knife." Gulrang started sobbing.

"And Diribani?" Ma Hiral demanded. "What about her?"

"I don't know!" Gulrang cried. "Nobody at the fort would tell me. One of my brother's friends cut me loose. He said my brother was dead. He said that I'd better run, or the soldiers would kill me, too."

"Why did you come here?" Tana asked. A whip snake flexed its tail, dark brown against the courtyard's reddish ground.

"To grind our hearts in the dirt, you wicked girl?" Ma Hiral would have slapped the kneeling Gulrang, but again Tana stayed her mother's hand.

"No!" Gulrang said. "I came to tell Mina Tana. In case one of the others had the same idea about her."

"Brother Akshath, protect us!" Ma Hiral folded her hands and lifted her face to the sky in prayer.

As when she first saw Diribani speaking gems and flowers, Tana felt numb. How could someone have attacked her sister? Naghali-ji was no crow god. Unlike Brother Utsav, whose favor was as whimsical as the wind, the snake goddess dealt fairly with her worshipers. Diribani had gotten good fortune. Hadn't she? Like a wheel with jeweled spokes turning, the possibilities revolved in Tana's mind. *Wisdom. Good fortune. Death.*

For either sister, or both? Tana had nothing; she didn't want to die. So she would have to be wise. "Thank you for the warning, Gulrang," she said. "Will you do me one more service?"

The girl averted her eyes from the two sand boas writhing on the ground. One twined around the other in a living knot. She wiped her wet face on her sleeve and faced Tana squarely. "Yes."

"Trade clothes with me," Tana said.

"Very good thinking," Nama-ji approved from her window seat. "No one will expect to see our snake girl dressed in a white coat."

Gulrang looked uncertain. It struck Tana that the two of them had quite a lot in common: cast from their homes, their work taken away, pursued by those who wished them ill. Not surprising if Gulrang hesitated to give up the last thing she could call her own.

Slowly, the girl nodded. "If Mina Diribani hadn't stood up for me, those soldiers would have ripped the clothes from my back and offered nothing but shame in return." Her chin lifted with the arrogance that had marked the Gulrang of old. "You people call us flesh-eaters. But our religion also condemns the murder of an innocent person. If my brother succeeded, he will suffer in hell forever. I pray that God will know the regret in my heart and judge me accordingly."

"Yes, yes. Change dresses now, justify yourself later." Ma Hiral shooed both young women into the empty house.

Tana took a clean blouse and red dress wrap out of her bag. It had been her idea, but she wasn't looking forward to trading with Gulrang. Traditional clothing was so much more practical than the invading white-coats' tailored things.

Prettier, too. The rich crimson shade of Tana's blouse flattered Gulrang's dark skin. Once Ma Hiral had helped her into it, the dress wrap's graceful drape disguised the girl's lankiness. She looked womanly, as elegant as a swan.

Until she walked across the room. Her long stride stretched the pleats around her waist. When she stepped on the skirt hem, the whole length came unwound and puddled at her feet. Gulrang flushed with embarrassment. "How do you keep it on?"

Ma Hiral tutted. "Small steps." She picked up the fabric rectangle and started over. "Tuck this end here, then pleat like so."

Tana, meanwhile, was swimming in her borrowed clothes. Gulrang's coat was far too broad in the shoulders; the sleeves dripped over her wrists. She sat on the floor, rolling the trouser legs so she wouldn't trip over them.

"Not like that," Gulrang corrected her. "Bunch the fabric around your ankles." She knelt and rearranged Tana's pant legs. "The idea is to keep your skin covered, not show it like a—" She glanced at her own bare arms and belly, and blushed deeply. "The shoulder laces adjust this way."

Tana held still as Gulrang tightened yellow ribbons over her arms and down the coat's side seams. She had thought the ribbons were just decoration. Had she ever really looked at a white-coat except with suspicion? Or cared about one? *Wisdom,* she reminded herself. If she and her sister wished to cheat death, they needed to pay more attention to the world around them. Tana ventured a few steps. The clothing felt tight against her skin, invisible hands squeezing her arms and legs.

"It's big on you, but not too bad," Gulrang said. "Try walking like you have an important errand and your lady will beat you for tardiness." She glanced apologetically at Tana's mother. "I know it's not what she's used to, but she looks silly, mincing along."

Ma Hiral snorted. "If stomping like a pregnant elephant gets her to safety, so be it."

Tana opened her mouth, then closed it again. When her mother looked at her, she shrugged. Big steps. She only had to wear these uncomfortable clothes for a little while.

Gulrang, too, was managing to walk without tripping over herself or unwrapping the garment. Tana pointed at the door. "You'd both better be going," her mother said with a sigh. "We'll send Indu to the temple grove with news of Diribani. The moment we know."

Tana nodded, her throat tight. She folded her hands to Gulrang.

Before the girl could leave them, Ma Hiral fumbled at her waistband, then pressed something small into Gulrang's hand. "For your voyage home," she said. "No, no. You take it. We'll be fine."

"Thank you." Gulrang bowed and walked away without a backward glance.

Tana hugged her mother fiercely.

"May blessed Khochari keep you safe between her palms until her will brings us together again." Ma Hiral dashed tears from her eyes. "What am I saying? The grove's not so far that these feet can't make the journey. We'll be together very soon, I'm sure." She led the way to the gate. "Don't forget your clothes or bedroll, daughter."

Tana hugged her mother, then picked up her belongings and waved to the neighbor. "Good-bye, Nama-ji."

"Safe travels, Tana." The gray-haired woman leaned out from her window and peered into the courtyard with professional interest. "That's a new ratter, isn't it? Eyo, grandson!" she called into the house. "Go down and open the gate for Hiral-ji, please. And collect that house naga, Indu. Your auntie was saying just the other day . . ."

With a final embrace, Tana left her mother at the neighbors' house and strode down the street. At any moment, she imagined fingers would point and voices shout "Impostor!" Maybe the jealous white-coat god would strike her for disguising herself as a Believer.

But no one seemed to take particular notice of her. A pushcart vendor spat at her feet; another berated her for blocking his way. At the next intersection, she didn't hesitate but turned east, toward Cow Gate, instead of south, to Horse Gate and the road to the temple grove.

Not wanting to argue and spoil their newfound harmony, Tana had let her mother think she would seek safety immediately with the priests and priestesses. In truth, she had no intention of leaving Gurath until she knew what had happened to her sister. Prince Zahid had promised to treat Diribani with honor. If he had failed that trust, he would answer for it.

CHAPTER ELEVEN

Diribani

GURATH looked smaller, seen from atop an elephant.

A little shaky still, but clean, fed, and dressed in borrowed finery, Diribani knelt in a corner of the howdah's curtained platform, among a group of older women. She lifted the gauze drapery just enough to peek out, hoping to distract her thoughts from what had almost happened back in the garden. And what *had* happened: a man's death. And its aftermath, upsetting in a different way, given Zahid's fury, Alwar's excuses, and Ruqayya's cool voice insisting that the regrettable incident not delay their departure. Diribani had searched her soul: Could she have done anything to prevent the man's death? She didn't think so, but the violence weighed on her.

She tightened her hold on the waist-high railing and forced her attention to the scene below. The fort receded, the ladies' quarter invisible beyond tall walls, the cannons so many dark twigs poking out of stone parapets. Gurath's customs house, marketplace, and warehouses, the oceangoing ships with their tall masts . . . all dwindled. The twisted length of the river San shone a dull green, like a basking snake.

Tana. Where was she, this sunny afternoon? In the short time they'd been parted, Diribani had stored up a hundred things to share with her sister. As the royal procession wound through the merchant quarter, Diribani searched the crowd of upturned faces. From up here, the people looked tiny, their cheers and shouts rising from little puppet throats. She couldn't distinguish her home from the anonymous walls facing the street. That tall pinkfruit tree might be the one growing in Trader Nikhat's courtyard, but it was gone in a roll of the elephant's broad shoulders.

The platform's motion, rising up and down, then tilting from side to side like the deck of a ship, made Diribani queasy. She leaned her elbows on a bolster and closed her eyes. When she opened them at the trumpets' brazen blare, the head of their long procession had already reached the parklike area just inside Gurath's easternmost gate. Cow Gate, dedicated to Mother Gaari, earth goddess, protector of the poor and helpless. The governor's escort would leave them here.

Diribani felt a moment of shock when the trumpeters rode straight through the gate without stopping. Of course, the white-coats didn't worship the twelve. But it felt wrong, to pass a goddess's shrine without offering even a flower. She parted the gauze curtains. Ignoring the older ladies' cries of consternation, Diribani folded her hands. "Please bless our party, Gaari-ji," she said softly. Several sprays of wheat stalks, heavy with grain, fell from her lips.

The she-elephant shivered at the kernels bouncing like hail off her gray hide. The mahout soothed her, and the enormous animal lumbered on.

"Safe travel, Mina Diribani!" A young man on a white mare waved at her. Diribani recognized Kalyan and Jasmine. She leaned out and waved in return.

Alerted to her presence, other townsfolk, too, folded their hands, smiling and calling their farewells. "Eyo, Mina Diribani."

"Remember us in Fanjandibad, Mina-ji!"

"Come back soon, diamond girl."

Most of the white-coats pretended they hadn't noticed her, but one girl stepped out from the shade of a rose arbor to blow kisses at Diribani's elephant.

Diribani's lips shaped Tana's name. But before Diribani could be certain she had really seen her sister dressed in overseer white, one of her companions hauled her inside and twitched the curtains together.

A ring of outraged faces confronted her. "Perhaps it escaped your notice that none of us are veiled?" one of the ladies said in an icy tone. "The curtains stay closed."

"Please excuse me, Lady Yisha," Diribani said.

"It mustn't happen again."

As the women murmured among themselves about the lilies and rubies at Diribani's feet, she settled back against the bolster. Had Utsav the crow god tricked her eyes? She had wanted so badly to see her sister one last time before what could be a long separation. She might have imagined the familiar features, the smile brilliant with affection—and relief, too, now that she thought about it. No, that had definitely been Tana, wearing a white coat. She had been standing a little way beyond Kalyan and Jasmine. Maybe the trader was teaching her to ride? That was the most likely explanation.

How did Tana feel, wearing the costume brought to Gurath

with the invaders? Diribani glanced down at her own borrowed dress wrap. Ruqayya must have sent one of her ladies to the marketplace, unless she traveled with a store of garments from each of the Hundred Kingdoms. The blouse was fine cotton, light as air against Diribani's skin. Embroidered irises in a maze of gold ribbon-work banded the dress wrap's length of butter-yellow silk. She felt a fraud in it, but her new maid's horrified expression when Diribani had suggested she return it to Princess Ruqayya and ask for a plainer one had convinced Diribani to wear it. The princess hadn't struck her as a frightening figure, but Diribani's circumstances were different from her maid's.

It didn't matter, since only these severe ladies would see her in it. Diribani hadn't decided whether their disapproval stemmed from her being a non-Believer, a commoner daring to wear a queen's dress, or a conjurer spouting flowers and jewels. They tended to ignore her, so she returned her attention to the countryside. Which, in its own way, was less than satisfying.

The howdah consisted of a platform with a tent built over it, the frame's four corners rising to a peak in the center. The thin fabric that covered it prevented people from seeing the unveiled ladies within, but also obscured the view out. The travelers passed through a misty landscape of shrouded fields and forest.

While admitting some air and light, the enclosure concentrated the mingled scents of sandalwood hair oil, the lilies and carnations Diribani had spoken, and a strong odor of garlic from the bread served at the meal just before their departure. It had tasted delicious, hot and puffy from the fort kitchen's brick ovens, then slathered with melted butter and herbs. The garlic, alas, lingered on the breath.

Lady Yisha smelled it, too. Her aristocratic nose wrinkled in disgust.

As Diribani watched, the courtier opened a wooden box on the carpet beside her. It unfolded into a portable desk, complete with paper, pen, inkstand, and flat leather-covered surface for writing. Lady Yisha composed a short note and tucked it into a purse whose long strap ended in a metal clip. One jeweled hand reached outside the howdah and clipped the pouch to the elephant's harness. "Eyo, driver," she called.

The mahout riding on the elephant's neck, below the platform, reached up for the pouch. He whistled. One of the servant girls riding alongside them guided her horse closer and caught the pouch the driver threw her. At least, Diribani assumed it was a servant; a scarf covered her hair and lower face. The royal party were more particular than Gurath white-coats about women veiling themselves. Even the servants covered their faces in public.

Not caring if it was low-class to admit her curiosity, Diribani put her face against the gauze fabric to see what was happening. The girl opened the pouch and read the note. She rummaged in her saddlebags, but didn't find what she was looking for. Diribani admired how the servant kept her balance on the moving horse, holding on with her legs and guiding the animal with just one hand on the reins. The white-coats' costume made sense, she had to admit, for riding astride. Perhaps she'd ask the princess whether someone could teach her. If Kalyan had given Tana lessons, Diribani could ride with her the next time they were together.

The girl approached another servant, with better luck. The pouch was filled, and the first girl rode back to the elephant. Instead of tossing the pouch up to the mahout, as Diribani expected, the servant held the strap out at arm's length and clicked her tongue.

Without breaking stride, the elephant picked up the purse with her trunk. As delicately as a woman clasping a chain at her neck, the elephant's trunk reached over her shoulder, found an opening between the curtains, and dropped the purse inside the howdah.

"Oh, well done!" Diribani clapped her hands. Outside, the mahout echoed her praise, calling God to witness his elephant's cleverness. The ladies tittered at Diribani's enthusiasm.

Except one. "Dried fennel?" Lady Yisha said reprovingly.

The other faces became prim again.

"Thank you, my lady." The pouch reached Diribani last. She, too, took a pinch of the aromatic fennel seeds between her fingers and chewed them.

Soon the garlic smell receded. The women made themselves comfortable on the carpets and cushions. Some dozed, some slept, a few gossiped quietly about people Diribani hadn't met. The southeastern road to Fanjandibad seemed drier than the road from Lotus Gate to Naghali's well. The puddles were farther apart, too. Diribani heard only a faint squelching as the elephant walked along. The howdah's rocking motion and the low hum of conversation combined to make her sleepy. As she relaxed against the bolster, Diribani realized that, for the next little while, nothing was expected of her.

She thought how pleasant it might be to ride like Ruqayya and the capable servant girl. Especially if the prince accompanied them to point out the landmarks. Zahid seemed like the kind of person who might know the history of each stone they passed along the road. And if he didn't, Ruqayya would twitch her fingers—flick,

flick—and summon a clerk to read them all the appropriate chapter in a book carried for the purpose.

Her last thought, before she drifted into a nap, was how swiftly the goddess's gift had changed her. Two days ago, Diribani would never have imagined herself conversing with royalty, let alone judging their potential as traveling companions. Ma Hiral's warnings aside, being a diamond girl wasn't so bad. Except when people tried to kill you for it.

Like a blow, memory struck. The blood, and the screaming. Diribani sat straight up. A sour taste coated her tongue.

"More fennel?" A lady passed her the pouch.

"Thank you." Diribani crunched the seeds between her teeth, hardly noticing the licorice flavor. She pretended that the ugly memories rising through her mind could be blown like smoke out the gauze curtains, to disperse in the afternoon breeze. Silently, she prayed to Sister Payoja, goddess of healing and peace, that, whatever his twisted reasons for attacking her, the deluded man might choose a better path in his next life. Then she prayed to Naghali-ji. *Give me the strength to bear your gift with grace.* If the goddess had arranged for Diribani to travel to Fanjandibad, she would find a purpose there, or perhaps along the way. She needed to pay attention, and hold herself ready.

Outside, a piltreet sang: "Lazy girl. Lazy girl, girl, girl." Cart wheels creaked, and marching feet drummed against the road. Insects buzzed in the fields. A frog shrilled; another answered. As its brothers and sisters and uncles joined in, a full-throated chorus rose from the flooded ditches. Comforted by the reminder of Sister Naghali's constant presence in their lives, Diribani's mind quieted. She slept.

CHAPTER TWELVE

Tana

TANA ducked under the arbor to collect her bedding, which she'd hidden behind a climbing rose. Thorns pricked her hands, but the pain didn't stop a grin from spreading across her face. Relief surged through her, washing the fear taste from her mouth.

Diribani was well, as glorious as the princess in a tale. The sun-colored dress wrap set off her dark beauty as it deserved. That handsome Prince Zahid had better watch his heart. Tana would bet a diamond of fifty ratis that, after several weeks' travel in her sister's company, he wouldn't care that she'd been born a commoner, and a non-Believer at that. Princess Diribani—why not?

Happily planning her sister's grand future, Tana waited for the prince's entourage to file through Cow Gate. When the governor's guard had also departed, she hoisted the bedroll onto her shoulder and turned south, toward Horse Gate. She'd taken only a couple of steps when she found an actual horse in her way. Face averted, Tana turned and hurried back the way she'd come, pretending she'd forgotten something.

Two steps, four steps. No buildings in the grassy area near Cow Gate. She made it past the arbor and dashed behind a tree, only to find herself nose to nose with Jasmine. The white horse whickered in greeting.

Cursing her own carelessness, Tana reached up to stroke the velvet nose. The white-coat disguise wasn't so good if a horse could catch her.

"It *is* you!" Trader Kalyan slid off the saddle and landed next to Tana.

At any other time, she would have been thrilled that he sought her out. Today she put him in danger. And why did he have to find her dressed like this? She was conscious of Gulrang's sweat-stained coat, the trousers crumpled and creased with bits of ground-in hay. Tana stepped back. She shifted to put the length of her bedroll between them.

Then, of course, she could see how fine he looked in court dress, a tan-colored coat which, unlike Tana's, fit him quite well in the shoulders. Light but not white, the color complemented trousers two shades darker. Had he been at the fort this morning, selling jewels to the visiting ladies? Perhaps he'd seen Diribani, or heard about the incident with Gulrang's brother. Tana lifted her eyes in hope and got an unwelcome surprise.

Amiable Kalyan wore the expression of a man who'd picked up a wolf snake and discovered he held a venomous krait. "What in Father Ghodan's name are you doing here? In their clothes?" he hissed. "You're going to the well this instant, Mina."

Tana frowned in surprise. She shook her head.

"Our house, then. My parents will make sure you get safely out of town. We know about the prince's order."

Again Tana shook her head. *No.*

"Haven't you heard?" Kalyan's voice lowered. "A white-coat tried to kill Diribani in the fort this morning. He didn't succeed, but rumor says the governor's furious. The prince's guest, attacked in Alwar's stronghold? If word of the scandal reaches Lomkha, the emperor might decide to appoint a more capable official."

Tana shrugged. Diribani was safe. And as long as Alwar didn't catch her, Tana didn't care about the governor's problems.

"Now Alwar's soldiers are going through the overseers' quarter, turning it inside out to root out any other plotters. He won't worry about insulting the nobles, even the revenue men and mint officials, not when his own neck's on the line. And you're wandering the town wearing their livery!"

Tana glanced around. They were outside, off the main street, with plenty of trees and bushes where a snake could hide. She decided to risk speech, though she turned her face away from Jasmine. "Thank you for the warning," she said softly. "I'm going to the temple south of Horse Gate; I'll be careful." A trio of lucky frogs landed—*plop, plop, plop*—at her feet. Jasmine snorted and tossed her head.

"Too risky," Kalyan said.

"Necessary," Tana contradicted him, though a part of her enjoyed his protectiveness. Neighborly protectiveness, she told herself. How could he know her feelings when she'd been so careful to hide them?

With the word, a golden-eyed tree snake had dropped to the ground, where it writhed in discomfort. Kalyan grunted. He handed Jasmine's reins to Tana. Scooping up the tree snake, he lifted it to a nearby branch, out of harm's way.

Kalyan was kind to everyone, snakes and tongue-tied girls included.

"I'll take you," he said.

"What?" Tana croaked in disbelief. Everyone in Gurath knew Jasmine and her rider. If Tana perched atop the trader's white mare, she might as well wear a sign that said *Look Here*. Besides, she might be dressed in the right clothes, but she didn't know how to ride. She thrust the reins at him. "No."

"You don't trust me?"

The accusation wounded her to the heart. Not trust him? She was trying to protect him! Her fingers dug into the bedroll. It gave off a faint smell of spices, and she breathed deeply. How typical of her luck, that this conversation was probably the greatest number of words they'd ever exchanged, and she'd spent most of hers arguing with him—while she was dressed like a stinking flesh-eater.

Kalyan's presence had always made Tana too shy to say much on the many occasions when her stepfather had consulted his friend and competitor. After the jewel talk was completed, the men would dismiss the girls and settle in to discuss politics over their coffee. Kalyan's younger sisters would carry off Diribani, whom they adored. If Hima, the eldest, wasn't present, Tana would make her way to the stables. She liked horses, liked their smell and how they didn't mind that a person was small and ordinary, as long as she remembered to bring them lumps of dark sugar.

And if Tana and Kalyan and Jasmine stood under this tree for much longer, somebody would wonder what the trader was doing with a disheveled white-coat girl. She couldn't risk setting free the dangerous snakes a long explanation might summon. Helpless to do more, Tana folded her hands to show she wanted only peace between them. She would have gone her way if Kalyan hadn't touched her arm. Lightly, but she felt it, even through her long sleeve.

"You think I'm an idiot, don't you?" His face twisted. "Good old Kalyan, rides his pretty horse around the town but can't tell a rough diamond from a lump of quartz."

Tana stared in shock. Where had he gotten that impression? Even if it were true, which it most certainly was not, why should he care about one girl's opinion? Her temper stirred. He had everything she had ever wanted: a family that loved him, rewarding work, the freedom of city and countryside both. She had just been separated from her family and sent into exile. How dared he judge her?

"I saw that report." His fingers brushed the back of her hand in trader-talk: *Sapphires.* "It was brilliant. A person with your skill doesn't belong in the temple, droning prayers all day."

Doubly unfair, that his touch burned like a hot spark. Tana shook her head, beset by a swarm of contradictory thoughts. Is that how he imagined her, hair shaved like a priestess? He had paid her a compliment. So why did she feel like throwing the bedroll at his head?

Kalyan misinterpreted her expression. "Go ahead, laugh. It's improper, speaking to you directly, but you're a levelheaded person. We're young, true. And I don't know the stones, not like you. But I'm a good listener. I know who's selling, who's buying, who can afford to pay for all the goods he's commissioned, and who'd pay more if he knew his competitor was interested. My family is well established. Please consider, Mina-ji. Between your talent, Hima's good management, and my contacts, we could be the most successful merchants in Gurath."

Tana wanted to shriek with frustration. This was hardly the time to discuss her employment, when any overseer who spotted her would likely drag them both to Alwar's jail. Not that she disliked Kalyan's idea. It would be perfect, actually. Servants could bring jewels to the well for her to evaluate. Hima and Kalyan might even visit, from time to time, and keep her company. And it was flattering to know that Kalyan respected her abilities.

Work that she loved, associates she trusted, a position of responsibility: All were within Tana's grasp. She needed to tell him how much she appreciated the offer. "Tell your father that once I'm settled by the well I'll be happy to work for you," she said, scattering several green frogs.

"Work for us? No." Kalyan sounded affronted. "We should get married."

Tana took a step back. "Married?" she repeated, breathless.

Like a figure from a nightmare, a long, dark shape reared up between her and Kalyan. The smooth black scales, the yellowish underbelly, and the wide dark neckband warned of what was to come: a neck swelling wide, the hood's paler ring pattern just visible in the shade.

Cobra.

It didn't matter why Kalyan had said it. It didn't matter how Tana's heart leaped at the prospect, or how it seemed most desirable at the very moment it was dashed from her. As if a blindfold had been stripped from her eyes, Tana saw that very clearly. She must have managed to conceal her feelings or he would have played on them, skilled negotiator that he was. The bald offer smacked more of business than of passion, but mutual ambition wasn't such a bad foundation for marriage. Once Ba Javerikh had died, Tana hadn't dared dream of that much. With her plain looks and small dowry, any husband willing to settle for her would have had little to give in return but a life of backbreaking work. Far less, certainly, than Kalyan offered.

But the goddess had changed her situation. Tana didn't need a cobra to remind her that those around her could be faced with mortal danger at any moment. How could Tana put people she loved at risk? The next thought hurt even more, but it was time she faced it.

No man would want to kiss lips that shed vipers and toads. Any marriage Tana undertook in her current state could be in name only. Wouldn't such a sham displease both Mother Gaari and Father Ghodan, not to mention Naghali-ji herself? Kalyan deserved better. Because she cared for him, she couldn't accept.

Step by slow step, Tana backed away from the cobra. Kalyan did likewise. Jasmine sidled behind him, her eyes rolling with fear. When they were several snake lengths apart, the cobra subsided. Black scales gleamed as it slithered under a bush and disappeared.

Letting her face show the answer she must give, Tana spread her hands wide. *Impossible.*

Kalyan nodded, his expression unusually serious. He folded his hands, then vaulted into Jasmine's saddle and rode away at a rapid clip.

Should she laugh or cry that her first (and likely last) offer of marriage had been abandoned in the next breath? It did hurt, that the suitor she had secretly dreamed of had retreated so quickly. But since Tana couldn't accept, at least Kalyan had saved his father the marriage broker's fee. It didn't require a professional matchmaker's services to understand that a cobra meant "no."

Tana's bag of clothing and bedroll weighed on her shoulder as though they had been stuffed with stones. Like her feet. Like her heart. She tried to compose her expression, pasting calm on a face that wanted to crumple. Shielded behind the bedding, Tana followed Gurath's back streets to Horse Gate and the road to the temple grove. She kept her mind occupied watching for white-coats, so she could keep away from them.

It served no purpose to dwell on might-have-been, or wonder how long Kalyan had been considering her as a possible bride. Since reading the sapphire report? Before? He'd never treated her with any special favor. Had he? Aware of him as she was, she thought she would have noticed. Had her own shyness blinded her? But, for however short a time, he'd held her in enough esteem to suggest there might be more than friendship between them. A tiny flame of longing lit within her. Tana wished she could ask Diribani. Could her sister have spoken to Kalyan's family about this and not told her?

When Tana realized she'd almost bumped into one of the governor's soldiers, she took herself sternly to task. The white-coat was picking his teeth with his dagger, not terribly fear-inspiring. But with only one question, her secret could be discovered. And Kalyan had called her levelheaded. Wouldn't he laugh?

She wouldn't think about him. How his eyes had darkened with concern when he recognized her. How he'd picked up the tree snake and carried it to safety. How he had sounded hurt, to think she mistrusted him. She wouldn't remember their every previous encounter and search it for a hint of his feelings, the way she'd examine a rough gem, teasing out the glory hidden within its heart. No, no, no.

How could she do anything else?

When she reached the temple grove, a priest whisked her inside. He answered her questioning look: "Trader Kalyan told us you'd arrive shortly, Mina-ji."

A good listener, Kalyan. He'd said so, and proved it true. Tana's disobedient heart melted anew at the gesture. He'd have guessed at the speculation her presence would kindle—a white-coat, visiting the home of the twelve?—and smoothed her way without being asked.

The priest hurried her past the worshipers' curious stares. They crossed the busy courtyard, weaving between the low arms of a many-branched fig tree. Tana smelled incense, fruit, and flowers. *Diribani.*

More than ever, Tana missed her sister's sympathetic presence. Tana couldn't confide Kalyan's proposal in a letter. Governor Alwar's spies might intercept the regular couriers traveling between Gurath and Fanjandibad, and Tana wouldn't repay Kalyan's kindness by exposing his family to official scrutiny.

The priest stopped in a patch of dappled shade. An older woman was dancing by a pool fringed with lotus blossoms. Her every movement was crisply defined as the edge of the white petals.

The priestess whirled a final time, then came to rest, arms falling to her sides like a bird's wings. "Peace to you, Tana-ji."

Tana folded her hands to the same priestess who had visited their home mere hours ago. "Peace, Ma-ji." A gliding snake coasted the short distance from her lips to wrap around a tree branch.

Tana's escort tripped over his own feet, his eyes round. The priestess, who had seen it before, smiled and dismissed him. The older woman straightened her orange renunciate's robe and motioned

Tana to a bamboo mat before dropping lithely beside her. They sat quietly, allowing the temple sounds, chiming bells and chanted prayers and animal noises, to fill the air around them.

"Lazy girl, girl, girl," a piltreet scolded. A pack of monkeys screamed insults at one another. Oblivious to their racket, a spider added a thread to her web. A peahen strutted past, gawky chicks scurrying after her.

"Why the white coat?" the priestess asked.

Tana twisted her hands together. "I was afraid of being recognized."

"Oh?" The woman extended her hand. Like a silver bracelet, the boa curled around her wrist. "Ch, ch," the priestess said. "Not so tight, friend." She put her arm in a patch of sunlight, and the boa released her, stretching out to soak up the warmth.

Tana explained about Gulrang's tearful arrival, the attack on Diribani, Kalyan's warning about the governor's activities. She left out the trader's offer of marriage, and the cobra, finishing with her other concern: "I'm sure the governor's men will be watching for me, and maybe worse. If Diribani's flowers and jewels maddened a white-coat enough to threaten her life, what about my snakes and frogs? Those people don't respect animals—they eat them! And although the prince saved us, he didn't make Alwar stop the bounty on snake skins."

As if to punctuate her words, a toad landed at her feet and croaked. Loudly.

"I'll be a constant reminder that Alwar isn't the only power in Gurath, even if he doesn't understand it. Especially if he doesn't understand it." Tana snorted. "I certainly don't understand it. Do you, Ma-ji?"

"No," the priestess said tranquilly. "But the gods' will may manifest itself in unlikely ways."

"There must be a reason." Tana leaned forward, nudging a ratter aside with her knee. "Naghali-ji can't have meant for me to cause trouble for my family, or sit at the well all day, speaking lucky frogs for children, house nagas for mouse-infested householders, and poisonous serpents to frighten everyone else!"

"And so?" The priestess waited, as patient as the tree under which they sat. A stripe-tailed squirrel chased another up the trunk. Hidden by dense foliage, the two chattered back and forth.

"I think I need to look for the reason," Tana finished.

"A pilgrimage? That's a traditional solution for those troubled in body or spirit."

"You think it's a good idea?"

"I think you must do as your heart guides you."

Color burned Tana's cheeks. The goddess had asked what her soul desired. *To keep my family safe* had been Tana's unvoiced answer. Naghali-ji had given her snakes. Now the priestess advised Tana to listen to her heart, and it told her to abandon the people she cared about. "Where should I go?" she said. Another ratter, long and muscular, curled beside her. A champion, Indu would have called it.

"There's a traditional answer to that question, too." The priestess stood and held out her hand. "Stay here until it comes to you. You're welcome to dance with us; perhaps that discipline will help."

Tana bowed her head. "Thank you, Ma-ji."

She meant to stay a few nights. But Tiger Month padded by on velvet paws, and she found much to do in the temple grove. When Horse Month galloped in, Tana's answer rode with it.

CHAPTER THIRTEEN

Diribani

B EFORE she could cover the yawn with her hand, Diribani's jaw cracked open. She closed her mouth just as Lady Yisha glanced over and frowned. The woman had a gift for catching Diribani in bad manners.

Diribani lowered her eyes in apology and turned to the gauzy wall of the howdah. Through the last days of Tiger Month, the elephant had carried them east, against the sun's path. The strips of jungle growth had thinned, then melted into vast fields dotted with laborers. They harvested the rice and cotton planted before the rains, or sowed wheat and barley. Trees lined the imperial road, providing welcome shade. The subsequent hours of travel through Horse Month's dry, pleasant weather were so much the same that Diribani gauged their progress by the size of the trees, which dwindled as they traveled from Tenth Province. Diribani wondered whether they'd find tiny saplings planted on the stretch to Fanjandibad. Carved from the last of the once-independent Hundred Kingdoms,

Eighteenth Province had been added to the empire at the beginning of the current emperor's reign.

This morning, the royal caravan had turned south to skirt the deep desert. As they left villages and cropland behind, flat terrain wrinkled into scrubby hills. Not much grew here but thorn trees and small-leafed bushes, from what Diribani could see through the canopy's fabric. The vegetation gave off a pungent, rather medicinal scent. A bird whistled, sweetly, its coloring too drab for her to distinguish against sparse gray-green leaves. Scorpion country, snake country.

What would Tana be doing now? The prince had dispatched several couriers to carry Diribani's jewels back to Gurath, and coin to start construction on a house by the stepwell. Ma Hiral would be in her element, situating walls for nicely proportioned rooms, directing the placement of doors and windows to catch the breeze, supervising the plastering and painting. Indu must be thrilled, too, Tana's gift the source of endless fascination. And her sister? Diribani imagined Tana enjoying the cool waters at the well, visiting with Geetika and Parul and Hima, surrounded by people who loved her, not these severe women who sniffed whenever Diribani opened her mouth.

Diribani wondered whether Tana had determined Naghali-ji's purpose for her gift. She was no closer to an answer for herself, though she had little else to occupy her thoughts. Also, she had discovered a potential flaw in the prince's resolution of the dispute in the street. After Zahid's intervention, the goddess's jewels flowed into Gurath through Governor Alwar's grasping fingers. Diribani couldn't imagine him using the proceeds to fund an animal hospital, or a school for poor children. Bigger guns for the fort, more likely. At best, he'd build inns for traveling merchants, to encourage them to trade in Gurath. Would Sister Naghali be displeased?

A movement outside distracted Diribani. She sat up and put her nose against the fabric. Let Lady Yisha frown. She must not know that her face had set in a habitual sneer, like a parrot's.

The petty thought flew out of Diribani's mind as she realized what she was seeing. "Gazelles!" she said. Yellow mimosa blossoms fluttered to the carpet around her. "Or antelope? Four, no, five! And there's another group, coming across the ridge."

Other ladies crowded to her side of the howdah, making the platform tip alarmingly before the far straps tightened against the elephant's side.

"Paper and pen!" Lady Yisha snapped her fingers. The lady sitting closest to the desk box opened it for her.

At first, the ritual of note passing had broken the monotony of travel; now Diribani wondered why they didn't just call out to their servants, and save everyone the bother of handing the pouch up and down. The women rode close enough to hear a raised voice. At Diribani's exclamation, one girl stood up in her stirrups and shaded her eyes to follow the ridgeline. With a whoop of excitement, she wheeled her horse and galloped toward the front of the caravan.

The gazelles' white tails flicked, flicked, just like Ruqayya's fingers commanding her servants. Since it wasn't very tactful, comparing any part of a princess to an antelope's backside, Diribani kept the thought to herself. She kept a lot of thoughts to herself, riding with Lady Yisha and her set. At the end of the day, Mahan and Zeen, the two stern women assigned to guard Diribani and her jewels, would have a scant handful of rough gems to collect for their box.

"Eyo, driver." Lady Yisha's message pouch went down; the driver whistled. A mounted servant claimed the pouch and read the note.

Until the gazelles swerved away from the caravan, they might provide a new topic of conversation. "Aren't they graceful?" Diribani said.

"Delightful," one of the ladies conceded.

"They do bounce so, you'd think it would shake up their insides," another said.

"Pepper, or tamarind sauce?"

Diribani silenced a groan. Once the ladies finished complaining about one meal, they speculated about the next, and whether it would suit their delicate digestions. What was the cook thinking? Too spicy, or not spicy enough, and, always, too much garlic. Nissa, the maid Ruqayya had assigned to Diribani, had told her in confidence that one pack elephant carried nothing but breath-freshening fennel seeds for the noblewomen's use.

"Spit-roasted," Lady Yisha said with unusual vigor. "I could fancy a bite of nice, tender kid with tamarind sauce." She actually smacked her lips.

Then Diribani realized that the ladies *were* talking about the gazelles. They were talking about eating them.

Her knuckles tightened on the platform railing as she closed her eyes and tried not to disgrace herself. That's why the servant had ridden to the front of the line, anticipating Lady Yisha's note. She'd gone to alert the hunters, in case they hadn't already spotted the herd—although it was more likely that the party's advance trackers and scouts had found them earlier, and driven the animals toward the caravan so more people could have a go at killing them.

Diribani couldn't bear to open her eyes and watch that graceful flight end in blood and death.

"Oh, good shooting," a lady said. "That makes three for the princess."

"Four, by my count," Lady Yisha corrected.

"As you say, my lady."

"What an archer Princess Ruqayya is."

Diribani opened her eyes. "Why don't they use guns?" she asked. Rubies gleamed among starflowers.

Disapproving stares swiveled to bear on her. "Guns aren't that accurate," a woman said, as if this fault could be laid, like so many others, at Diribani's feet.

Lady Yisha sniffed. "And it would hardly be sporting. Which reminds me. Have I told you about the time my grandfather killed a tiger with only a broken spear-butt?"

As the other ladies demurred, they made themselves comfortable in a way that suggested to Diribani that they *had* heard the story. And that it was long and tedious, like so many of the noblewoman's reminiscences. Diribani no longer wondered why the woman's daughters and sisters traveled separately.

If Diribani had made friends who were traveling in other howdahs, she would have asked Ruqayya for permission to switch places. But unless they were ill, the younger, livelier women all rode horses. "To escape our mothers," one had giggled to Diribani at a meal. "Praise to God, the littles stayed in Fanjandibad with their nurses this year, or I'd have been stuck in a howdah, too, wiping sticky faces and bottoms. Ugh."

"Praise to Her Highness, rather." A young woman raised her

cup in salute. "I heard she's the one who refused permission to the pregnant ladies and young mothers this time."

"Well, she would, wouldn't she? After her sister died on the last trip, and the baby, too," another said. Then she had stared into her cup, as if she'd spoken out of turn, and the conversation had shifted.

As Lady Yisha droned on about the tiger, Diribani braced herself against the howdah frame and looked out. White tails flashed in the distance, so not all of the gazelles had been killed. Enough fallen bodies lay on the sparse grass to make Diribani grateful, for a change, that the curtains clouded her view.

The thin fabric didn't obscure Prince Zahid, riding past marching men, oxcarts, camels, and elephants toward a veiled figure just now unstringing her bow. Her crisp movements were as distinctive as his prancing bay. Flick, flick, she directed servants to collect the gazelles, and turned to exchange words with her brother. The scarf hid her face, but every line of the princess's body radiated pride in her deadly accomplishments.

Disgust flared before Diribani's conscience pricked her. Why shouldn't Ruqayya be proud of her skill? If she hadn't been so handy with her knife, or her brother with a sword, Diribani wouldn't have the luxury of being disgusted by their ferocious ways. When the man had attacked her at the fort, she certainly hadn't remembered any of her temple training. Rather than trying to escape or deflect the attack, she'd huddled against the fountain like a rabbit in short grass, as if stillness would give her safety.

It was all very well for a sheltered Gurath girl to congratulate herself on achieving some harmony with her fellow creatures. Diribani had learned a little, listening to the other young women talk over meals in the princess's tent. Ruqayya's ancestors had lived a nomad's life, in terrain more barren than this, and relied on their hunting skills to feed their children. Although their dominion over Diribani's people had begun generations ago, the emperor's throne hadn't passed peacefully from one occupant to the next. Perhaps a white-coat princess didn't dare trust in the goodwill of others. Diribani tried to imagine drawing a weapon and actually using it against another person. The thought made her stomach cramp in knots.

When Naghali-ji had asked her at the well what her soul desired, *beauty* was Diribani's answer. And she'd already received it. What could be lovelier than a flower? No, whatever the goddess intended for Diribani to learn from her gift, she was sure it didn't involve choosing a path of violence.

Ruqayya mopped up gravy with a piece of bread. "Lentils and yogurt and sliced cucumber again, Mina Diribani? You'll blow away, like a leaf!" Fingers snapped in one of her characteristic gestures.

"I don't believe so, my lady," Diribani answered. She shook her head at Nissa, who was trying to slip a spoonful of gazelle stew onto her plate.

"The broth will strengthen you." Since Nissa had the princess's support, the maid dared to argue. "I picked the meat out," she coaxed.

"No, thank you." Diribani declined with a smile and two lotuses.

"Our gentle flower girl," Ruqayya mocked. She stretched her arms over her head and leaned against the bolster, relaxed as a hunting cat. Their caravan had stopped for the night. Lamplight reflected off the royal tent's crimson walls, warming the princess's dark skin and waking purple lights in her curly black hair. In these private quarters, Ruqayya and her friends had shed their coats and wore sleeveless cotton tunics over their trousers. "You don't eat meat, you won't join us for archery or knife work—"

"I saw her slap a mosquito," a girl piped up, to general laughter.

"Can't you defend yourself at all?" Ladli asked, more scornfully. Tall and fit, the same age as Diribani, the young noblewoman was second only to Ruqayya in skill with a knife. Or so it had seemed to Diribani, watching them practice.

She might have turned aside the question with more smiles and flowers, as she usually did. Tonight the memory of the fleeing antelope woke a contrary impulse. "Defend? A little."

"With what, a garland of flowers and a few rough rubies?"

"Not usually, no." Diribani drew in a steadying breath. That barb had been aimed with malice. Ladli must have heard about the incident with Captain Tashrif. Diribani hadn't crossed his path since that afternoon in Gurath, but the soldier might not have been as discreet as Prince Zahid about how, exactly, Diribani's gift had come to the prince's attention. "I did study dancing at the temple."

"Warfare with bells and drums? That explains much of your history," Ladli drawled.

This time, the other girls' laughter sounded uneasy. Diribani's people had been conquered, but she was the princess's guest. This conversation pushed good manners to the edge of acceptability.

Ruqayya lolled, as indolent as before, though her eyes were intent. "Really? I've heard of temple dancing but never had the opportunity to see it."

"I should hope not!" Ladli exclaimed. "Our pure, devout princess visit an idolater's temple, to be bitten by snakes and crapped upon by pigeons?"

Even Diribani smiled at the accurate imitation of Lady Yisha's scandalized tones. The older woman might have thought it, but she would certainly never say anything so vulgar out loud. "I'm not as good as my sister, Tana, but I learned the basic steps."

"Will you show us?" Ruqayya asked.

"Dance for you? Here?" Diribani looked around the tent. "I suppose. A drum would help. As I said, I'm not an expert."

"Oh, yes."

"My maid drums."

"Mine, too."

Chattering like nesting birds, the young women summoned servants to fetch the instruments and clear the serving dishes. The two guards who followed Diribani everywhere picked up flowers and gems, recording the latter and securing them in a locked box. Then, with professional interest, they smoothed the carpets over the ground in the center of the large tent, leaving no uneven ridge or pocket to trip her.

Diribani knotted her long hair at the nape of her neck and asked Nissa to retrieve the mended pink dress wrap; all the clothes Ruqayya had provided were too grand to risk tearing. In preparation for dancing, Diribani rearranged the fabric so it resembled a pair of baggy trousers rather than the usual draped skirt. She shortened it, too, to just above the ankles, and dispensed with the shoulder drape. After conferring briefly with Ruqayya and then the two drummers, she was ready.

The other young women had gathered in a circle at the edges of the tent. Their maids packed in behind them, faces alight with the prospect of entertainment after the day's ride. When the princess had taken her seat among them, Diribani stood in the middle of the empty space, folded her hands, and prayed silently. Now was not the time to speak, scattering tiny hazards for her bare feet to find. *Manali-ji, Naghali-ji, sister goddesses of love and wisdom, guide my steps.* She nodded to the first drummer.

The heart drum sounded. Diribani relaxed; the woman had understood her instructions. Slowly, Diribani bent into the dance's opening movements, designed to warm muscles, focus the mind, and stretch the limbs for the faster sequences to follow. When she'd finished a complete repetition and saluted each of the twelve sacred points of the compass, she signaled to the second musician.

The spirit drum had a higher, thinner tone, but this woman, too, proved an artist. Her capable fingers made the rhythm skitter like gazelles leaping.

Diribani inclined her head to Ruqayya. As they had arranged, the princess tossed a wooden practice knife to the girl who had sneered at Diribani earlier.

"Attack her, Ladli," the princess said.

Ladli had caught the dagger, but at the command, her fingers fumbled it. "What, my lady?"

"You wanted to see her defend herself," Ruqayya said. "Go on. We're waiting."

"Yes, my lady." The young woman jumped to her feet and stabbed the wooden weapon at Diribani.

But Diribani had entered the discipline of the dance. The heart drum steadied her; the spirit drum lightened her step. Centering herself, she extended her awareness within the boundaries of the tent. With ridiculous ease, she evaded the dagger.

Her opponent overbalanced and almost fell. A couple of onlookers jeered, but Ruqayya shushed them, as Diribani had asked.

No matter where one performed it, ritual dance was a sacred undertaking, not like the white-coats' armed contests, where the object was to draw blood. A petitioner worshiping the twelve in any form—prayer or music or dance—sought to invoke their harmony.

Ladli feinted, then stabbed again, harder. The thrust would have bruised Diribani's ribs if she had been there to absorb the blow.

She wasn't.

The other girl hissed with surprise. She tried again. Missed. Each failed attempt made her angrier and more determined. But not successful. Like water, Diribani flowed around her.

When Ladli was wiping away tears of rage with her fist, her body stiff with frustration and shame, Diribani moved to the next stage. As she had been taught, she began to teach. Lightly, she tapped Ladli's elbow, back, thigh, shoulder, showing her where she was out of balance.

The moment Ladli stopped trying to strike Diribani and started imitating her steps, Diribani slowed deliberately, to show her. She started with a simple foot-pattern and danced away to let the other girl complete a rotation once by herself. Legs, heart, spirit, all leaping like a running deer.

Ladli had stopped crying. Her expression resigned, she finished her circle and raised the dagger in salute. To her surprise, Diribani's empty palm was already there to meet it.

Diribani smiled encouragement, her feet still moving in slow, rhythmic steps.

Ladli's face tensed with concentration. Like Diribani, she kept dancing. With a sudden motion, the dagger sliced sideways. Again, Diribani's hand touched it. Ladli's expression became even more focused. Inward, Diribani was glad to see—where her attention belonged. While the girl's feet carried her in a tight circle, the dagger flashed out unpredictably. Always, Diribani anticipated it.

Sweat beaded on their faces as they circled. Diribani knew her muscles would be complaining later, but this was so much fun! The musicians were as talented as temple players, which helped. The spirit drum sped up. Ladli's dagger followed; Diribani extended her senses and matched it. Up, down, sideways. Over her head, behind her knees. The sides of the tent seemed to pulse with the beat of the drums, the rhythm of women breathing in unison.

And one man.

At some point, Prince Zahid had stepped inside the tent. His privilege, as Ruqayya's brother, but one he had seldom exercised. He stood, unnoticed as a shadow in the corner. Until Diribani caught his eye.

Their glances locked for the tiniest instant. The admiration she read in his face jolted her out of step.

Slap! The dagger missed Diribani's hand and tapped her on the elbow. Startled, she lost her place in the rhythm. She tripped, then tumbled—slowly, gracefully, inevitably—over Ladli's hip and landed in a tangle of pink fabric at Ruqayya's feet. Smiling through her panting breath, Diribani sat up and folded her hands to her opponent.

No, her partner. Ladli bowed and handed Diribani the dagger hilt-first, to signal surrender. The drummers ended in a flourish. Diribani turned to include them, too, in her appreciation, as the other women clapped their hands. Laughing and exclaiming, they crowded around the dancers.

Ladli bent over at the waist, breathing in gulps as if she had just run a race. She shook her head. "I couldn't touch her, until she let me."

Diribani peeked at the corner of the tent, but Zahid had gone. "As I said, I'm not very good. Tana can keep up for hours."

"If you're not forbidden to teach us *flesh-eaters*"—Ruqayya used the rude word deliberately—"I would be honored to learn from you."

"And I," Ladli said.

"I would be happy to teach anyone who likes," Diribani said. Carnations fell into her lap. She handed one to Ladli. "You did very well for your first practice." Her legs unfolded. "Oof. I'll pay for this tomorrow. It's better to stretch first."

"It looks like fun," a girl said.

"Hard work," another demurred.

"Both," Diribani answered them truthfully.

"Tomorrow." Ruqayya directed a servant to begin extinguishing the lamps. At the signal, the other women put on their coats and head scarves. Like giant moths, they drifted off to their sleeping tents.

Diribani paused to refold her dress wrap into the usual skirt-and-shawl drape. Nissa brought her slippers.

When they were alone except for the maids, Ruqayya spoke. "You were distracted at the end."

"Yes," Diribani admitted. The warrior princess missed nothing.

"Be careful," Ruqayya said.

Of her brother, did she mean? Or of Diribani's own wandering attention? She stepped into her slippers, thinking about how a spark of intention could leap the greatest distance. About distraction, and danger. Fierce Ruqayya wouldn't warn her of shadows.

"Good night." Diribani folded her hands to the princess and followed Nissa's lamp into the darkness.

CHAPTER FOURTEEN

Tana

THE metal blade slid over Tana's scalp. She knelt on the bamboo mat, her hands clasped in her lap. Long black locks slithered over her shoulders to land, limp and lifeless, on the ground. Coolness followed, the wind's playful touch tracing naked skin. Though she had agonized over the decision, the sensation itself was pleasant. Tana peeked at her reflection in the basin of water. Her neck seemed longer, her ears more delicate, without hair to hide them. She looked smaller. Older, or younger? She couldn't tell what others would make of her appearance. Her mother, she meant. Her sister. *Kalyan.*

Unvarnished honesty, that was her new plan. She had forged it in weeks of temple service and nights of dancing. With the gift of snakes and toads, Naghali-ji had separated Tana from her family, her home, and any possibility of a normal life. In return, the goddess offered her devotees three choices. Tana had escaped death; good fortune eluded her. So she had decided to go in search of wisdom.

Diribani's gift had taken her far from Gurath, though never far from Tana's thoughts. Perhaps Tana's fate, too, lay elsewhere.

The first step was admitting how little she possessed. The shaved head, the orange renunciate's robe, the small bag and wooden begging bowl were just the outward signs of a truth she had accepted in her heart. It had pleased the goddess to strip Tana of everything she valued. So she would search until she discovered what Naghali-ji wanted her to have, or learn, or do.

"Wash, please," the priestess said.

Tana bent over the basin, bracing her elbows to face her reflection full-on. Two determined dark eyes stared back. At their fierce expression, she almost jerked away. Deliberately, she closed her eyes and splashed the water over her bald head. Her hair would grow back. Until it did, she would have to get used to this hot-eyed, egg-headed girl.

The priestess handed her a drying cloth and small clay pot. "The skin will be tender. You don't want to burn, the first few days." She rubbed her own bronze scalp. "Try and keep to the shade."

"Yes, Ma-ji." Tana spread the salve on her skin. It smelled like coconut. She stowed the jar in her bag. "I'm ready."

The priestess accompanied her to the temple gate. Tana took a last look at the bustling complex. She had enjoyed caring for the injured animals and learning more about snakes from the priests. She had served meals to the pilgrims, and, in the evening, danced under the stars to the heart drum and spirit drum. Every word she spoke, each toad and snake, reminded her that she had unfinished business with Naghali-ji.

Tana's mother had visited the temple and begged her to reconsider. But Tana knew that every day she delayed meant another chance the governor's spies might find her. The sooner she left, the sooner the priestess could tell Alwar that Tana had become someone else's problem. The thought made her smile, a bit grimly.

"Peace, Tana," the priestess said. "May the twelve guide your steps."

"Peace, Ma-ji," Tana replied. A lucky frog leaped onto the priestess's bare foot. It rested for a moment, then hopped across the courtyard, delighting several children who were waiting for their father to finish praying at Brother Vilokan's shrine. Tana hitched her bag over her shoulder and stepped into the street. Instead of walking through the city, she circled the walls. A network of footpaths bordered the cultivated fields and jungle thickets around Gurath. Eventually, she found her way to the royal road.

While she was dancing one night, the question of where to go had answered itself. As Tana had saluted each of the twelve directions, she had almost laughed out loud when her feet turned east-of-north, the point of the compass dedicated to Naghali-ji. What could be more obvious? She even had a guide. Tana could follow the river San to its source.

Her pilgrimage had begun with auspicious weather. Washed by the rains, the sky was as yet unclouded by the dust that hotter months would bring. Sunlight poured down on groves of mango and pinkfruit, palm and nut trees. The hemp blossoms glowed golden. Wheat and barley ripened in shades of delirious green. Until the emperor's road turned due north to Lomkha, it ran by the San. Tana walked along the shady bank, enjoying the breeze on her scalp.

Birds who had spent the rainy season elsewhere were returning to Tenth Province. Near the river, Tana heard the whistling of duck wings, the cries of curlews and pipers, and, once, the squawk of a disgruntled night heron. Great flocks passed overhead, fly-catchers, finches, swallows, and starlings. Where the smaller birds flew, others followed: eagles and falcons, buzzards and kites. In the shadow of the hunters' wide wings, doves ceased their cooing, quail their chuckling, green parrots their screaming, and mynahs their chattering. Only the frogs in the ditches and the insects in the fields continued shrilling and buzzing, unconcerned.

People, too, were taking advantage of the fine weather and improved roads. Farmers harvested the rice, millet, and sugarcane sown before the rains. Trade caravans set out from Gurath for the empire's most distant corners. Before Tana left the temple, couriers had begun to come from Prince Zahid, laden with jewels for the governor, and, more precious to Tana, letters from her sister. Ma Hiral had brought them to share with her.

Together they had read of Diribani's travels, and how she was teaching the white-coat girls to dance. But a whiff of sadness hung between the cheerful lines. Surrounded by the Believers' different customs, attitudes, clothes, and even food, Diribani clearly missed her family and home.

Tana thought that loneliness made another bond between them. Naghali-ji's gifts, though so different, had parted them with equal swiftness from the lives they knew. Tana wondered whether her journey would take her as far as her sister's. The manner of it was certainly more modest. On foot rather than elephant-back, she shared the road with long lines of camels and oxcarts. Later in the year, the tramping of so many hooves would raise clouds of choking dust. For now, they packed the dirt into a hard, flat surface.

Outside artisan and farming villages, gangs of children waved and called to the caravan drivers. Once the wagons had passed, they'd dart into the road and fill their baskets with ox dung left behind, to be dried in pats on the village walls and burned for fuel. The only cart they left alone was a corpse wagon, carrying the dead to the cremation grounds outside the city. That driver commanded folded hands and respectful silence.

The shade trees along the road belonged to the emperor. It was forbidden to raise an ax against them, but dropped branches were free for the taking. As she walked, Tana met girls and boys collecting wood to burn and thin branches to repair shutter lattices. Many people asked for her blessing. She folded her hands and smiled. It was still early in the season for pilgrims, but she had seen a few other orange robes on the road. As long as Tana didn't speak, she blended in, one more traveler going about her business. With every step from Gurath, she felt freer.

The soft light of late afternoon gilded the treetops and cast the road in thick shadow when she reached a village she recognized. Tana had visited Piplia before with Ba Javerikh and Diribani. The headman was a master gem-cutter who had left Gurath to teach the trade to his extended family. They had built a nice well here, too, if she remembered correctly. A bath would soothe her aching legs. She'd stopped several times to rest, but her feet weren't yet used to walking all day.

Food first, her stomach informed her. Tana made her way to the grove in the center of the village and sat down in the grass. She leaned against a tree trunk, scratching her back against the rough bark. A sweet smell made her look around, then up. She'd chosen a cork tree: Dangling clusters of long-throated white flowers had released their twilight fragrance. She sniffed with appreciation.

Placing her begging bowl on the ground in front of her, she sat and waited.

Within moments, the first child spotted her. Curious eyes peered from behind a mango tree. Feet pattered in the grass, and then came the familiar shout: "Ma, there's a pilgrim." How many times had Tana heard Indu say exactly the same thing?

Soon a young girl brought her a cup of tea. A boy followed, bearing rice cakes spread with butter, and slices of dried mango. "There was soup earlier, but we ate it. Sorry, Mina-ji."

Tana smiled and folded her hands. She sipped and ate, enjoying the peaceful scene. Men and women were returning from the fields or the well, tired and dirty or laughing and clean, depending. A horse whinnied; a cow lowed in answer. Dogs barked from the courtyards they defended. As daylight faded, doves cooed sleepy songs in the branches above her. Tana heard the *rackety-rack* noise of grinders and cutters slow, then stop. In the workshop, artisans would be cleaning their tools, sweeping up the dust, and returning the gemstones to their marked pouches. Each one must be accounted for at every stage, from mine to finished ornament. The familiar sounds made her feel at home.

"Peace to you, pilgrim." The headman's wife appeared, resplendent in a melon-colored dress wrap. She carried a pot of spicy lentils. Ladling some into Tana's bowl, she leaned closer to study her face in the dim light. "Mina Tana?"

Tana rubbed her bald head. "I'm surprised you recognized me, Ma-ji." A green frog fell from her lips and hid, its color indistinguishable from the grass.

"Aaah!" The woman hugged her pot of lentils to her chest. "It's true, then, what we heard. You'll honor our house tonight, Mina

Tana? My husband and his guest will want to hear the story from your own lips."

"Outside is better for talking," Tana said. "And I don't mean to burden you with more visitors."

"It's no trouble," the woman assured her. She eyed the snake at Tana's other side. "That ratter, is he spoken for? With the white-coats' bounty, it's difficult to get a healthy house naga."

Tana shook her head.

"Please excuse me." The woman hurried away. "Vilina," she called. "Vilina, bring the snake basket."

Tana ate her lentils. The snake stretched lazily, as if it found its new existence good. Tana watched it over her bowl. As long as a house naga appeared at least once in a conversation, it seemed that people would excuse Tana's other shortcomings.

But when the horse whinnied again, Tana stiffened. Dropping the begging bowl, she crept to the edge of the grove and peered around a tree at the headman's compound. Through the gate, a white shape was visible, ghostly in the twilight.

No ratter could excuse Tana's stupidity. What else could she call it? Lulled by the day's lack of event, the stroll through a peaceful countryside, Tana had jeopardized her entire plan to slip unnoticed out of Gurath. Like a fool, she had stopped at a village where she was likely to be recognized. She had spoken. She had even disregarded Jasmine's familiar whinnying. How many people rode white horses to a gem-cutters' village? She couldn't bear another argument with him, or, worse, uncomfortable constraint.

Tana slipped between the trees and made for the well. Unlike Gurath's large open tank, this one was a single shaft dug deep into the earth. A small pavilion marked the flight of steps leading down.

Lamps glowed in their niches, illuminating the snake curves painted over the doorway. As Tana remembered, a decorative stone border surmounted the pavilion. Flowering vines wound up the pillars and spilled across the roof. Through the years, the stems had grown thick and woody, strong enough to support her weight.

Grateful for the concealing darkness, Tana climbed up to the roof and wormed her way under the vines. Generations of children had played here, leaving nests lined with mango pits, empty nutshells, cracked clay cups. Birds twittered at Tana's intrusion, but soon quieted.

She'd been just quick enough. A lantern glowed by the headman's gate. It bobbed through the grove to the flowering cork tree. To judge by the voices, the ratter had been secured, and Tana's begging bowl discovered. She recognized the headman's voice, and his wife's. But the person calling her name most loudly was Kalyan.

CHAPTER FIFTEEN

Diribani

DIRIBANI opened the tent flap and turned her face to the morning light. Briskly, she rubbed her arms, bare under the iris-banded dress wrap. The cool season had stolen upon them, or perhaps it was the increasing elevation. Over the last few days, they'd climbed out of desert scrub and wound their way upward to this high plateau. The fort of Fanjandibad waited at the far edge, where, Nissa had told her, the landscape changed again. Soon she would see it. Surely then she would know why Naghali-ji had sent her so far from home.

"Your slippers, my lady."

"Thank you, Nissa. I keep forgetting." Shoes looked odd under a traditional dress wrap, especially one as splendid as this. Diribani missed the reassurance of earth under her feet, but in the thorny countryside she had been persuaded to adopt the custom.

"And your scarf."

Diribani shook her head. "Oh, I think I'll be warm enough inside the howdah."

Still, Nissa held out the length of fine white cotton. "Your *head* scarf, my lady."

"My what?" Two narcissus flowers and a large emerald bounced off the tent flap. Standing just outside the opening, the guard Zeen reached out and caught the stone.

"For our arrival in Fanjandibad," Nissa said. "The riding animals are stabled inside the first gate, so we have to dismount and walk through the fort grounds to the palace. Four hundred steps, from the outer wall to the ladies' court! It always seems like the longest part of the journey. I can show you how to wrap the scarf now; or, later, perhaps one of the other ladies . . ." Nissa's voice trailed away as she read Diribani's expression.

"I'd rather not cover my face with that scarf," Diribani said distinctly. "Thank you."

Nissa looked at Zeen, as if for support.

The guard's impassive face didn't change. She bent and picked up three small bloodstones, entered them in her ledger, and handed them to her partner, Mahan, who carried the locked box.

"But, my lady," Nissa persisted, "we all veil in Fanjandibad when we're outside the ladies' court. It's the custom."

"Not my people's custom," Diribani said. A spray of jasmine added its perfume to the chilly air.

Nissa held her ground. "Her Highness said you should have it."

"Then I had better discuss it with her." Gingerly, as if it were a venomous snake, Diribani took the length of white cloth. Tana had worn the Believer coat and trousers, which made sense for riding. But this! Surely her sister would be as disgusted as Diribani by the suggestion that she cover her face. And she'd not hesitate to make that clear to her host, princess or no.

Diribani shouldered her way outside the tent, past Zeen and Mahan. The guards fell into step behind her. Nissa followed them. Marching the short distance to the royal tent, Diribani might have felt ridiculous about her entourage. Anger didn't leave much room for embarrassment.

As was usual in the morning, the red cloth door panels still hung undisturbed to the ground. Diribani hesitated, then sat a polite distance from the entry. The guards stood to one side. Nissa hovered, wringing her hands.

The camp bustled with the usual routine of meals and washing and exercise, the shouts of soldiers drilling, the smell of millet porridge and horse, the clang of pots, and the bellowing of hungry oxen. Today the familiar sounds seemed infused with a fresh energy. If all went well, this time tomorrow they'd be waking up in Fanjandibad. First Camp might be there already.

The prince's caravan traveled in grand style. There were actually two of everything: royal tents, cook tents, wash tents, teams of draft oxen and pack elephants, cooks and soldiers and laborers. The royal party traveled short days so the camps could leapfrog each other. While one packed up behind them, the other prepared for their arrival. This was Second Camp. First Camp would have hurried past them in the night, to alert the fort's resident staff that the prince was on his way.

As the sun climbed, Diribani attracted her share of curious glances and amused comments. Ruqayya's manner, though never less than regally courteous, tended to crispness in the morning hours. People with questions or requests usually waited until later in the day to address her. Meanwhile, the princess's maids came and went, slipping inside the red tent with basins of water and steaming cups of tea. One of them must have told her mistress about the petitioner outside.

"Come," an imperious voice called.

Diribani's stiff knees popped audibly as she got up, but she waved away Nissa's offered arm.

Ladli, returning from the direction of the latrine pits, beat an imaginary drum on her thigh. "Pa-pum, pa-pum." She lowered her head scarf to grin at Diribani. "Braving the lioness in her den? Remember, mindfulness is all."

Diribani returned a rueful smile, hearing her own instructions quoted back at her. In the dancing the previous night, Ladli had bested her three times, and Ruqayya once. These white-coat girls were so quick, they had risen to the limit of Diribani's ability to teach. Ladli's teasing reminder was useful, though. Matching wits—or wills—with Ruqayya was like facing a steel blade, not the usual wooden practice ones. Diribani stepped into the tent and waited for her eyes to adjust to the rosy light inside.

Ruqayya sat on a bolster while a maid arranged her curly hair into a braid for riding. A white brocade coat hung over her shoulders; the long rope of pearls had reappeared, looped several times around her neck. She held a clay cup between her palms. Chin lowered, she breathed in the fragrant steam. "Yes?"

"Peace to you, Your Highness." Diribani folded her hands. "I've come about the head scarf."

"What about it?" Ruqayya said. "Assuming your head's the usual size, the scarf I gave Nissa should fit."

Diribani squared her shoulders. She set the scarf on a cushion. "Thank you, but it won't be necessary."

"Necessary?" The princess gulped her tea and shoved the cup at a maid. "What about respectful? What about prudent?"

When Diribani didn't answer, Ruqayya twitched loose from the woman braiding her hair to prowl up and down the carpet. "Fanjandibad is a small island of Believers in a sea of your folk. Within its walls, our people take religion very seriously. Outside her home, an unveiled woman risks public shaming. Do you want to be called names? Spat upon?"

"No." Diribani looked the princess in the eye. "But I will endure it before I'll cover my face." Chunks of turquoise thumped onto the roses and irises scattered across the carpet.

"Why so stubborn, flower girl?" Ruqayya chided. "We don't force you to renounce your idols or eat our meat. Humor me in this one thing. Bend a little for the sake of harmony, as you're so fond of telling us."

Again, Diribani's own words taunted her. How could she make the princess understand? "When your brother invited me to Fanjandibad, he promised my stepmother I would live in comfort and honor. As to comfort"—Diribani gestured at the luxurious tent, the plates of food on Ruqayya's table, her own silk dress wrap— "you couldn't have been more generous. And honor? All these weeks, not a single person in your party has accosted me for a jewel. But even to repay your kindness, I cannot dishonor the twelve."

"Can't or won't?" Ruqayya snapped.

Diribani answered gently, but firmly: "Won't."

"Must I spell it out for you?" the princess growled. "You're our guest. Anyone insulting you will be punished."

"I'm not asking," Diribani began, but Ruqayya overrode her.

"How will your conscience balance that? Will you come crying to me when your tender ears are assaulted with the screams of men being whipped? They would be guilty of upholding their own beliefs by chastising an immodest woman, and yet Zahid will put them to the post."

Diribani stared at the carpet. The thought of covering her face— like a corpse—made her ill. But which would the gods count as the greater sin? Adopting the white-coats' unpleasant custom, or causing others to be injured when she could prevent it? She tried to think what Tana would do.

"Good morning, ladies." Prince Zahid's voice surprised Diribani into looking up. He'd come into the tent with a cup of tea in each hand. He held them out to his sister and her guest. Diribani accepted, but Ruqayya shook her head.

"I can't drink and pace." The princess's lips twitched in a smile. "Tell me you've come to talk sense into your hardheaded holy woman. She won't wear a head scarf."

"I'm not a holy woman," Diribani insisted.

Ruqayya flicked her fingers. "Fine."

"Since we've settled *that* issue to everyone's satisfaction," the prince said, "tell me, Mina Diribani, is it the practice of modesty or the scarf itself that you object to?"

Diribani sipped her tea. As usual, the prince's presence distracted her. It was as if the force of his personality swept across her like an actual current. Her skin tingled; the blood pumped more energetically through her veins. She found it hard to concentrate on the question.

Ruqayya paced. Zahid swirled his cup. He watched the steam rise up as if he had all the time in the world to settle this dispute.

"We, too, value modesty, but define it differently," Diribani said, feeling her way through the tumult in her body to an answer. Peonies, ashoka blossoms, and a spray of orange lilies punctuated her words. "For us, modesty doesn't mean covering the skin with cloth to avoid inspiring envy or desire in others. If I wrapped my face in that fabric, it would suggest I was ashamed of the features Father Ghodan and Mother Gaari had given me."

"So, if there were a way to convey respect for our beliefs without wearing a head scarf specifically, you'd do it?"

"I think so," Diribani said cautiously.

"Let's try this." The prince handed his cup to a maid and approached Diribani. "A most ingenious garment," he said in conversational tones. "If, for example, you take the end that falls over your shoulder—may I?"

Diribani's breath caught. She nodded.

Zahid lifted the strip of yellow silk. He draped it over her hair and forehead, then passed the free end loosely across her chin and back over her shoulder, like a shawl.

Intensely aware of his hand brushing her ear, Diribani held tight to her empty cup. As a talisman, it didn't work very well. Her mouth was dry, her skin fluttery where he had touched it.

The prince stepped back. "What do you think?" he asked his sister, but looked at Diribani.

She glanced away. The improvised scarf wasn't confining, but with only her eyes visible, she felt they were too transparent, as if to make up for the expression concealed by a fall of yellow silk. She didn't want Zahid reading a message she wasn't ready to share with him. If she even understood it. A person couldn't fall in love with so little encouragement—a few words, a speaking glance. Could she?

Attraction, that was all she felt, and perfectly natural, Tana would say, that the foreign prince intrigued her. He had saved their lives. He had treated them with respect. And his lightning intelligence made the young traders Diribani knew seem impossibly dull and provincial. Perhaps, she thought wildly, she should have wrapped the scarf around her head altogether and let Nissa lead her from the tent like a blind woman before Zahid could touch her.

Unveiled, Ruqayya's face held the same concentrated stillness it had held the night she had warned of distraction. The first night Diribani had danced for them, when the prince's appearance had surprised Diribani into carelessness. *Trouble*, the princess's expression said. Her voice, however, was cool and assured. "Unorthodox, but not objectionable. Mina Diribani?"

"I will wear it this way, if it pleases you."

"Thank you," the prince said. His breath touched Diribani's cheek.

He smelled like spicy tea, and horse, and man. A dangerous combination for an unsophisticated Gurath girl. Even as she told herself she shouldn't, she breathed deeply.

"Then perhaps I may continue with my interrupted meal?" The princess flicked her fingers. "Out, the pair of you. And do have your maid clean up my floor before the petals are ground into the carpet, Mina Diribani."

"Yes, my lady."

"We hear and obey," the prince said. He smiled at Diribani.

She bowed her head, and escaped from the pair of them.

CHAPTER SIXTEEN

Tana

B IRDS weren't the only creatures sharing the well-pavilion roof with Tana. As the evening advanced, a family of tree mice woke in their nest in the corner. For a while, they chittered grumpily. One sniffed around Tana, but found nothing to interest it. The rest left her alone. Intent on the night's foraging, they climbed up and down the vines. Tana tied her drying cloth around her head to shut out their noise. Even so, she slept badly, plagued by dreams she couldn't remember when she woke. Bats fluttered above her, squeaking as they chased moths and insects. By ones and twos, the tree mice returned, leaves rustling around them.

Tana half woke at the racket, then burrowed deeper under the leaves. When the muffled sounds of trouble reached her not long after, she thought it was the tree mice stirring again. Then a shrill cry of fear penetrated her sleepiness. Dogs barked, an angry chorus.

Tana slid the cloth from her ears and into the bag she was using for a pillow. Without moving, she listened. The sky was dark, though a gray tinge in the east smudged the stars. A horse bugled alarm. Tana crawled to the edge of the roof and parted the curtain of vines with her fingers.

In the direction of the village, torches flared. Their ruddy light illuminated figures moving against the mud-brick walls. Steel helmets reflected the torchlight; long blades glinted like metal splinters. Soldiers, going from house to house. At this distance, Tana only got confused glimpses, but what she saw frightened her. Men and women holding children were being driven from their homes, herded like animals into the central grove. Then their livestock, too, followed: oxen and water buffalo mostly, with a flash of white that might have been Jasmine. Or a light-colored cow. Tana couldn't see what was happening under the trees, but she could hear the wailing. And her name, shouted in unfamiliar voices.

The soldiers were looking for her.

When they didn't find her in the headman's house, they set his roof on fire. Mud bricks didn't burn, but thatched palm fronds ignited in a fountain of hissing sparks. Orange flames tongued the darkness. A new note of despair issued from the villagers' throats.

Shaking with dread and helpless anger, Tana put her head down. She considered showing herself so the soldiers would spare the rest of the houses. But if it were proved, not just suspected, that the headman had sheltered her, his punishment might be worse than damage to his home. So she remained where she was, wondering whether cowardice or common sense kept her hidden.

She had the chance to speak. Torches approached the well; she smelled burning resin and saw the light flicker through the concealing vines. A couple of the soldiers went inside, to judge by the sound of clay pots being smashed below her. Attracted to the torch light, moths gathered. Wings brushed Tana's hair. Then the entire bat colony converged on the moth banquet. Tana heard their leathery wings flapping, the high-pitched squeaks, the men's cursing and tramping feet. The torches retreated. She stayed hidden.

From the village, more shouting, more wailing. A dog's yelp stopped abruptly. With a loud crackling, another roof caught fire, and then another. Closer, whips snapped and oxcarts creaked. Shouted orders cut through the babble of voices, followed by a strange clanking noise. The sky was getting lighter. She might be discovered, but she had to know. Tana pushed up on her elbows and peeked through the vines. What she saw made her bite hard on her fingers to keep from crying out.

The adult villagers had been chained in lines, five or ten together, and attached to the oxcarts. Lanterns fixed to the carts' wooden sides shed a feeble light over the nightmare scene. Children rode on their parents' shoulders or ran alongside, clutching at their clothes. Tana glimpsed the headman's stocky form, but she couldn't tell whether Kalyan was among them. Soldiers rode ahead and behind the oxcarts. Some drove the farm animals. One led a riderless horse, briefly silhouetted against a lantern.

Horror choked her. Hadn't the soldiers done enough? Rousting people from their beds, breaking their things like the clay pots at the well, setting fire to the houses . . . after they'd looted them, probably. Why did they have to take the people away?

So they won't tell.

The answer came to her, as cold as a stone lodged in her throat. The soldiers weren't returning to Gurath; the sad procession was headed the other way. If Tana guessed rightly, these poor people would be marched to one of the white-coats' country estates. Alwar didn't want word to get out that his men were chasing Tana in spite of the prince's order to leave her alone. Tana breathed a quiet prayer of gratitude to the twelve that Diribani was safe with the royal party.

The governor must have known when Tana was at the temple. She had moved freely around the compound, where multitudes attended to pray or dance or study. Ma Hiral brought Diribani's letters. Pilgrims stayed at the lodging court; children attended lessons. Even white-coats brought sick and injured animals for the priests to treat. Strictly speaking, Prince Zahid had told Tana to leave Gurath. He had also said that the emperor would frown on the civil authorities' interfering in a local religious matter. Sending soldiers to one of Gurath's temples couldn't be hushed up. But a night raid on an artisan village far outside the city gates? Who would know it wasn't bandits attacking Piplia for the gems the workers cut and polished?

Shame coiled in Tana's belly. She had underestimated Alwar's hatred for Naghali-ji's gift of snakes. He must have stationed someone to watch for Tana by the temple gate. She hadn't worried about pursuit, foolishly congratulating herself on the disguise of a shaved head and pilgrim's orange robe. But hidden among the travelers on the road, a spy could have seen her go to the village with her begging bowl and hurried back to alert the soldiers.

If Tana hadn't spotted Jasmine, the governor's men would have found her exactly where they expected, sleeping at the headman's home.

As she reproached herself, the world around her turned to shades of gray. A cock crowed. He sounded forlorn, as if suspecting that nobody would feed him today. Tana gathered her resolve. She had better get on with it.

She climbed down from the roof. Inside the well, she gritted her teeth against the pain of clay shards that stabbed her bare feet. She drank, then washed stealthily in the small bathing pool. Emerging a short time later, she found a thick mist shrouding the trees. It tasted of ash and felt clammy on her bare head. But it was her friend, she reminded herself. It would help hide her.

She picked her way up the path, stopping often to listen. Birdsong greeted the dawn, cooings and cluckings, whistlings and the piltreet's "lazy girl, girl, girl." Inside the village, Tana crept along the walls. Scenes of destruction played out in every home: cooking pots overturned, bedding slashed, farm implements broken and the pieces scattered. The headman's workshop was the worst. The valuable drills and tools were all missing. The wooden benches had been smashed, then set on fire. Soot smeared the walls, which were fringed with scorched thatch and open to the sky. Tana's bare feet left gritty black prints. When she noticed it, she grabbed a fallen palm frond and dragged it behind her. The deception wouldn't fool a serious tracker, but it should make it less obvious that one person, at least, had been here shortly after the fire.

When she found the dead dog outside a house, a scrap of white fabric caught in its teeth, Tana crouched next to it and cried. Tears ran warm down her cheeks and dripped off her nose. With sorrow came anger. Anger at the soldiers for killing the dog. At the governor for ordering them here, at the spy who had watched her. She was furious with herself, too, for not considering the possibility of pursuit, for putting innocent people in harm's way. *Kalyan*, her heart mourned. What had happened to him?

Deeper still, where she could hardly admit it, Tana was angry with Naghali. The goddess scorned her pilgrimage, strewing devastation in Tana's wake. Many of the villagers had seen her; they had no reason to lie about that. The soldiers would be searching the roads for a bald-headed, orange-robed, stupid girl who spoke snakes and toads.

Tana hiccupped and wiped her eyes on the robe, now stained with soot. Inside the house, Tana found a worn yellow dress wrap and shawl, not too badly singed. She took off the pilgrim's robe and put on the dress wrap, tying the shawl over her shaved head. If the morning stayed cool, nobody would find it strange. Kneeling by the household shrine, she prayed to Brother Akshath that the war god recognize the dog's courage and speed his rebirth. She hoped the brave soul might protect his own more successfully in his next life.

Under the shrine, Tana noticed the broken pieces of a house naga's pot. The ratter lay a short distance away. Its head had been severed from its body in a display of cruelty that made the tears start again. Crying, she bundled the dead animals into her discarded robe.

Judging from the broken, unfired pots littering the courtyard, the next house belonged to a potter. The kiln wood stacked along the wall had burned to a deep bed of coals. Tana raked them together to make a pyre for the bodies. On it, she also burned two more dead dogs, a chicken, and all the village ratters. The soldiers had broken the pot under every household shrine and killed any house naga sleeping inside. The smell of cooking flesh made Tana retch, but she didn't leave the village until all the dead had been burned. By the time the morning fog cleared, the betraying column of smoke should be gone.

After Tana had dealt with the bodies, she washed again. Then she returned a last time to collect what food she could find: a bag of dried chickpeas, another of rice, and some dried fruit. Occupied in her sad work, she felt her resolution harden like a clay pot in the flames.

She wouldn't wear a pilgrim's orange robe or beg for food in Naghali's name any longer. She wouldn't speak and let one more snake fall from her mouth to be cut up by the governor's butchers. Tana could no longer call her flight from Gurath a pilgrimage. Not after this. The goddess might have turned her back on Tana, but Tana would keep faith with the people who had been taken in her place. If she had to walk all the way to Lomkha, she would find them.

And she would send word to Diribani, in hopes that her sister could convince Prince Zahid to punish Tenth Province's lawless governor and set his captives free.

CHAPTER SEVENTEEN

Diribani

I trust you'll be comfortable here," Ruqayya said. Fingers adorned with rubies and pearls waved Diribani through an arched doorway and into the suite of rooms.

"It's lovely." Diribani left her slippers at the door. Her bare feet sank into the carpet. A flower design woven in tones of pistachio, melon, and berry, it gleamed with the sheen of silk. Diribani wanted to kneel and touch it, but after the morning's difficult interview, she preferred not to play the country maid where a passing courtier could see.

Although the younger ones had gotten used to her, Lady Yisha and her friends continued to treat Diribani with condescension, as if she were a superior type of conjurer, producing more than the usual silk scarf from her sleeve. *Someday,* their expressions said, *you'll slip, and we'll understand how the trick is done. Then we'll ship you back to the dusty town His Highness plucked you from. In the meantime, it amuses him to honor you, and suits us to indulge the royal whim. As long* as Diribani remembered her manners. The prince ate first, always, and then the princess, and then the rest of the court.

With Ruqayya strolling behind her, Diribani walked through the suite. She wished Tana were with her to admire the carpets scattered over floors of inlaid marble, plastered walls painted in shades of cream and tea, the mirror-encrusted dressing room. Tall windows set with intricate stone screens overlooked the rest of Fanjandibad. Diribani saw the fort's grand audience hall, soldiers' barracks, stables, prayer halls, and other buildings they had passed on the long climb up the hill. Four hundred steps, Nissa had said, from the gate in the massive walls to the palace at the top of the hill. Diribani's knees still felt them.

One of those buildings would be the artists' workshop. She couldn't identify it from above, though she lingered at the window for an extra moment. As she turned back inside, a young woman whisked out the door, her arms full of bedding and gauzy clothing. Diribani recognized the maid. After a moment's reflection, she wished she hadn't.

"These are Lady Yisha's rooms?" she asked her hostess.

"They were," Princess Ruqayya said. "She'll be moving in with a cousin, on a lower floor."

"It's kind of her to give up her apartment for my sake," Diribani said.

"Not a bit," the princess returned. "You should have seen her face when I told her. She'd have had her elephant hoist you up by the neck and drop you in a ditch outside the walls if she thought I wouldn't find out." A trill of laughter issued from Ruqayya's lips. The sound was so unlike her usual straightforward manner that Diribani stared. "Never fear. Everyone knows you're under our family's protection. And Yisha was getting rather tiresome, acting as if her father was chief adviser to God Himself, not a mere emperor." The princess bared her teeth in a fierce smile. "A taste of humility will improve her character."

Humility? Or humiliation? Diribani didn't ask.

Entering the fort's gates had changed Ruqayya, and not for the better, as far as Diribani was concerned. The princess's manner had become both more arch and more cryptic. That one speech seemed to contain several warnings, but Diribani wasn't sure what kind exactly, or how many. Again, she missed her sister. With her skill at marketplace bargaining, Tana would be better at deciphering Ruqayya's underlying message.

If anything, her hostess's conversation reminded Diribani of an elaborate sweet the cooks had served recently. Layer upon layer of pastry, chopped nuts, and honey syrup surrounded a caramelized sugar wafer sharp enough to cut your lips unless you knew to eat it by nibbling around the edges toward the center. If Ladli hadn't warned Diribani to eat it slowly the other night, blood would have flavored her portion. Diribani's hand fluttered to her mouth to cover a grimace. "The rooms are so large for one person," she said. "I wouldn't mind sharing."

"You'll get used to it, I assure you." Again, the princess laughed, but then her plucked eyebrows drew together in a slight frown. "I can't let a well-born girl live with you, my dear. Your, uh, gift—you must see how the situation would give rise to jealousy and mistrust. Also, it would put your guards in an awkward position."

"My guards?" Diribani braced for another unwelcome revelation. She glanced over her shoulder. Sure enough, Zeen and Mahan were standing by the door. Lilies, orchids, and precious stones dotted the carpet where Diribani had walked. At any moment, one of the women would be retrieving the gems, noting them in her ledger, and putting them in the locked chest. They left the flowers for Nissa to clean up.

"I mean," Diribani said, "on the road, it seemed practical. But surely there's no one inside the palace who would do me harm."

"Little innocent." Nudging jewels and flowers aside with her embroidered slipper, the princess moved closer to whisper in Diribani's ear. "Learn quickly; the travel idyll is over. Why do you think Zahid and I live in this barren flypit of a district?"

"Because of the diamond mines? And it's a position of great responsibility, overseeing the seat of justice on the southeastern frontier . . ." Diribani's voice trailed off.

Ruqayya tossed her head. She kept her voice too low for any but Diribani to hear the anger in it. "Before the cool season ends, I imagine you'll have produced as many diamonds as these mines. No, it's because our elder brother doesn't want us exerting any influence over Father. Those who keep us company are either suspect themselves, or paid to spy on us, or both." Her lip curled. "Have I frightened you? Good. Remember the assassin in Gurath. Revenge, greed, necessity: Any could be your undoing. Only think. One of the gems you spit so casually would secure an ambitious man's future."

Diribani swallowed the ugly taste in her mouth. "Thank you for your counsel, my lady." Lotus flowers drifted to the floor.

"It would reflect poorly on our supposed trustworthiness if something happened to you in the heart of Fanjandibad, wouldn't it?" Ruqayya primped in a mirror, adjusting her dark curls. "I believe Governor Alwar would ride his horse directly into my father's throne room in Lomkha if Zahid's couriers stopped delivering that lard pudding's share of your jewels."

"Lard pudding?" Diribani said.

"Why, how very undiplomatic of me. Never mind. It's a nasty dish." Ruqayya clapped her hands, effectively changing the subject. "Nissa."

"My lady?" Diribani's maid dropped the bag she was carrying and bowed.

At court, white-coats didn't fold their hands to show respect, Diribani had noted. They bowed, more or less deeply, depending on relative rank. Lady Yisha had resented Diribani from the first day, when she didn't know enough to bow. And now Diribani had taken her rooms. Was this her new fate, to make enemies without understanding what she was doing wrong?

Like a rose's thorn, danger accompanied the fragrant petals of Sister Naghali's blessing.

The princess flicked her fingers at the maid. "I charge you with ensuring that Mina Diribani lacks nothing suitable for her station."

And wasn't that nicely stated? Diribani thought. Ruqayya used the traditional honorific "mina," not the court's "lady," since Diribani wasn't nobly born. That way, others weren't offended that she'd been granted a status she didn't deserve. And if Diribani appeared to presume, the princess could blame Nissa for not following her instructions.

"Yes, my lady." A deeper bow.

"Then I will leave you both to get settled," Ruqayya said. "Rest, if you like, and wash off the road dust. The baths are on the lowest floor; Nissa will show you. Since the weather's fine, we'll eat this evening on the upper rooftop terrace."

"Thank you, Your Highness." Instead of bowing, Diribani folded her hands, Gurath-style.

Ruqayya's lips twitched, but she didn't comment on the minor rebellion. At the door, she spoke briefly to the guards, then called out again to Diribani. "By the way, Mahan and Zeen have their orders. My brother has proclaimed that, unless given expressly by your hand, the jewels that fall from your lips are to be considered royal property. Their theft is punishable by death."

"What?" Diribani couldn't contain her dismay, even as a particularly fine piece of jade plunked onto the carpet. "But he said that Fanjandibad didn't covet Gurath's gift, that the jewels would go to Tenth Province and glorify Naghali-ji."

"And so they will. Zahid's word is law." Princess Ruqayya gestured in graceful apology. "But people can be so undisciplined. Especially those who don't believe in your Gurath gods and goddesses. This way, no one will be tempted to tuck a diamond into her coat sleeve. For her dowry, or to pay off a father's debts. Don't you agree, Nissa?"

"Yes, my lady." The girl stared at the carpet, where real flowers overlaid the woven ones. Her expression did a poor job, Diribani thought, of concealing raw terror.

"I'm glad we understand one another," the princess purred. In a sweep of white brocade, she left the room.

The moment Ruqayya's voice could no longer be heard issuing orders to the servants in the corridor, Diribani snatched the nearest three gems from the floor. She dragged her maid by the elbow to stand in front of the guards. "Mahan, Zeen," she said, "I want you to witness that I am presenting Nissa with this ruby, sapphire, and emerald." As she named each stone, she set it deliberately on the girl's moist palm. "She may dispose of them however she chooses."

"Yes, my lady."

"As you command, my lady."

Diribani couldn't tell whether her bland-faced guards approved or disapproved of her action, and she didn't care. She had to assume that they would report each word she spoke, down to the last rati, to Ruqayya.

"A thousand blessings on your head, my lady." Nissa had fallen to the floor and was pressing kisses to the carpet at Diribani's feet.

"Eyo!" Diribani said, disconcerted out of her temper. "Stop that, please. I should have thought of it before." She should have thought of a lot of things, but, as Tana would say, it was no use standing on one leg to kick yourself for being clumsy; you'd fall over for certain.

As Diribani extracted herself from Nissa's effusive gratitude, the ever-present knot of loss tightened in her chest. In these palatial rooms, every comfort—suited to her station, of course—could be enjoyed at the snap of her fingers. And yet it seemed a wasteland in comparison with the humble house in Gurath. There a few bare rooms had contained people who loved her.

At least Tana and Ma Hiral had each other. Diribani didn't even have news of them. Without benefit of imperial courier, their letters had yet to catch up with her. The court ladies were relieved to be home, but Diribani felt so lonely she would have been glad to find a house naga's clay pot under the window. She hadn't noticed one as she walked through the palace. Perhaps white-coats who didn't kill snakes on sight kept them in the kitchens. Diribani wouldn't have minded banishment to their fair-minded company. You knew where you stood with snakes. Unlike courtiers, ratters made no distinction in their treatment of the humble and the mighty. They hunted as happily for a farmer in his hut as for an overseer in his mansion. More happily, probably. Farmers had fatter rats.

Diribani tried to imagine Lady Yisha attempting to intimidate a house naga. The thought lifted her spirits until bedtime, when she lay on soft sheets and stared at the moonlight filtered by stone screens. What was she doing here?

CHAPTER EIGHTEEN

Tana

FROM dusk to foggy dawn, Horse Month to Monkey Month, Tana followed the kidnapped villagers across Tenth Province. As if transporting a herd of valuable wild elephants, the soldiers moved the people and their livestock after dark, from one walled enclosure to another, along the emperor's road.

Thick evening mists favored Tana's pursuit. Bare feet quiet on the hard-packed dirt, Tana maintained a discreet distance from the creaking carts. Her shawl and the walking kept her warm as she plodded along, listening to the cries of owls and other night hunters. A distant howling alarmed her, but the pack of wild dogs didn't approach the mounted soldiers. Leopards posed a greater danger. Several times, she heard the distinctive barking cough. Ahead, torches flared and men shouted. Tana quickened her pace. More than discovery, she feared straggling behind, lest a big cat mark her as easy prey.

When dawn broke, she scouted her surroundings for a safe

place to eat, wash, and rest. Tana had never traveled so far from home. If she hadn't been worrying about the others, she would have enjoyed her morning and evening glimpses of the countryside. Gradually, the road curved north, away from the river San's marshy course. As the ground became higher and drier, the coastal landscape of fields carved from jungle changed. The vegetation thinned. In place of great mango, pinkfruit, and tamarind groves, scrubby trees and bushes poked out of the soil. Fewer people lived in the northeastern part of Tenth Province. They seemed poorer, scratching out a living from fields pinched between walled whitecoat estates. The powerful artisan guilds didn't extend this far, making craft enclaves less common. Tana rarely saw the vivid swaths of dyed fabric drying on a village's mud-brick walls, or heard the distinctive rattle of gem drills and polishers. Even the region's stepwells were plainer affairs, large open tanks without the shade pavilions of Gurath's sacred well.

Whenever Tana entered one of the small market towns, she looked at the goods for sale. The stalls of common household items and food told the same story: poor-quality cloth, rough baskets, crude wooden tools. At home in Gurath, market tables were heaped with foodstuffs. Ordinary dried beans came in many shades of yellow, brown, red, and dark purple. Here, vendors displayed bins of common red lentils alongside grit-flecked rice, a few vegetables, and wild greens.

Only one kind of stall showed an abundance. After the first horrified glance, Tana averted her eyes from the tables where the local white-coat officials paid out Governor Alwar's bounty on dead snakes. Disgust hardened Tana's determination not to speak and give these people more creatures to kill.

Unsurprisingly, given the cruel slaughter of ratters, their prey had multiplied.

It turned Tana's stomach to see the evidence everywhere. In town, gnawed rinds, husks, and droppings littered dusty streets. In the countryside, she heard rats rustling and squeaking in the undergrowth. After an inquisitive mouse stuck its nose in her ear and woke her, she stopped using her bag for a pillow. Instead, she wrapped up her supply of dried chickpeas and fruit and slept curled tightly around it. If she had had a snake basket like Indu's, she might have been tempted to carry a house naga to patrol during the day, while she rested. But she knew people would remember a girl traveling with a snake, and she wanted to pass unnoticed.

She succeeded almost too well. Although Tana of course spoke to no one, the talk she heard in the markets was all of taxes, wheat blight, and the putrid fever infecting estates and villages. None of the vendors cared about a traveler who had nothing to buy or sell, no news to trade or diversion to offer. Tales about the toad girl and the diamond girl hadn't reached this far north. Even when Tana's shawl slipped off her head, the stubble there attracted no more than brief sympathy. Louse infestations, she discovered, had caused many people to shave their heads. Sleeping by day and walking by night, she might have been a ghost wafting after the kidnapped villagers.

Until the afternoon she overslept, and lost them.

Just past the white-coats' way station, the road forked. Tana couldn't tell which direction the party had gone, but at first she didn't worry. Then the road split again. She hurried through the misty darkness, first one way, then the other, then back to the starting point. The emperor's road was easy to find, because of the double row of shade trees that lined it. Since they had followed it this far from Gurath, Tana ran along it until her side hurt, and then walked for hours without hearing the familiar creaking carts or horses' hoofbeats. When dawn brightened the eastern sky, she saluted Mother Gaari with regret. She had chosen the wrong road. They had turned off somewhere, perhaps even reached their destination.

Not knowing what else to do, Tana retraced her steps to the way station. That day, she didn't sleep, but haunted the closest market town, listening for news of them. Without success. She walked again down the roads that had been so confusing in the dark, past the high walls of several white-coat estates. For lack of a better idea, she returned to the biggest one. Circling around it in the late afternoon, she noticed a patch of uncleared brush opposite an open gate. Women were leaving the estate, their bent backs eloquent of time spent toiling in the fields.

The women scattered before a government courier who rode his horse out at a rapid pace. The distinctive red and white stripes of his saddlecloth gave Tana the first encouragement of a long, dispiriting day. This estate had business with Lomkha, or Gurath's fort, or both. Only high officials were allowed to send messengers who took priority on crowded roads. She might still hear something of the vanished artisans if she could get inside.

Once the light faded and the gate closed, Tana wormed her way into the bushes until she found a sheltered spot under a ledge. Chewing the last of her dried fruit, she drifted off to sleep. If the estate hired day laborers, she'd apply for work. She'd watch, and listen. She wouldn't give up until she found her people, including Kalyan.

Especially Kalyan.

Tana shoveled filth for days.

Getting inside the immense walled property had been simple, though her jaw had clenched in fear every time someone looked at her twice. Shivering in her clammy dress wrap, she had lined up with the local women at the side gate in the early morning. As they gathered outside the wall, the rising sun burned off the mist. The gate opened; one by one, women filed through it.

At the guard post inside, a clerk sat at a table. His ledger was open to a page filled with columns of numbers. Tana held her breath. Would he see her as a fugitive or simply another poor young woman here to work in the fields?

"Day labor pays two coppers, plus the midday meal," he droned. "Wash off the mark, you don't get paid. Understand?"

When Tana nodded, the clerk added a number to a column. She had watched the other workers, so she knew to hold out her arm, which looked naked without her two gold bangles. The clerk inked the same number just above her elbow. "Cow barn," he said, and jerked his head. "Next!"

Tana followed the vague direction to a maze of long, low buildings. On one side, fields of barley and peas alternated with wheat. Bright spots of color marked women crouching to pull weeds from the young plants. Trees screened the estate's other half from view. Tana kept her head lowered as she glanced around; she didn't want to be caught acting like an obvious newcomer. She smelled cow and reached a doorway.

A bored-looking overseer stood beside it, running a leather whip through his fingers. When he pointed with the whip handle, the motion pulled his white coat snugly over a round belly. Tana took a shovel from a row of tools hanging on wall pegs. She walked through the door. Muck squished under her bare feet. The stench made her eyes water.

"That's ten," the overseer shouted to the gate clerk. "All I need today."

As the women inside had already done, Tana hitched her dress wrap above her ankles. Their task wasn't complicated. She helped herd forty or so cows through a wide arched opening into a court-yard. By stringing a rope across the opening, two women stopped the animals from wandering back inside. All ten women shoveled cow dung and fouled straw into baskets, which they dumped on a pushcart.

Tana quickly fell into the rhythm of the work: Shovel. Carry. Dump. Would her mother and Diribani laugh or cry, seeing her doing this kind of work?

The overseer sat on a bench with his feet propped on a barrel, out of the filth, and snapped his whip at flies. His aim was good; Tana figured he had plenty of practice. He didn't care whether he startled the workers. After a while, Tana stopped jumping at every hss-CRACK!

The women, mostly Ma Hiral's age, didn't talk much. Their dress wraps were faded and patched, like the one Tana had borrowed from the artisan village. Several wore shawls or scarves to keep the flies off, so Tana's covered head wasn't conspicuous. None of them had dowry bangles. Given other resources, they wouldn't be work-ing so hard for the pitiful wage. The previous night, Tana had tucked her own bangles into her bag, which she had hidden in a fig tree not far from the gate. She had picked one whose branches stretched over the wall, so she could retrieve the bag from either side.

When the women had cleaned the barn, spread fresh straw on the floor, and replenished the water troughs, they herded the cows inside. Then they took their shovels, baskets, and pushcarts to the next building. Shovel. Carry. Dump.

Walking across Tenth Province had strengthened Tana's legs, but her shoulders and back burned from the unaccustomed shoveling by the time a loud clanging noise signaled the noon meal. She stretched and followed the others, hoping to see more of the place, or at least hear the local gossip. Surely the arrival of a whole village's worth of people, in chains, accompanied by their animals and escorted by soldiers, would have caused comment.

To her disappointment, the barn and field workers were herded—much like cows—into yet another empty courtyard. A woman had just finished sweeping it. When she dumped her basket on the closest pushcart, Tana was sorry to see that the refuse included rodent droppings. On the bright side, the overseers didn't make them sit in filth. The workers lined up in rows. Each person received a bowl of rice with some mushy vegetables and gray broth slopped on top. From the scraps of talk Tana overheard, these women walked quite a distance every day from huts and villages in the countryside. Most, she gathered, were widows, without family to support them. None had much interest in her or in the Believers who employed them.

Only the promise of the courier she had seen leaving the estate brought Tana back to the side gate the next day, and the next, after teeth-chattering nights spent outside. She didn't know what else to do. The regular servants were all white-coats, who looked down on the day laborers. She couldn't ask anyone what she wanted to know, but at least her silence raised no awkward questions: Commoners weren't expected to speak, just to work.

Frustration smoldered inside her. She had started out on a pilgrimage, and ended up a drudge. She'd surrendered her former dreams, her community, her gold bangles. Her hair. Was this her punishment, to labor like a mute beast, far from her home and family? If her mother saw Tana's hands now, what would she say?

What Ma Hiral always said, probably: *Why can't you be more like your sister?*

And Diribani, at the ladies' court? She wouldn't be washing in ditch water. The palace baths would have scented soap, soft drying cloths, and a maid to help with the tangles. Not that Tana's prickly stubble needed combing.

She stabbed her shovel at a pile of dung. She had to find Kalyan and the Piplia villagers. If Tana's work pleased the overseers, maybe they'd send her someplace more interesting than the cow barn. Someplace she might overhear a nugget of gossip. Until then, she had a task to do.

Shovel. Carry. Dump.

CHAPTER NINETEEN

Diribani

COOL, dry days sharpened to frost-flecked mornings, and Diribani drew flowers.

She filled page after page with sketches: tulips with their fringed bells, freckled orange lilies, the four square petals of a pink blossom whose name she didn't know. If Naghali-ji withdrew her gift, Diribani could share the images with her family after the flowers had faded. She wished she had more to show for the goddess's blessing. The grand plans she had once laid out for Ma Hiral seemed farther away than Gurath itself.

The jewels left her the moment she spoke them, to be secured in a guard's box and sent to Tenth Province's governor. Not that Diribani required any for herself. Princess Ruqayya was the soul of generosity, showering her with beautiful clothes and gifts. As a royal guest, Diribani was free to eat with the court, sleep in her elegant rooms, or wander through the gardens. But with a palace to run, her hostess had little time to spare for the diamond girl. Prince Zahid, too, seemed in constant motion, meeting with advisers and administrators throughout the area. Diribani rarely encountered him. Except in her dreams, where he was a regular visitor.

The court ladies mostly concerned themselves with their families. The scholarly pursued their studies, the religious spent time at the prayer hall, the vain practiced elaborate beauty rituals. Even Ladli was busy with her own affairs. Temple dancing, it had been suggested, wasn't an appropriate pastime for pious young ladies.

A couple of letters had arrived for Diribani with a trade caravan from Gurath. Tana was serving at the temple grove while she, too, struggled to find the deeper purpose of her gift. Old news by now, written weeks earlier. Diribani hoped her sister had since met with more success than she. Casting about for occupation, Diribani started riding lessons.

She also visited the court artists. In the large, spacious workshop, she felt almost at home. Engrossed in their work, the artists paid no attention to her lack of rank or title. Even the novelty of flowers and jewels didn't distract them for long. Each artist, she discovered, had a specialty. Some painted portraits of nobles riding elephants or horses. Others depicted scenes conveying the grim spectacle of battle or the luxury of palace life. Again and again, Diribani found herself going back to the albums illustrating the empire's plants and animals. Perhaps art would be her life's work? At least it might fill more of the hours as she waited for Naghali-ji's purpose to be revealed.

"First, you must observe," one of the masters had suggested to her. "The eye and the heart, as much as the hand, guide the brush."

He also gave her a list of materials. One cool morning, Nissa accompanied Diribani to the market stalls inside the fort's main gates. Separate from the palace on top of the hill, and the military and administrative buildings that occupied the middle section, the lower part of the fort was as busy as a small city, with residences, shops, inns, and prayer halls. Unlike Tenth Province's, Eighteenth Province's administration didn't offer a bounty on dead snakes, so she was spared that grisly sight. But, like an ear of ripe wheat in a cotton field, Diribani's gold dress wrap stood out from the white coats. As she had promised Zahid and Ruqayya, she had thrown a lightweight wool shawl over her hair and across her chin when she left the palace. Still, people stared.

When she returned to her room, she questioned Nissa. "The vendors all acted as if I planned to steal from them. Other court women paint—it's not so unusual."

"Oh, my lady." Her maid was still catching her breath from the climb up the hill. "Half of them think you're a witch."

"And the rest?"

"They'd as soon see you talk flowers and jewels and make up their own minds." Nissa arranged the jars of pigment in a niche. "Why *don't* you ever speak in town?"

Diribani smoothed the sheets of paper. "It's bad enough having Zeen and Mahan follow me everywhere. Can you imagine if they started walking on either side, one hand stuck under my mouth so no jewels were lost in the street? Or maybe"—Diribani snorted, struck by the absurdity—"I should hang a bucket around my neck to catch them."

Nissa giggled. "How about a silk feedbag? We could match the colors to your dress wraps, and set a new fashion. All the court ladies will want their own."

"Lady Yisha can carry fennel seeds in hers." Diribani brandished a bunch of wood violets at her maid. It felt good to laugh, safe in her peaceful room, away from the townsfolk's suspicion and the court ladies' indifference. She sat at the low table under the window, heaped violets and carnations and poppies in a bowl, and sketched.

"Very pretty." Nissa clasped her hands. "My father works in colored stone, did I tell you, my lady? If you wanted one of your drawings inlaid in white marble, he could do it."

"Hm." With a fine brush, Diribani applied pigments to the paper. She looked again, trying to capture the delicate grades of color. The poppy needed a darker orange along the edge of the petal, where it shaded to red. "Thank you, Nissa. This design might suit a silk panel, too, don't you think? Princess Ruqayya suggested I decorate the rooms, but I hadn't really . . ." Her voice trailed off. *Thought I could bear to live so far from my family* was the way she felt. "Decided how," she finished, more diplomatically. The truth, if not all of it.

"Yes, my lady." Nissa seemed to understand what her mistress wasn't saying.

A rapping noise startled them both. Ladli stood at the door, her face animated. "Come out with us," she said. "The miners found a big diamond. A hundred ratis, my maid said."

"A hundred?" Diribani measured it with her fingers. "That's the size of a duck's egg!"

"Her Highness says we can attend the presentation if we hurry. Get your riding gear and meet us at the stables. Hurry!" Ladli repeated. She disappeared, and soon thereafter they could hear her fist banging on the next door.

"Presentation?" Diribani asked. Nissa bustled around the room, collecting trousers, long-sleeved tunic, flared coat, and shawl. The court tailors had made a riding costume especially for Diribani. It was the same cut that the other women wore, but in pale shades of yellow and green so she wouldn't be mistaken for a Believer. A few girls had looked enviously at the results. So far, none had dyed her own white coat.

"Any diamond over ten ratis is presented to the emperor. Prince Zahid will accept on his father's behalf," Nissa explained. "The finders get a big bonus, and, no matter which of them came up with it, all the workers get a feast to celebrate, and a paid day off at the emperor's expense."

"Doesn't he usually pay their wages?" Diribani changed her clothes. "I thought the mines belonged to the crown."

"Yes, of course." Nissa held out her coat. "But the actual work is done by your people. Merchants lease plots, hire the workers, and return a tithe of the value mined. Plus any stone over ten ratis, like I said. The emperor pays fair value for it, but it can't be offered to anyone else."

"A hundred ratis! How my sister would love to see such a gem." When Diribani thought of Tana, her pleasure in the outing dimmed. Her sister hadn't answered any of her recent letters. The prince's couriers had taken jewels to Gurath every few weeks. So far, they had returned with bland communications from the governor, assuring them that Tana remained in seclusion at the temple grove. A small house was going up by the stepwell. None of the couriers had seen Tana or her mother there. But, Diribani told herself, it wasn't likely a Believer would visit a temple grove, so she needn't read anything sinister into her sister's silence.

"And there's fireworks," Nissa went on, not noticing Diribani's distraction. "We'll be back at the palace by then, and can watch from the terrace. The show won't be quite as good as the prince's birthday." She separated Diribani's hair into sections and began braiding it. "Almost, though."

Diribani brushed poppies off her lap. "So when may we look forward to the really excellent fireworks?" she teased.

"Prince Zahid's birthday? Just when the weather's turning from bearable to too hot. That would be your"—Nissa counted on her fingers—"Moonbird Month. Not too very long from now: We're halfway through the cool season already."

"Really?" Diribani twisted to look out the window. "I was waiting for it to get colder."

"Not in Eighteenth Province," Nissa said. "You're ready. Oh, boots! Here. You go down with Mahan and Zeen—I'll meet you at the stables. Have the grooms give you a poky horse, my lady. You want a plodder, not one of Lady Ladli's fire-breathers. The road is steep."

The trail dropped so precipitously that Diribani clung to her horse's mane, afraid she would pitch forward between the animal's ears. She might not have agreed to such a rough ride only for the sake of seeing a big diamond, since small ones fell from her lips every day. But for a chance to watch Zahid, even at a distance . . . At last Diribani understood how Tana felt about Kalyan. The hours between their meetings seemed endless, and yet, in his presence, confusion often tied her tongue. Then she'd spend days thinking of the brilliant things she should have said—to make him laugh, to make him notice her—while not sure exactly what he felt in return. She knew it for foolishness, but that didn't change her body's response.

The horse stumbled, pulling Diribani's attention to her immediate surroundings. When she felt safe enough to steal glimpses at the countryside, the contrast amazed her. Thickly forested hills descended in ranks from the flank of the plateau. The gorges between were so steep it looked as if a basket of giant serpents had fallen to earth, then thrashed their way toward the sea, cleaving the earth in their wake.

Not serpents, Diribani corrected herself. Streams. Water ran deep in the valleys, showing glints of green through the dusty foliage. Ruqayya's party, with servants and armed escort, claimed the narrow trail; women carrying jars on their heads stood aside. Partway down, when Diribani's thighs were aching from the effort to stay on her horse, they turned off the trail to traverse the side of a hill. The trees opened up, giving Diribani her first glimpse of a diamond mine.

It looked like a giant latrine pit, was her first thought. Ugly, barren, and swarming with flies. No—those were people, their skin burned dark by the sun, and coated with dust. Before she had traveled much farther, Diribani felt the grit settling on her, too. She licked her dry lips.

Nissa couldn't have seen the motion under Diribani's loosely draped shawl, but the maid kneed her horse over to hand Diribani a water pouch. "See the banners?" Nissa pointed. "Workers will have roped off an area for us, and set up tents for shade."

Gratefully, Diribani sipped the water. "How do they find the diamonds?" Honeysuckle sifted into her shawl. Lacking the threatened feedbag, she had tucked her head covering into her coat collar. This way, she could retrieve any gems she spoke and put them in her saddlebag for Zeen to collect later. The flowers she stuck in her horse's mane. "There's dirt everywhere."

As they picked their way through piles of stone and swarms of people, Nissa explained: "Each team has a digging spot. The men break up chunks of rock with their pickaxes. Women and children carry the baskets of rubble to a clay-lined pit. They flood the pit, drain it, and winnow out the sand. Then they rake what's left, and pound it smaller."

"With those wooden mallets?"

"Exactly. Then they rinse it again. They may have to repeat the steps a few times. Finally, they go over the gravel, looking for diamonds."

It looked to Diribani like hot, backbreaking work. "There must be thousands of people here. They don't travel from Fanjandibad every morning. Where do they all live?"

"The villages are that way, I think." Nissa gestured. "The merchants are responsible for the workers' huts and food."

"And water?" Diribani saw young women and girls trudging along the edge of the clearing. They carried large clay jars on their heads. Their backs were straight, so as not to spill the water, but thin shoulders slumped, and dusty arms hung fatigue-limp at their sides. Diribani's neck ached in sympathy. Most of them were her age, or younger.

"They must bring it up from the river." Nissa stood in her stirrups. "Can you ride a little faster, my lady? We don't want to be late."

"The river at the bottom of the gorge?" Diribani said. The note of horror in her voice brought Zeen at a trot. When the guard saw nothing amiss, she eased her horse back. "The trip must take half a day. Why don't they have a stepwell, closer?"

"Too expensive, surely, when people can walk to the river for nothing." Nissa dismissed the idea. "The ground's so hard up here; only diamonds pay for the digging."

The words echoed in Diribani's ears. *Only diamonds pay for the digging.* Obviously, the miners couldn't afford to build a stepwell, and their merchant employers didn't choose to. Why should rich men care how many hours of labor were added to a poor girl's lot before she could perform the simplest of household tasks? Bathing an infant, cooking lentils, brewing a pot of tea to warm a cold morning—all required clean water. Diribani knew; she had hauled enough for her own family. And a stepwell was more than a water supply; it was a chance to meet with friends or just take a quiet breath in a long day of chores.

The merchants might not care, but Diribani did. And, thanks to the goddess's gift, she had access to plenty of diamonds, enough to build the empire's most expensive stepwell. Diribani sat straighter on her horse. Now she knew why Naghali-ji had sent her here.

CHAPTER TWENTY

Tana

AT last, the estate's hiring clerk sent Tana to the mare barns. Far grander in design than the cow barns, they were built of stone instead of mud brick, with a stall for each animal. Tana fought to keep her expression blank when she saw a red-and-white-striped saddlecloth hanging on a stall door. This must be a regular courier way station, and the property owner an important—as well as wealthy—individual. Whoever he was, he kept his horses in elegance. Trees graced the central courtyard, along with banks of hardy flowers that reminded Tana of Diribani, and a fountain that overflowed into two shallow canals. But even though they were much fancier, the horse barns smelled the same as the cow barns, and attracted as many flies.

Tana gathered that dung sweepers weren't permitted to touch the valuable mares; stablemen were supposed to lead them outside while the stalls were cleaned. This morning there was only one groom, a Believer boy of twelve or thirteen. He kept her and the other workers waiting in the main aisle while he returned a mare to her stall.

"Why are these women standing about?" A booming voice made Tana jump.

"Sir, sorry, sir." The groom closed the stall door and rushed past the clump of women leaning on their shovels, heads bent. He bowed to the overseer, a barrel-chested, bandy-legged older man with a whip tucked into his belt. "The rest of the fellows are still in quarters, sick as dogs. My lady sent her own physician. Putrid fever, he said."

The sweepers sidled away from the groom, their shovels clinking on the floor. Behind their backs, free hands cupped like lotus flowers, invoking Sister Payoja, goddess of healing.

The overseer fingered his whip handle. "*All* of 'em?"

"Yes, sir. He dosed them, but meanwhile there's just me."

"And you are?"

"Atbeg, sir."

The overseer grunted in annoyance. "Well, Atbeg, show me the new girl."

Alarmed, Tana peeked up through her lashes. Her racing heartbeat slowed down when she realized that the white-coat wasn't talking about her.

The groom hurried to a door at the far end of the row and stepped inside the stall. Hooves thunked on the floor, and Atbeg could be heard soothing the stall's restless occupant. "Come here, pretty. Little pearl, little snow blossom. Mind your manners, Mina; you know me."

The mare might have known Atbeg, but she liked Tana better.

Mincing out of her stall, Jasmine saw her friend and made straight for her. She dragged the groom along with her.

"Courtyard's this way, you cow," he said, but the mare didn't stop until she reached Tana's side. Atbeg puffed out a frustrated breath. "Sorry, sir. I'll bring her outside."

"This will do." While the overseer ran his hands over the mare, Jasmine lipped Tana's head scarf.

Exultation sang in Tana's heart. If Kalyan's horse had arrived recently, he couldn't be far. Thank the twelve, she must have picked the right estate. Unless he'd been injured, or worse. But Jasmine looked healthy; perhaps her master had been well treated also. Tana patted the mare's silky neck for comfort. Unobtrusively, she thought, but when the overseer finished, he spoke directly to her.

"Good with horses, are you?"

Tana cast her eyes down as if she were too shy to speak.

The barrel-chested man grunted again. "Show me you can lead the mare out and tie her up and I'll add a copper to your wages."

"But, sir . . ." the groom began.

Tana didn't give Atbeg a chance to finish his sentence. She rested her shovel against a wall and twitched the lead out of the boy's hand. Tugging on the strap, she walked toward the courtyard. Calm as milk, Jasmine followed. Tana tied the mare to one of the posts and left her with a final pat.

Inside the barn, the overseer was examining another mare while Atbeg stood by. "The black's still favoring her left foreleg," the older man said. "I want you to add the new white one to the courier rotation. And you"—to Tana—"do what the groom here tells you."

Once the overseer was satisfied that Tana could follow Atbeg's directions, he went off to inspect the other barns. Tana's fellow sweepers shoveled out the empty stalls without looking at her, as if worried that, like putrid fever, her extra responsibility might be catching.

For Tana, the day passed quickly. She hadn't worked with horses before, just visited Trader Nikhat's. But they didn't frighten her. By watching the white-coat boy, she learned that confidence was more important than strength in getting the mares to do what she wanted. For a chance to find out what had happened to Jasmine's rider, Tana would have volunteered to tend Prince Zahid's hunting cheetahs. Fortunately, Atbeg didn't expect her to ride the mares. She had only to guide them from stall to garden courtyard, and back to a clean box. The animals humored her. Sister Naghali might have turned her face away, but others of the twelve smiled. Tana breathed a silent prayer of thanks to Father Ghodan, the horse god, for his kindness.

The overseer returned late in the afternoon, as the other sweepers were putting away their shovels. Heads bowed, the women eased down the aisle, ready to collect their wages from the gate clerk and go home. The overseer snapped his fingers at Tana. "You, girl. Stay."

She folded her hands and lowered her gaze against a spurt of glee. If the white-coat had a task for her inside the walls, she could see more of the compound, maybe spot some trace of the kidnapped villagers. Where, oh, where had Jasmine's rider been taken?

The burly man waited for the sweepers to leave. He tugged at his coat collar, as if the white fabric itched. "So, Atbeg?" he demanded.

"Sir, they did finish cleaning this barn." Atbeg sounded apprehensive. "If the men are on their feet tomorrow, we'll make better time with the others."

"Don't count on it," the overseer said flatly. Sweat gleamed on his forehead. He wiped it with his sleeve. "The fever's vicious. It's spread to the kitchen and house servants, too. Out flat, most of 'em."

Tana made the lotus sign behind her back.

"Almighty God protect us," the groom muttered.

"One man's burden is another's blessing." The overseer laughed without humor. "You're promoted, Atbeg, to acting head groom in charge of the mares. You'll be responsible for this barn, including any courier mounts that arrive, and the foaling barn, too."

"Yes, sir!"

"Don't go back to your quarters until the other men are better. This barn's stocked with bags of dried peas, wheat, and salt. Good enough for my lord's beasts, and you, too. You'll find cooking pots and blankets in with the travel gear in the storeroom. Eat here, wash here, and sleep in the foaling barn. Understand?"

"Yes, sir." Atbeg sounded subdued.

"You, too, sweeper girl. Eat here, sleep here. Obey Atbeg."

Tana nodded.

"Don't talk much, do you?" The overseer pulled at his collar. "Makes a refreshing change."

"But, sir!" Atbeg exclaimed. "She's a filthy dirt-eater. And a girl. They can't be *grooms*."

"Word of God." The overseer frowned at Atbeg. "She's healthy enough to lift a shovel and a bucket. Unless you want to care for all the mares by yourself?"

"No, sir."

"It's just for a few days." The overseer fumbled in his coat, then tossed a copper coin in Tana's direction and another at Atbeg. From the groom's delighted expression, his was silver. "No trouble with the girl, eh, Atbeg?" The overseer wiped his face again. "My

lady's a stickler about the local women, our kind or dirt-eaters, doesn't matter. Leave 'em alone."

"Of course, sir."

Atbeg didn't need to sound quite so . . . *repulsed*, Tana thought. Then she remembered she had spent days shoveling muck and sleeping in a nest of leaves. She couldn't smell herself, but others might not be so lucky.

"Good." The overseer put his fist to his mouth and left abruptly. Tana wouldn't be surprised to learn that he was headed for his own bed. Via the latrine pits.

Atbeg polished the coin on his sleeve. He stopped when he noticed Tana watching. "I'll show you the grain bins so you can make us porridge. I have to see to the brood mares."

Tana nodded.

"Wait till my father hears. Acting head groom." The boy flipped his coin and then tucked it into his belt.

She wished him joy on his promotion. Tana was sorry for the sick people, of course, but if illness had so disrupted the household that lowly day laborers were trusted with valuable livestock, who knew what else she might manage? As the overseer had said, a burden for one might mean a blessing for another.

That night, Jasmine received a thorough brushing and an extra measure of grain.

CHAPTER TWENTY-ONE

Diribani

SHE found Zahid on the rooftop terrace, deep in discussion with Ghiyas the steward and a tall man Diribani didn't recognize. The stranger's occupation became clear from the snatches of conversation that reached Diribani's ears as she and Nissa strolled at the far end of the terrace, waiting for a chance to approach the prince. A builder, it appeared; the men were talking about where to put a new palace, adjacent to this one and connected by gardens.

Diribani wondered why the prince was considering it, when this one was so large and so lovely. Her thoughts skittered like squirrels. Other grand houses ringed the fort grounds. The nobles' wives and daughters spent time in the ladies' court, but slept under their own roofs. Did Zahid want a place for his family, when he married? Had he chosen a bride? That news would set the palace abuzz, but Nissa hadn't mentioned it. And a palace would take time to build. No immediate plans, then. Diribani wiped damp palms on her skirts. She had business with the prince; best keep her mind on that.

The steward's narrow face was familiar, though it was most unusual to see a man other than Ruqayya's brother inside the ladies' court. On the other hand, this terrace did have the best view of the fort grounds, and the guard at the bottom of the stairs had warned them about the prince's guests. Like the other women guards, Zeen didn't veil, but Nissa had put on her head scarf. Diribani rearranged her dress wrap in the agreed-upon style.

The coldest part of the year was passing at a tortoise's imperceptible pace. Today, instead of frost, thick dew beaded the terrace's potted palms and roses. Servants hadn't yet brought out carpets and cushions, and the broad expanse was empty but for their two small groups. So as not to stare at the prince, Diribani leaned on the railing and looked in the other direction, where the land dropped sharply. "Can we see the mines from here, Nissa?"

An orchid fluttered over the railing. Zeen cleared her throat.

Diribani's maid joined her. "It's still a bit misty. This time of year, you get a better view later in the day. But it's that direction." She pointed to one of the narrow valleys, where the fog was lifting in white wisps from the trees.

This time, Diribani turned her head before she spoke, to let Naghali-ji's gifts drop to the terrace. Zeen could collect the jewels later. "Where the fireworks were coming from last night?"

"Exactly."

"Good morning, ladies."

Nissa bowed and backed away. Diribani schooled her expression to serenity before she turned. Ridiculous, the effect one person's voice could have on someone. "Good morning, Your Highness."

The steward and builder had gone. The breeze played with Zahid's dark hair. It fluttered Diribani's dress wrap around her face and stirred daffodil petals at her feet. The prince picked up the bright-yellow blossoms and set them on the railing. "Did you enjoy the fireworks?"

"Yes, very much." Diribani shot a sly glance at Nissa. "Though I understand they're better in Moonbird Month."

"Moonbird?" The prince sounded puzzled. Then he laughed. "Oh, *those* fireworks. I must admit, they're my favorite part of the day's events also."

"Why is that?" Diribani asked.

The prince smiled at her. "Because then I know it's almost over."

Diribani kept her voice light. "Is it such hard work, celebrating your birthday?" An emerald and a ruby plinked onto the terrace.

"Long," the prince said. "And some of the customs are more entertaining than others."

The humor in his voice encouraged her to ask, "Like what?"

"The weighing, for one." Zahid sighed so mournfully that Diribani burst out laughing.

"Why, do they weigh you against your brothers and sisters, to see who is more valuable?"

The prince's expression set her off again. "That's a fine idea," he said. "I'll suggest it to Ruqayya. Usually, I sit by myself in a scale pan. Guests put gifts in the other pan, and when the scales balance, the offerings are distributed to the poor. I can't get up and join the feast until that happens."

"I'm sure it doesn't take long," Diribani said, scattering peony blossoms and little lumps of turquoise.

"That depends on how my sister has rigged the scales." Zahid's voice was dry. "She likes to make me wait, so I have to ask Ghiyas to bring a couple of bolts of fabric or sacks of grain to add when the gifts are drying up."

Diribani was touched that he would admit his counterstrategy to her. It sounded like something Indu would do. "We won't let you miss the feast," she promised.

The prince put his hand over his heart and bowed. "Thank you."

"I do have a favor to ask," Diribani said, before he could go.

"Name it."

Diribani fancied she heard a note of reserve. What favor might he be reluctant to grant her? She chose her words carefully. "I'm glad that Naghali-ji's jewels are returned to Tenth Province, but I would like to keep some out." She gestured at the stones lying at her feet.

"You have before, without asking my leave," he said.

Zahid didn't look at Nissa, but Diribani was aware of her maid holding her breath. She spoke slowly, feeling her way. "Princess Ruqayya said I could make a direct gift if I chose."

"Yes," he said.

Behind Diribani, Nissa breathed again.

"But I don't want to give these away. I want to sell them."

Zahid's expression lost all its humor. "Why?"

A prince's voice, not a friend's, had asked the question. She mustn't forget. To her, the jewels were a miracle. To him, they represented something else. Diribani had the sense she was pushing a big rock uphill, but she forged on, spraying bloodstones and diamonds between them. "I want to build a stepwell for the miners. So they have a place to wash, at the end of the day. So their wives and daughters don't have to climb up and down to the river. Tenth Province has plenty of wells; Governor Alwar shouldn't feel cheated."

"You want to build a well near the mine?" the prince repeated. His face gave her no hint of his opinion.

What was the matter? Did he believe her idea ill-advised? Was he insulted that a newcomer would suggest the imperial mine wasn't run properly? Except that the merchants were responsible for the workers' villages, Nissa had said. So Diribani hadn't insulted his oversight of the mines. Had she? She was committed now; she had to continue.

"If the ground's too hard for digging, perhaps one of those valleys could be dammed?" Diribani went on in a rush. Gemstones pattered onto the terrace. Flowers landed with softer thumps. "Those water jars looked so heavy, and the path is so steep, and the girls are working so hard. . . ."

"I think it's an inspired idea."

His face was still stern, but Zahid sounded so positive that Diribani blushed. "You do?"

"Yes." He clasped his hands behind his back and began to pace.

Like his sister, Diribani thought. She hurried to keep up. "So you'll help me value the stones and trade them to pay for the materials and workers?"

"Of course. In fact, the crown will match your gift."

"Oh!" Diribani smelled narcissus and violets. "Will it be that expensive?"

"Costly enough," Zahid said. "But the project will benefit our subjects. Also, His Excellency Governor Alwar will complain less if we don't completely halt the flow of jewels to Gurath."

"It won't affect your building plans?" When the prince glanced at her, Diribani confessed, "I overheard you and the other men talking."

He shook his head. "The well should be started first, to capture next season's rains. The other project's not as"—he seemed to be searching for the right word—"pressing," he concluded, with an enigmatic twist of his lips. "I'll have Ghiyas call the interested parties to meet with us after the midday meal. Would you mind explaining to our builders about the wells in Gurath?"

"I'd be happy to," Diribani said. "If you like, I could sketch the different designs. Gurath has a big open tank, but other villages in Tenth Province have a single closed shaft. Your builders can decide what will be best for the site."

"Wonderful." The prince smiled at her with such warmth that Diribani feared she might melt at his feet.

Later, as Diribani swam in the palace baths, she remembered that look. Like a miser with a secret treasure, she held the memory close. Down in the underground bathing chamber, oil lamps and candles lit stone walls hung with mango- and pomegranate-colored fabrics. Herbs burned in metal dishes, sending curls of scented smoke into the humid air. The pool's azure tiles gleamed; light reflected off moving water. Diribani thought it was like swimming through twilight, or dawn, with the chatter of women's voices replacing the birds' usual chorus.

This cool evening, the few ladies present had clustered around one of the heated pools. A maid played a stringed instrument, the sound rising and falling under the splashing noises and quiet laughter. Diribani had the long pool to herself. Stepping into it, she had sucked in her breath at first, but as she swam, she warmed up. And after the day's activity, she couldn't sit still and listen to gossip. She had to move. *Inspired*, he'd said. *Wonderful*. Diribani ducked her chin to hide a monkey grin from Nissa and Mahan.

Zahid had liked her ideas. He'd listened to her, and so had the other men in the room off the Hall of Public Audience that afternoon. She'd shown her drawings to builders and merchants, secretaries and officials. Now she was grateful for all the time she'd spent carrying water from Gurath's stepwell. She'd noticed quite a lot in those daily trips: the stone blocks' proportions, and how the stairs were laid out so that the water could always be reached as the level rose and fell with the rains. She'd drawn the traditional two lamp niches, and even the serpent form over the entry pavilion's door. That had raised a few eyebrows from the white-coats, and approving nods from the merchants whose workers would use the wells.

Diribani extended her arms straight out and pushed through the water. Other women were dressing now, their maids gathering cosmetics and drying cloths and pitchers of fruit juice, trays of sweetmeats and salted nuts. The mellow light didn't change, but the large room quieted. Diribani kept swimming.

Many of the noble ladies climbing the stairs to their apartments had commissioned gardens and tombs, prayer halls and markets, but Diribani was the first to suggest building a stepwell for commoners in Eighteenth Province. Without the prince's support, she didn't think she would have gotten such a respectful hearing—especially after the men had seen her speaking flowers and jewels. Again, Zahid had set the tone. He didn't appear to find it remarkable, so they didn't, either. Diribani had even heard a builder joke to the secretary sitting next to him that they should ask the Gurath girl more questions and take her answers for their first payment.

Mahan had heard the man, too—Diribani saw her guard's lips twitch with amusement as she noted Diribani's diamonds and amethysts and rubies in her ever-present ledger. This afternoon,

Diribani had spoken enough to satisfy anyone's curiosity, and to make a start on the amount required. Nissa had been the silent one. Head scarf hiding her features, she had stood nearby, ready to replenish ink and paper when Diribani wanted to illustrate an answer. There had been a lot of questions, and the best ones were Zahid's.

Unlike some people, he raised obstacles to plan around them, not to prevent the project from going forward. He invited discussion and paid attention, reminding Diribani of Kalyan. Good listeners, both, though Diribani found Zahid's intensity far more compelling than the Gurath merchant's easygoing temperament. A successful trader had to satisfy both buyer and seller. A prince could command.

Was that why Zahid's approval delighted her so much? Because it wasn't lightly given? Or perhaps the fluttery, excited feeling that had sustained her through the meeting came from her impression that his regard extended deeper. It might encompass not only her ideas, but the mind they came from, the body and spirit that nourished them. She turned on her back and floated in the middle of the pool to consider the question.

She felt that way about him. Hands, mind, heart, all wanted to please him. And not just because he was a prince, the ruler who could help or hinder her building project. Well, him, yes, but also Zahid the laughing brother, the man who treated non-Believers with respect. Zahid who smiled at her and said *inspired*, in that voice she heard in her dreams.

How Tana would tease. Falling in love with a prince, and daring to think her feelings might be returned? She, a merchant's daughter! Above all, though, Tana would want for her sister to be happy. As Tana was, Diribani hoped, safe in the temple grove, surrounded by the music and comforting ritual of worship, the company of family and friends. Not like here, where Diribani moved alone through her splendid surroundings, forever longing to see the one person who made her feel completely alive.

Could this be another facet of Naghali-ji's gift? For a humble Gurath girl to catch a prince's eye? Perhaps her influence at court might be turned to others' benefit, and soften the Believers' attitude toward the conquered people they called "dirt-eaters."

Diribani took a deep breath and sank underwater as if she could hide from thoughts that nibbled like little fish. Dangerous thoughts that started with *if only*, and *one day, perhaps*. Her hair swirled around her face, blotting out the candle flames that twinkled through the water like distant stars.

Someone grabbed a fistful of her hair and yanked, hauling Diribani coughing and sputtering to the surface.

"My lady!" Nissa knelt at the edge of the pool.

Diribani spat water and pushed wet hair out of her face. Next to her, Zeen stood chest-deep in the pool. Her soaked white coat stuck to her body, outlining more dagger-shaped lumps than Diribani had ever noticed when the guard's clothing was dry. Emotions flitted across the woman's face, relief and then irritation, before Zeen's expression smoothed into the usual hard-eyed watchfulness.

"Eyo, flower girl!" Ruqayya's voice echoed across the bathing chamber.

Diribani turned to see the princess sitting in one of the smaller pools. Curls of steam wreathed her body. Flattened by the weight of water, dark curls straggled over Ruqayya's bare shoulders. A light-colored paste was smeared over her face, emphasizing the dark hollows of her eyes. She beckoned.

"I was fine," Diribani muttered to Zeen and Nissa, and handed her silent guard a lump of jet-black onyx and a purple tulip. She swam to the stairs at the far end of the pool, Zeen squelching after her. At least the other noble ladies had gone; only Ruqayya was present when Diribani's guard had fished her out. Diribani shivered as the cool air struck her bare flesh. Not waiting for Nissa to drape the drying cloth around her, Diribani obeyed Ruqayya's flicking fingers and stepped into the small pool. Heated water stung her skin. "Ah!" Diribani yelped quietly, and eased into it.

The princess slid down the tiled bench until she sat neck-deep. She leaned her head against a padded mat, and her maid resumed combing out the long curls over a brazier of herb-scented smoke. "Do tell me," Ruqayya said lazily. "Why do you wear jewelry to bathe?"

"Jewelry?" Diribani said. Poppies floated on the water, red petals spread like skirts. The princess lifted a languid hand from the water and bent her wrist. "Oh, the bangles!" Diribani laughed. "Habit only. We don't think of them as jewelry."

"What, then?" Ruqayya asked.

"It's my dowry." Diribani turned the bracelets around her wrist. "Married women wear them on the right arm, unmarried girls on the left."

"Ah," Ruqayya said.

"You don't have a similar custom?" Diribani asked.

"Displaying our worth on our sleeves? No."

"It's not boasting," Diribani said, too surprised by the scorn in the princess's voice to take offense. "Girls wear gold to prove they can be trusted with the family purse. In difficult times, a woman can sell a bangle to feed her children." As Ma Hiral had done for her and Tana.

"Not unreasonable, I suppose," Ruquayya said.

Diribani was glad for the chance to ask a question of her own, since the princess had raised the subject. "How are matches arranged among your people?"

"Families consult a marriage broker," Ruqayya said. "For the nobility, that's usually a woman from the ladies' court, preferably a high-ranking one. The contracts can be complicated, and family alliances must be approved by the emperor."

"You're one of the royal matchmakers?"

"Ha." Ruqayya snorted, then continued more thoughtfully. "I could be, though no one's consulted me since we were sent to Fanjandibad. Why, have you a client in mind?"

"Not today," Diribani said, dropping sapphires and honeysuckle, "but someday I might ask you on my own behalf."

"No, flower girl. Not today." Ruqayya's voice held no answering humor. "Not ever. You didn't imagine you'd be allowed to marry? Oh. I see." The princess sounded weary, and three times her age. She snapped her fingers. "Leave us," she commanded. The maids bowed and withdrew to the stairwell, leaving the large bathing room empty but for the two of them. Even so, Ruqayya moved down the bench, closer to Diribani.

Diribani stared at the princess. She hadn't thought Ruqayya would offer her brother outright, but to say that Diribani couldn't marry *anyone*? Never have a husband and children and a home? She hadn't been in a hurry to take on those responsibilities, but she had assumed that one day . . .

The princess spoke so low that her breath barely stirred the water. "Your religion and your family's lack of influence don't signify. It's your gift that makes you too great a prize," she said. "While you're a ward of the crown, Father, through Zahid, controls your diamonds and jewels. Whether they're spent in Tenth Province or Eighteenth Province, the wealth benefits the empire. But if you were to suggest marrying anyone but my brother Jauhar, the crown prince, he would have you killed at once rather than give Zahid such a political advantage." Her voice dropped again—soft, like a snake's hiss. "Zahid cares for you—as do I—too much to wish either fate upon you."

Diribani knew that Ruqayya meant her warning sincerely. But she couldn't help fixing on the two words that struck her heart with a thrown dagger's force: *Zahid cares.* Because he cared, he would not admit it and make Diribani a target of his elder brother's jealousy. The pang this understanding caused her must have been reflected in her face.

Ruqayya reached out and grabbed her shoulder, nails digging into Diribani's bare skin. "If you esteem Zahid as I believe you do, you won't sign his death warrant with yours by giving him any encouragement."

"I don't—"

"Jauhar will kill him." Ruqayya's voice was so etched with grief that it startled Diribani out of her preoccupation. Tears leaked out of the corners of the princess's eyes, cutting tracks in the powdery cosmetics that covered her face. "The lust for power has consumed our elder brother and left nothing but a husk for a heart. Don't tempt him to prove it."

A weight greater than the heaviest water jar bowed Diribani's neck. "Then what will become of me?"

"Why, nothing." Ruqayya recovered her composure. She splashed her face, washing off the paste and, with it, the tear marks. "You'll stay with us, an honored guest. Build your stepwell, paint your flowers. Royal princesses in the direct line don't marry either, you know. A person can learn to occupy herself with art and music, prayer and good works. In time, she accepts the idea." With every word, the princess pushed an anguished woman behind a careless façade. "Eyo," she called out.

The maids returned to dress them. The interview had ended.

Diribani bowed her head. She did have the stepwell task to finish. She had her painting. But would living for years in the walled beauty of the ladies' court steep her, too, in bitterness? If the bathing room hadn't been empty, would she and Ruqayya have had such an honest conversation? At moments like this, Diribani missed her sister so sharply it felt like an actual wound in her chest. Tana wouldn't lie to her as the princess just had.

To be fair, Ruqayya hadn't overstated Zahid's danger; Diribani believed that all too well. But Ruqayya's own dreams—who had crushed them underfoot, as she had dashed Diribani's? The princess might have gotten used to her fate, but she hadn't embraced it. When she let her guard down, the pain showed through.

Though Diribani's racing mind hardly let her sleep that night, she didn't have to worry that Zahid might read any of her new understanding in her expression. He didn't come to the rooftop terrace again. And a week later, when preparations for the stepwell were under way, he rode out of Fanjandibad at the head of his troops to deal with a border uprising.

She wouldn't see him again for months.

CHAPTER TWENTY-TWO

Tana

SICKNESS muffled the estate's usual sounds and smells,
silencing voices that would otherwise have been raised in
instruction or argument. Within days of Tana's new assignment,
most of the resident white-coat servants had taken to their beds.
No one drove the bullocks, so the sugarcane presses fell silent. The
fires went out under the syrup-boiling kettles. Smoke still rose from
the kitchen fires, but the fragrance of fresh-ground coriander, mustard, and ginger was replaced by the odors of charred lentils and
sour milk. Tana decided that there must be enough healthy dairy
maids to milk the cows—or the bellows of distress would have dis-
turbed the entire compound—but not enough to keep up with the
work of turning milk into butter, cheese, and sweetmeats.

Inside the barn, the unnatural quiet wasn't as noticeable. The
young groom worked the sweepers and Tana to exhaustion. She
assumed he was trying to earn a permanent promotion through
the cleanliness of the floors and good condition of the animals. The

burly-chested overseer hadn't visited since Tana's first day, but Atbeg acted as if he might appear at any moment. Two of the regular grooms had staggered back to work. They spent as much time leaning on the horses as brushing them. Atbeg didn't reproach them.

Tana was kept busy sweeping and shoveling and leading horses to and fro. When a courier arrived, she walked his sweat-streaked mare around the courtyard while the man took his message pouch to the main residence.

Atbeg rushed past Tana, a red-and-white-striped saddlecloth draped over his shoulder. "Don't let her drink too much," he ordered.

Tana dipped her head in acknowledgment. This wasn't the first courier horse she'd walked cool, but outsiders always made Atbeg jumpy. The groom saddled and led out a bay mare just as the courier returned. Without a word to anyone, the man swung onto the fresh mount and galloped off, clearly hoping to outride the putrid fever that had overtaken the estate. Glancing after him, Tana noticed the gate guard snap to attention, then shake his fist as the rider's dust enveloped him. She turned back to a frowning Atbeg.

The groom crossed his arms over his skinny chest. "We're out of clean saddlecloths," he complained. "The washerwomen must be sick, so you'll have to do it, dirt girl. Give yourself a scrub while you're at it. You're probably giving the horses fleas." He sniggered at his own joke.

Tana went in search of the cloths. In a room where saddles, bridles, and other gear were stored, she found a huge pile of dirty linens on the floor. There were far more than she could carry, even in one of the large wicker baskets stacked in the corner. She heaped five of the special courier saddlecloths in a basket and hoisted it onto her head. In the stable's main aisle, she hesitated, looking for the groom. Would Atbeg expect a dung sweeper to know where the laundry area was?

She did, as it happened. The past few nights, as soon as the waning moon rose, she had crept out of the barn to prowl around the estate. Once the mists descended, she hadn't worried much about anyone's noticing. Atbeg slept in a different barn. The few resident workers not suffering from putrid fever had to do the tasks of many others. The moment they were dismissed, the estate's servants probably dropped into their beds. And, unlike the white-coats' clothing, Tana's faded, dirty dress wrap blended into the shadows.

She had kept clear of the main house and the servants' rooms behind the big kitchen courtyard, where people might emerge to visit the latrine pits. That had still left a number of buildings to explore. The estate was bigger than most villages, a maze of mud-brick and stone structures, courtyards, gardens, fields, and pathways. Her nose had identified the vinegar smells of the dyeing and weaving rooms, and steered her around a stinking leather tannery. Rats had left their nasty traces outside grain storehouses and dairy buildings, the sugarcane press and fruit-drying racks. Just the previous night, she'd ventured far enough to spot a tank-style well on the opposite side of the estate. And still she hadn't found those she sought.

"Wait, you." Atbeg sounded harassed.

Tana turned, moving slowly under the basket's weight. Five saddlecloths were perhaps too ambitious a load to carry on her head. Would he notice if she put one back?

The groom opened a door and jerked his thumb inside the stall. "Take a clean pushcart, not the dung hauler, and do all the cloths at once. The washers use the tank by the east gate." He pointed. "Keep clear of the main house, and make sure the cloths are dry before you bring 'em back, or they'll smell, and you'll have to do the job again."

Tana set down the laundry basket and heaved sacks off the push-cart Atbeg had indicated. Rats had chewed holes in the corner of several bags. Dried peas trickled onto the floor. Tana swept them up and wrestled the pushcart out of the storage room. She loaded it with more baskets full of dirty saddlecloths, but the baskets stood so tall she couldn't see over them. She rearranged the load to leave a gap down the middle. The cart's bamboo frame proved light yet sturdy. Once she got it rolling, she pushed it quickly out of the barn.

The estate displayed a painting's vivid colors: green barley and wheat, mustard blooming yellow. Along the field's margins, orange poppies shook their skirts at purple linseed and shy white wild-flowers. Birds sang and whistled, busy with nest building.

That's when the deserted aspect of the place struck her. There should have been four times as many people in the fields, and more walking between the various buildings. Tana glanced over her shoulder and pushed the cart faster. The sun shone on her head. A crow cawed. Tana's palms sweated on the pushcart handles, raising blisters by the time she reached the tank.

It was constructed like Gurath's stepwell, but smaller, and with-out the shade pavilions. And, of course, it lacked the two lanterns honoring Naghali-ji. If there had ever been a snake image here, the white-coats had smashed it. At the nearer end of the tank, two nicely dressed Believer girls Tana's age squatted to slosh coats and trousers in the water.

One stood and stretched at Tana's approach. Dark eyes judged her.

Tana straightened, aware of her dress wrap's filthy hem. The shawl tied over her head wasn't much cleaner, spotted with hay and dried horse slobber.

Before she could unload her baskets, the young woman pointed across the water. "Horse blankets get washed on that side."

Tana leaned into the pushcart, puffing with effort to get it rolling. One basket tipped and knocked over its neighbor. She stopped the cart and fixed them. She preferred not to drop the baskets into the well and give the maids another reason to mock her.

The standing girl spoke to her companion, loud enough for Tana to hear. "My lady may need us to do laundry for a little while, but we can't be expected to associate with field hands."

"Stupid dirt-eaters." The other tossed her head. Her dangling earrings sparkled in the sun.

Tana gritted her teeth and shoved the cart forward. As never before, she could appreciate what Diribani had endured from haughty Gulrang and the other girls. Of course, Tana wanted these two to think her too afraid to talk back. The more people considered her a pair of strong arms and legs, with only enough sense to follow orders, the less they expected her to speak. It was just that she had been playing the part of a nobody so long that her spirit, like her aching hands, chafed from the work. The rude girls might have been more respectful had Tana been wearing her dowry bangles. Unlike those flashy earrings, her bracelets weren't cheap twisted wire and glass.

Then Tana recognized her own folly. Diribani's bangles hadn't stopped the Gurath white-coats from taunting her. Besides, girls so conscious of their appearance might have wondered why anyone possessed of two gold bracelets was sweeping dung, the lowest of all possible occupations. Why encourage them to ask questions she had no intention of answering?

The far end of the tank had stone ramps instead of stairs, so Tana was able to push the cart quite close to the water level. Unfortunately, a herd of goats must have been the most recent visitors. Clumps of coarse hair, leaves, and twigs clogged the waste channel. She hiked up her dress wrap, hoisted the first saddlecloth, and waded down the ramp into cleaner water. Cold nipped at her legs. Washing wasn't pleasant in Cow Month.

Despite the shoveling she'd been doing, this work made her arms and shoulders tremble. When wet, the saddlecloths each weighed far more than a shovel of muck, and she had thirty or so to clean. Her legs and feet were quickly chilled. Her fingers wrinkled into raisins, while the blisters stretched and popped as she scrubbed at ground-in stains. The two snippy girls laid wet clothing out on the stone steps to dry, and left. An older woman came and rinsed out a basketful of kitchen towels. She, too, ignored Tana.

Tana arranged the dripping saddlecloths over the slanting upper edge of the ramp. She found rocks to anchor the corners, so the padded cloths hung in crooked lines. The couriers' red and white stripes angled down to meet the plain colors of the regular saddle-cloths. From a distance, the ramp would look as if it had been strung with signal flags.

When the meal bell rang, she entertained the thought of visiting the day laborers' courtyard, just to eat something besides plain boiled peas or wheat, but she was too tired to make the effort. Atbeg would make her cook for him later, anyway. As the overseer had ordered, the young groom kept strictly to the stables.

Tana did take advantage of the deserted tank to wash herself and her clothes, the dirt-crusted dress wrap and shawl. Her hair had grown; short dark strands stuck out from her head. Shivering, she draped wet fabric around herself and splashed out to stretch full-length at the top of the ramp. She hoped the sun-warmed stone would dry her backside while the breeze dried her front.

Wistfully, she picked at the loose skin of her popped blisters and thought of the field workers' rice and soup. Thin as it was, the broth had started with a curry leaf, some sliced vegetables, or a handful of lentils before they dissolved in discouragement, unequal to the task of flavoring an entire pot.

Her thoughts wandered farther—south and east, to Fanjandibad. What might Diribani be eating today?

Tana considered the question seriously and came up with buttered rice, puffy bread with garlic, eggplant fried in hot mustard oil. Spiced lentils, cucumbers in yogurt, crispy chickpea fritters with tamarind sauce. Hot, sweet tea. She almost moaned with longing, but couldn't stop torturing herself. For dessert? Sliced pinkfruit, or maybe milk fudge topped with crushed pistachios. Her mouth watered. While Diribani made friends at court and ate delicious food, Tana hid among the white-coats and swept filth. To what end?

Lying here, limp as a wilted onion, Tana hadn't much but clean saddlecloths to show for her labors. Shame nagged at her. Some rescuer she was, thinking of food at a time like this. She should concentrate on saving Kalyan and the Piplia villagers, not her stomach.

She gazed at the trees sheltering the main house. Perhaps that was where she needed to go. Did the white-coat estate houses have dungeons, like the fort? Or had the people been taken to one place, and their livestock to another? How could an entire village vanish in the night? Like smoke, Jasmine's rider continued to elude her.

Odd, that. Kalyan usually popped up at exactly the moment you wished he wouldn't. And then he asked you to marry him.

Tana's lips curved in reluctant amusement. Utsav the crow god must be dogging her steps, turning every situation on its head. The trickster brother of the twelve never slept.

At the thought, Tana noticed a young woman in a dirty blue dress wrap. She carried a jar on her head and another in her arms, with a covered basket balanced on top of that. Though she came from the direction of the kitchens, she wasn't headed to the courtyard where the field hands ate. Her destination seemed to be a fruit orchard. Instead of cutting straight across a patch of close-cropped sugarcane, the way Tana would have if she was loaded down as this girl was, she followed the longer dirt path along the edge of the estate wall. Her gait was the final oddity that made Tana sit up on her elbows and stare. As the girl shuffled along, she raised more dust than two bare feet should account for.

Curiosity beat out fatigue. Tana tied her almost dry shawl over her head. She shook out her damp skirts and hurried to meet the girl, who allowed herself to be relieved of one jar and the basket. Her gaunt, weary face was vaguely familiar, though pocked with insect bites, inflamed and oozing.

Falling in next to her, Tana glanced down and caught her breath. Her heart beat faster. No wonder the girl shuffled: An iron chain stretched between two ankle cuffs.

She showed no sign of recognizing Tana, but staggered on, empty hands dangling at her sides. They walked deep into the orchard. Screened by leafy orange, pinkfruit, and mango trees was a windowless, mud-walled compound. The girl pushed open a latticed door.

The stench inside rocked Tana back on her heels; she almost

dropped what she was carrying. Fouler and more throat-closing than the horse or cow barns, these dim rooms stank of human waste, illness, and misery. Tana clutched the jar and basket to her chest. Eyes watering in disgust and pity, she crept after the other girl, who hadn't flinched, or even seemed to notice.

Inside, four arcaded halls surrounded a central courtyard. Voices coughed and babbled with the disordered talk of fevered minds. If Tana ignored what her nose and ears told her, she could imagine how the building might once have been a pleasure pavilion, given its secluded location, the rooms' elegant proportions and tall carved pillars. Now light leaked through holes in the thatched roof, revealing fragments of colored tile and peeling plaster. Water trickled over a jumble of stones in the central courtyard, the sad remains of a fountain. Instead of silk carpets and gauzy hangings, inlaid furniture and urns full of flowers, the space was divided by scarred wooden workbenches. Rats scurried across the filthy floor; flies buzzed over squat clay pots. Tana tried not to look inside them. But she had to look at the people.

Grubby children surrounded the young woman in the blue dress wrap. Many showed telltale signs of putrid fever: an angry red rash on arms and legs, a rasping cough, fever-bright eyes, and cracked lips.

"Vilina, Vilina." They begged and cried and tugged at her skirts.

"Get your bowls," she said. "Ma-ji will share it out."

Tana couldn't understand why the adults sitting at the benches or lying on the piles of dirty bedding followed the girl with their eyes only, until she saw that their right ankles were chained to the benches. Mounted on the work surfaces were tools she recognized: drills and saws, buffing wheels and polishers.

She had found her lost artisans. Fury mounted with every step Tana took. Alwar had been even more calculating than she could have guessed. These workbenches hadn't been built in a day or two. The soldiers must have been instructed to kidnap the villagers whether or not Tana was found among them. Still, she felt responsible for leading the soldiers directly to Piplia.

She stifled a bitter laugh as another thought occurred to her. Perhaps it wasn't only her fault that the people had been taken. Some share of blame belonged to Diribani. Or, more properly, to the goddess who had "blessed" them both. The diamond girl's rough gems needed to be cut and polished for the most profitable trading. How like Tenth Province's greedy governor to decide he needn't pay guild rates for the work.

Alwar had stolen a village-full of artisans and spirited them off to some relative's country house. Well away from Gurath, he could work them in secret, without any guild inspectors demanding appraisal fees.

Tana set the covered basket and jar on the workbench next to Vilina's jar and backed out of the way. Intent on the food, the people ignored her while the headman's wife spooned out rice and thin soup into the children's bowls, topping them with a flat, round biscuit.

As she stood near the wall, searching the dimness for Kalyan, Tana breathed through her open mouth. The room's evil smell coated the inside of her throat and settled on her skin. She'd need to wash again before she returned to the mare barn, or Atbeg would know she'd gone somewhere she had no reason to visit.

No reason? Every reason. People were dying here. Their dignity, as much as their suffering, brought tears to Tana's eyes. Instead of gobbling down the food they were given, the children carried the bowls to the workbenches. Men and women divided the biscuits, shaped the rice into balls, and shared them out. Many people were too weak to sit or stand. Family members knelt and fed them, tipping the broth into mouths stretched wide with pain. Each low, rasping cough twisted Tana's heart.

A woman moaned, twitching on her bedroll. A child scratched listlessly at her flea-bitten arms. As everywhere on the estate, there were plenty of rats. Where rats went, fleas followed. A furtive noise caught Tana's attention. Two rats were sidling along the wall to the darkest corner, where several shrouded shapes lay, unmoving. Tana's fists clenched as she counted five: three the size of children, and two adults.

Was Kalyan one of them?

Desperately, she searched for another explanation. He had little skill at gem-cutting. He was a trader, not an artisan. Perhaps the white-coats were keeping him somewhere else. At the main house, maybe. She'd go there next. She'd do anything, look anywhere, as long as she didn't have to pull the cloth from one of those still forms and see his face.

One of the rats stood on its hind legs and sniffed, as if preparing to climb over the bodies.

The people's souls were gone, already embarked on new lives, in new bodies. Tana knew those empty shells wouldn't care about rats crawling on them. But she did. With an angry cry, Tana untied her shawl and flapped it.

One rat fled, chittering abuse. The other, bolder one defied her. Tana advanced, snapping her shawl. The cloth almost touched the matted black fur before the animal gave way. She chased it out the door, into the orchard. The rat vanished into a hole in the ground, its bare tail flicking an insulting salute.

Tana tied her scarf around her head. She panted, inhaling great gulps of fresh air as the tears ran down her cheeks. When she heard the creak of cart wheels, she ducked into the shelter of the doorway.

Approaching the building was a pushcart covered with a heavy cloth. The cloth was dyed a green so dark it could be mistaken for black. The color of a serpent's hide at night, of deep water and death, the shade sacred to Naghali-ji. This would be the corpse cart, come to take the five bodies to the cremation ground. She glanced up. Her fingers closed hard on the splintery door frame, but she disregarded the pain.

Thin as a skeleton, Kalyan strained between the cart's two handles. Step by slow, wavering step, he pushed the cart to the door. His gaze was fixed on the ground, as if he didn't trust his balance.

Tana could hardly believe her eyes. Gone was the wealthy, carefree young trader. He'd been ill, seriously so. The rags of his once-fine clothes hung from his shoulders, and his halting gait made her bare feet curl in sympathy. Unlike Vilina, he didn't wear chains. If he'd been hobbled, Tana doubted he could have managed the cart. An overseer must have decided Kalyan was too weak to get far. Or else the white-coat didn't want to spare one of the estate's few healthy servants to deal with non-Believer dead.

Kalyan's condition brought home to Tana the extent of the plague. As with the people inside, suffering had stamped his expression, adding a profound dignity to a face made for smiling.

Not that he was likely to smile at Tana. Not when she and her sister were the cause of this pain.

How he must hate her.

CHAPTER TWENTY-THREE

Diribani

WASPS drove Diribani into the Believers' prayer hall. The stinging insects had come out of their cool-season sleep and built nests all around the fort grounds. In response, Princess Ruqayya dispatched workers with long poles to detach the constructions from eaves and doorways. Much like the border uprising that had called Prince Zahid from Fanjandibad, the resulting skirmishes were brief, but fiercely fought.

It was Diribani's bad luck to be passing the Hall of Public Audience when a servant knocked a large nest from a column. The papery comb landed on the ground and split like a melon, disgorging wasps like yellow-and-black-striped seeds.

"Run, my lady!" Nissa darted ahead of Diribani and opened the door to the nearest shelter, which turned out to be the prayer hall. With Zeen hard on her heels, Diribani ran inside. A few wasps pursued them through the arched doorway, but Nissa grabbed Diribani's hand and tugged her to the left, around a lacy stone screen. "The ladies' side," the maid whispered. "We leave our shoes here."

Diribani stepped out of her silk slippers and looked around in curiosity, for she had never been inside a prayer hall before. It was an empty, light-filled room, the exact opposite of the temple groves she was used to. The home of the twelve was as lively as a market-place. Between the sound of drums and the scent of incense, temple groves offered a feast for the senses. People decked the images of gods and goddesses with garlands of flowers and placed offerings of fruit and grain at their feet. Animals wandered freely through the trees, as welcome there as the worshipers, chanting priests, and dancing priestesses.

But, just like their clothing, the white-coats' prayer hall was deliberately plain. Nissa and Zeen took a few steps into the room. Zeen pulled a length of fine muslin from her sleeve and draped it over her head. Both women knelt and closed their eyes.

Diribani followed their example, though she peeked out from under her lashes. She felt twitchy. However did these people catch their god's attention? Where were worshipers supposed to direct their prayers? She didn't see any images or altars, or any priests to lead the worship. Plain blue and gold tiles alternated in the tall vault of the ceiling; white marble faced the walls and floors. The wasps' faint buzzing intensified the oppressive quiet of the place.

Then, as she looked around, Diribani noticed the details. Bands of intricate cream-on-white geometrical designs surrounded the doorways and high arched windows. Light shone through the carved stone screen dividing the men's and women's areas. It cast delicate shadows of vines and flowers on the floor, almost like a temple grove's dappled shade.

The longer Diribani sat there, the calmer she became. It was like sitting inside a giant pearl. In time, the silence took on the same quality she had noticed at Gurath's well, the morning she met Naghali-ji there. As if someone were listening, the prayer hall's peace invited confidences, coaxing Diribani's worries to the surface of her mind. Foremost was the fact that she'd had no word from her dear ones—Ma Hiral, Tana, or Zahid. She knew there was nothing she could do but wait, so she had tried to ignore her fear. In this quiet, light-filled room, it welled up like water and spilled out of her. But not, she thought, into nothing.

She closed her eyes and sensed an invisible force flowing around her, as if the Believers' prayers ran together in a river, and carried her heartfelt wishes for her family's and the prince's well-being along with the rest. The river didn't judge her. She was present; her silent voice, too, would be heard.

Opening her eyes, Diribani felt lighter, as if her water jar of worries had tipped over and spilled its contents into the current, where they had been washed away. How odd, that she could almost feel Naghali-ji's hand on her head in the middle of the white-coats' prayer hall.

Next to her, Nissa sighed deeply, as if she, too, had been relieved of a burden. Diribani glanced over and met the maid's inquiring look. They both stood. A few other women had come in, bare feet soundless on the marble floor, and knelt some distance away. Quietly, Diribani and Zeen followed Nissa to the entry and retrieved their slippers. As she passed the screen, Diribani peeked into the men's section. As far as she could tell, it was the same as the women's, with white floors and walls saturated with the sunlight streaming in through the tall windows.

What had she expected? That the men would get carpets and cushions while the women knelt on stone? No, the two sections were equally plain. Like their clothes, she realized with a start. As they emerged from the prayer hall and started up the steps to the palace, Diribani turned to Nissa. "Why do you all wear white coats and trousers?"

"To match the marble, you mean?" Her maid giggled. "Not exactly, my lady. In the poorer neighborhoods, prayer halls are built of mud brick, like everything else."

"But the custom is based on religious teaching," Zeen said behind them.

Diribani and Nissa both spun around. Zeen hardly ever volunteered information; it was as if a stone column had spoken. The guard straightened, dropping a ruby and topaz into the bag at her belt. "It's to remind us that all souls are the same in God's eyes," she explained.

"But Princess Ruqayya wears white brocade, and you—" Diribani bit her lip, afraid to insult them.

"Wear white cotton?" Zeen finished dryly. "If we were all perfect, we'd be walking in God's garden already."

"There'd better not be four hundred steps to God's garden," Nissa muttered. Then her eyes widened and her shoulders hunched, as if she were expecting a blow. Zeen snorted, but didn't comment.

Diribani dropped the subject of religion, in case she'd made Nissa uncomfortable. But as Cow Month ambled along, she found herself returning often to the prayer hall. She did ask Ladli about it, at a noon meal after the wasp incident.

"Mind?" Ladli's brows arched in surprise. "Why should we mind? As long as you don't wear shoes inside, or"—her eyes narrowed with mischief—"bring any animals with you."

"The wasps followed us on their own," Diribani protested.

The young noblewoman selected a piece of milk fudge from a silver tray. "So I heard," she said.

"But should I ask Princess Ruqayya's permission?" Diribani glanced down the table, over the carnations scattered around her plate.

As she often did these days, the princess was eating alone, barricaded behind a pile of papers, her inkstand, pens, wax, and seal. Behind her stood three maids, head scarves draped over their shoulders, waiting to carry her messages to every corner of the fort.

Ladli tapped her fingers on the table. "I wouldn't bother her. She's doing both Steward Ghiyas's job and her brother's. The more prayers for their success, the better."

Diribani's soup slopped in her bowl. She set it down and licked dry lips. "Is there bad news from the border?"

"Oh, the usual." Ladli sipped her tea. "My brother reports their progress as slow but steady, with bloody fighting in pockets. He thinks they'll be home for the prince's birthday."

Diribani shredded a marigold. "That's weeks away."

"Mm, about when it's getting too hot to keep fighting," Ladli said. "One way or the other, they'll be back."

"Oh, I hope so," another girl said from across the table. "We can't have the Mina Bazaar without His Highness."

"And His Highness's friends." The girl next to her split a pink fruit into segments. She winked at Diribani. "Including a certain—"

"Sh!" her neighbor hissed. Jeweled fingers flew up to cover the speaker's mouth. "Do you want my mother to hear?"

"What's the Mina Bazaar?" Diribani asked.

"A palace tradition," Ladli explained. "On the princes' birthdays, their sisters and their friends set up stalls in the garden. The boys have to bargain for the things they want."

"When the princes are young, we offer toys and sweets," the girl eating the pinkfruit said. "For someone Prince Zahid's age, it's armor, jewels, paintings."

"And sweets," the other girl said.

They all laughed. "Boys are never too old for sweets," Ladli agreed.

At the end of the table, Ruqayya glanced up from the letter she was reading, but didn't ask them to share the joke.

Despite the princess's earlier assurance that Diribani would get used to life in the ladies' court, her loneliness intensified. The only good thing about Zahid's continued absence was that Ruqayya had given Diribani permission to install her birthday gift in the prince's suite. As promised, Nissa's father had executed one of Diribani's flower drawings in a large panel of white marble and colored stone. Diribani had been pleased with the effect, and hoped the prince would enjoy having a garden vista from his room no matter what the season.

It was supposed to be a surprise, but many of the servants had stolen inside to see it. Their descriptions inspired some palace ladies to decorate their rooms in a similar fashion.

When construction noise and dust enveloped the palace, Diribani escaped outside. In the fleeting cool of the morning, she wandered the fort grounds. Followed by her maid and guards, she visited the library and prayer hall, artists' workshop and marketplace. Beyond Fanjandibad's walls, a golden blanket of mustard flowers spread across the plateau. Cereal crops ripened and were cut, husked by tramping cattle, and winnowed with the help of the blustery winds that heralded the hot season's arrival. As if the birds felt that burning breath on their necks, flocks gathered to fly north.

During the increasingly sultry afternoons, when workers set aside their chisels and hammers so the palace ladies could rest, Diribani paced the covered galleries, as restless as a hunting cheetah on a jeweled leash. She watched the birds, wishing she could fly, too. But, rather than following them northward, she would go northwest to Gurath's temple grove and Tana. Or east to the border, and see what was happening with her own eyes.

One day, Ladli caught her at it. Taking advantage of Diribani's preoccupation, the older girl walked up behind her and tapped Diribani's shoulder.

Diribani whirled, but Ladli danced out of reach, her feet moving in a familiar pattern. "You should have caught me," she teased. "Out of practice, teacher."

"Don't expect me to dance without drums," Diribani said.

"Hah," Ladli scoffed. "You don't need musicians for this. It's all the outward show with you people."

"What do you mean?" Despite her initial protest, Diribani rearranged her yellow dress wrap for dancing. The gallery was wide enough, and empty.

The other girl thumped her chest. "Heart drum, spirit drum. They're inside you, silly. Only listen."

Challenged, Diribani matched her steps with Ladli's. The palace drowsed around them, with most of the ladies escaping the heat in the shady garden or the bathing room's cool pools. As in the prayer hall that first time, the silence felt awkward. Diribani wished she had the drums' help to keep her feet moving steadily. Sweat gathered under her arms and behind her knees.

Ladli's left hand swept out. Diribani missed seeing it, and took a glancing blow on her elbow. Her dance partner's mocking expression goaded her to keep going.

What would Tana say if she knew a pampered palace beauty had mastered dancing without drums? If Ladli could do it after a few months' practice, Diribani would, too. She listened as hard as she could, trying to hear what the other girl heard. In the garden, a peacock screamed. Down a corridor, a woman scolded her maid with equal harshness. Closer, Diribani's feet struck the floor. Her breath hitched in her throat. Under those noises, a thread of sound reached her ear. Soft, but steady. She almost—There.

Her heartbeat.

Heart drum. Heartbeat. Diribani flushed with chagrin. How had a white-coat understood this mystery before she did?

When Ladli laughed, Diribani realized she had said the thought aloud. "Because you people don't shut up," the other girl said cheerfully. "You talk and sing and dance and carry on. Listening is *our* practice." Again, Ladli thumped her chest. "Why do you think prayer halls are silent?"

"I don't know," Diribani said humbly. She kicked a couple of rough diamonds out of the way. Honeysuckle perfumed the air.

"We pray quietly so we can hear God answer. This isn't so different. When you listen with your body and mind, not just your ears, you can hear what your partner is about to do."

As she danced, and listened, Diribani fancied she *could* hear what Ladli was thinking. Beyond the mischief in her voice, beyond the rhythm of their feet striking the floor, Diribani caught an echo of intent. Her hand flew up and met Ladli's, palm to palm.

"Better, flower girl," Ladli teased.

"Thank you, knife girl." Diribani picked up the pace. Her partner matched her. They whirled like twin dust-clouds, hands flashing out to meet each other in flight. Dancing, Diribani had no room in her mind to worry about the continuing silence from Prince Zahid.

And Tana.

CHAPTER TWENTY-FOUR

Tana

PUSHING the corpse cart, Kalyan trudged toward her. Tana's feet stuck to the ground. She couldn't move, trapped between the wretched villagers inside and the man who knew—who better?—that their hardship was partly her fault. Tana steeled herself for the scorn, the disgust, that must follow when Kalyan looked up and recognized her. He shuffled forward. With every dragging step, her anguish increased. How thin he'd become!

Naghali-ji would have done better to kill her that day at the well, before the taint of death could spread to others. What purpose had her dark gift served, except to make others pay for Tana's failings?

A few paces from the doorway, Kalyan wheeled the pushcart in a half-circle and came to a stop. His back to her, he bent across the cart. Slowly, he folded the dark-green cloth, furling it over the sides. Then he stood for a while. He might have been praying. He might have been gathering his strength for the grim task ahead. Finally, he straightened, turned, and saw Tana.

She didn't expect his reaction. She certainly didn't deserve it.

Without hesitation, Kalyan opened his arms wide. Tana fell into them. He staggered back, into a mango tree, and slid slowly down the trunk without letting go of her. They sat together in the dirt.

She had intended to be dignified. Instead, she wept into his shoulder. Crying didn't bring toads and snakes, as long as she didn't speak words. So Tana choked and sobbed for the disaster she had caused. She'd imagined that, with Diribani's help, she could lead the people away in a glorious rescue, make all right again, like a princess in a tale. The reality was uglier. By the time Tana walked to the palace in Fanjandibad and told her sister, these sick people might all be dead.

And she was a fool. So stupid, to be happy in the arms of a man she couldn't have. Even if, thank Manali-ji the love goddess, he didn't seem disgusted by her presence. Tana's scarf had slipped to her shoulders, and Kalyan was stroking her short hair. If only she could talk to him!

Well, and why not? Tana's common sense asserted itself. They were alone among the trees. If Tana could speak anywhere on the estate, this was the place. And inside her, beneath the crying, disordered mess of a girl, a plan was taking shape, like a jewel forming in the burning heart of the earth. Even as she wept, Tana considered its many facets. *Wisdom, good fortune, death*: It needed all the goddess's attributes. If Naghali-ji withheld one, the plan would fail.

And Tana wasn't going to worry about that. If Kalyan had a better plan, he would tell her. Reluctantly, she extricated herself from his arms. She had to assume that the biggest obstacle between them still existed. Who knew what kind of creatures would follow her explanation?

She didn't go far, kneeling in the dirt next to him. "I'm so sorry, Kalyan-ji."

"You found us! I can't imagine how." Kalyan touched the lucky frog that had landed on his knee. Dark eyes searched Tana's. "But you mustn't blame yourself. Are you responsible for the soldiers' actions? Or for the fever? The twelve guide our fates."

"Alwar's men followed me to Piplia." A whip snake slithered on the ground between them.

"Maybe," Kalyan said. "But they would have come sooner or later. The governor's been trying to disband the artisan guilds since the day he was appointed. Weavers, ironworkers, dyers—there have been rumors of other villages gone missing. Before the guild masters could denounce him, they needed proof."

"I had thought to tell Diribani and get her help with the prince," Tana said, "but I don't think we have time. If the Jewelers Guild knew about the Piplia villagers' imprisonment, they could appeal directly to the emperor, couldn't they?"

"Yes." Hope strengthened Kalyan's voice. "Will you tell them?"

"You mean, will I take my friends to shock the Believers in Lomkha?" Tana waved at the snakes and toads collecting around her. "No, you'd better do it. Your father's a well-respected guild member; the court officials will believe you. And since you're not chained, it will be easy to get you out of here."

He frowned. "At a slug's pace, I'm afraid," he said. "Or maybe this handsome ratter will carry me."

"I was thinking you might prefer to ride Jasmine." Tana grinned at his surprise. "I'm working in the barn where she's kept. The grooms are mostly sick. You could ride out tonight."

"The guards will chase a horse thief."

"Not if he's disguised as a courier."

Kalyan's bony fingers plucked at the rags he wore. "In this?"

"Two girls were washing white coats and trousers at the tank. We'll find a pair for you."

Kalyan thought about it. "How will I get into the stables?"

"I'll smuggle you in under the clean saddlecloths, in one of the big laundry baskets. Atbeg, the boy who's acting head groom, thinks too much of himself to put them away. He'll expect me to do it, and I'll make you a hiding place in the storeroom. Only for a few hours." A toad blinked at her, unconvinced, but the trader was nodding agreement. Tana went on. "You'll leave with the sweepers. The gate's open while the guard watches the clerk count out the day laborers' wages. Ride away without stopping, like couriers always do."

Kalyan's fingers drummed on his leg. "You'll come with me, of course."

"No. Even if I could ride, couriers travel alone."

His face tightened. "It won't work. If I disappear, the overseer will kill Piplia's headman and his wife. He warned me when he unlocked my ankle cuffs yesterday morning."

"Oh, did I forget to mention?" Tana said. "You'll be dead."

"What?"

Giggles threatened to break through the tragic expression Tana had assumed. "Alas, your fever worsened," she said sadly. "Vilina will complain about how her parents made her take all the bodies, including yours, and burn them at the cremation ground. I'll borrow her blue dress wrap, shuffle like she does, and push the cart. White-coats will keep their distance, you know they will, but anyone who sees me will confirm her story." She looked down at the ground. A sand boa stretched, displaying handsome scales. "I'm afraid you'll have to ride in the cart, too, under the cloth." With the bodies.

"And?"

"Along the way, I leave you at the tank, where the clothes are drying. While I'm gone, you bathe and dress and load the clean saddlecloths for me. I'll push the empty cart here, give back Vilina's dress wrap, and meet you at the tank."

"Very well. But you'll leave me at the well *after* we go to the cremation grounds. You're not doing that job by yourself. I'll change while you're returning this cart."

Grateful for the suggestion, Tana looked up through the trees, marking the sun's progress across the sky. "We've got to hurry. The saddlecloths will be dry soon."

After the sweet fresh air, the stink inside the makeshift prison smelled worse than ever. Tana hated to put on the stained blue dress wrap, especially when she had just gotten clean. But she hoped its bright color would draw the beholder's eye enough that nobody would notice the girl inside.

While the families wept, Tana and Kalyan picked up the bodies and put them in the cart. Vilina wasn't much help, and Tana wondered how Kalyan would have managed alone. His skin had an unhealthy tinge when she rolled the cloth over the top of the cart, but he winked bravely at her.

As she had predicted, the few people who noticed her kept well away from the corpse cart. The cremation ground was a deserted patch of bare dirt just beyond the estate wall. White-coats wouldn't want commoners holding death ceremonies on their land. The closest gate was unlocked, but barred with a heavy log so it could only be opened from inside the estate. Lengths of wood and dry brush had been stacked nearby. Tana and Kalyan built the pyre, then laid the bodies carefully on top. Local villagers must have brought the wood, built the small shrine, and supplied its burning lamp with oil.

His voice somber, Kalyan said a prayer over the bodies. Together, he and Tana lit straws from the lamp and touched them to the dry brush. Withdrawing to a respectful distance from the flames, they waited for the cleansing fire to reduce the bodies to ashes.

Whether as a result of the sad task they had shared or the unexpected embrace in the orchard, Tana sensed that matters had changed between her and Kalyan. They hadn't discussed his earlier marriage proposal, Tana's refusal, or the cobra that had intervened. They didn't need to. While she spoke toads and snakes, he wouldn't try to change her decision. But he looked at her with a deep interest, unlike the pleasant face he usually showed to the world. Despite their grim surroundings, delight rose within her like the rain filling a tank with life-giving water. Tana had kept her love a secret for so long. Allowing it to surface in her own eyes and smile felt deliciously freeing. As they worked, he had found excuses to touch her hand, to tuck wisps of hair behind her ears. Tana stifled a snort of affectionate laughter. Trust Kalyan to figure out how to court a girl even on the cremation ground!

As the fire burned, he told her more about what had happened to the artisans. From the moment of their arrival, they'd been closely watched. Except for the chains, and the lack of privacy, they hadn't been badly treated at first. Food came regularly, with sweets for the children when the workers exceeded their quota of jewels cut and polished. Sweepers emptied the slop jars, aired out the bedding, and kept the floors clean.

They had their first inkling that trouble had struck the estate when the clerks failed to appear with the daily packet of rough gems. Cooks no longer brought meals, and the sweepers stayed away. The bolder children crept out at night, stealing into the kitchens for food. Even in their isolation, illness had struck the artisans, as Tana had seen. Eventually, an overseer had remembered the people sequestered in the grove. Ill himself, he'd come and unlocked Vilina from her bench. He had secured the free end of the chain to her other ankle, so she could fetch their food. That was the last they'd seen of the white-coats, until another man had come the previous day. He'd unchained the dead—and Kalyan—and told him where to find the corpse cart.

Tana prayed she would never remember the rest of that day.

With every breath, she feared discovery. Her hands burned from pushing the carts, the skin raw and red where the blisters had popped. When she returned to the barn with Kalyan hidden in one of the big baskets, Atbeg complained about how long she'd taken. Finally, he and the other grooms went off to the foaling barn. The sweepers, too, put away their shovels and departed. Kalyan helped Tana saddle Jasmine with courier gear and pack a bag with a cooking pot, dried peas, and travel biscuits from the stores.

"You needn't stay here any longer," Kalyan said softly. "Alwar's actions are so outrageous that the guild's petition is sure to prevail. It will take time, though. Negotiations always do."

Tana shrugged. She didn't speak inside the barn.

"It's not safe. You could be discovered." He clasped her elbow, and Jasmine butted Tana's shoulder, as if to add her own encouragement. "Promise me you'll go. There'll be a temple grove along the main road. I'll find you. Or Jasmine will," he said, as his mare whuffled at Tana.

She didn't plan to abandon the villagers, but she nodded. Much as she longed for him to stay, to put his arms around her again, he had to leave. This was the most dangerous element of her plan. If Kalyan was stopped going through the gate, both of them would be discovered, and all hope of rescue lost. She urged him up on Jasmine's back.

"I'll see you soon," he repeated, and smiled down at her. "Don't forget me, toad girl."

Agreed. She tapped his hand in trader-talk. Loitering in the doorway, she signaled behind her back.

Kalyan straightened, putting on an arrogant manner to hide his weakened state. Looking neither right nor left, he rode straight at the gate. Tana held her breath. The white mare's hooves struck the ground. Ten strides from the road, and freedom.

Five.

The guard glanced up. Tana's nails bit into her raw palms. Three paces.

"You could walk her to the road," the guard grumbled loudly.

Like the other couriers, Kalyan paid no attention. He rode on, leaving the man to cough and wave away the swirling dust.

Tana sagged against the door frame as relief weakened her knees. Kalyan faced a difficult ride, but with the protection of the courier's disguise and his own quick wits, he should succeed. The one great fear eased, smaller irritations began to jostle for her attention. She scratched a fleabite on her arm. Her stomach growled. Her hands throbbed. Before Atbeg could return and catch her idle, Tana went to start a pot of wheat porridge and put away the clean saddlecloths.

One by one, the more senior grooms returned to work, displacing young Atbeg. The boy who had once protested Tana's presence now begged to keep her assigned to the barn, mostly so he'd have some-one to order around. Tana didn't mind. She preferred sleeping in the barn to outside in the brush. And it was easier to keep an eye on the artisans from inside the estate walls.

When Atbeg noticed Jasmine's absence and queried Tana, she pointed to a red-and-white-striped cloth and then in the direction of the gate.

"Courier took her?" He scratched his head. "Wonder which one he left in trade."

Tana tensed, but another groom called Atbeg's name and the boy didn't pursue the question.

By day, Tana walked horses, shoveled dung, and kept out of the grooms' way. At night, she stole out to the orchard. She could do little for the people there but empty waste jars into the latrine pits and bring fresh water to bathe the victims' cracked skin. She helped however she could, and retreated to the barn to sleep.

Crow Month flapped by on sullen wings. Then, one afternoon, she could no longer ignore the heat crawling along her own skin.

When evening's cooler air brought no relief, Tana forced her-self to think. She should run. Now, tonight, before she got sicker. Before the fever affected her mind and she could no longer control her tongue. Before she spoke frogs and snakes and the white-coats realized who she was.

She grabbed a water sack and a pouch of travel biscuits, though she wasn't hungry. Creeping along the estate wall in the dark, she found the gate, and then the tree where she had hidden the bag with her dowry bangles. The bark scratched her hands and bare feet as she climbed. It took a long time to reach the bundle, longer than it should have, and Tana was frightened by her dizziness as she half slid, half fell down the other side of the wall.

After gathering her meager supplies, she slung the bag over her shoulder and walked down the road. While she still commanded her shaking limbs, she meant to put all possible distance between herself and the white-coats. If the twelve smiled, she'd find a temple grove before dawn. If not, she'd go to ground like an animal and wait for the fever to pass.

One thought kept her feet moving, hour after hour. Kalyan had promised he'd find her. Naghali's gift might betray Tana, but Kalyan never would. She held that knowledge, even though she felt her head might split from the pain echoing inside it. She walked on. The moon peeped between the clouds. Tana walked. She'd show them. She'd look death herself in the face and spit to express her contempt. Tana shook her fist at the goddess. Weren't toads and snakes frail flesh, like her own? Not anymore. She was stone. Adamant.

The road forked. She chose the narrower way. Dust puffed under her feet. She smelled mango flowers; the sweetness tugged at her. Night birds screeched. She walked on. Her eyes fluttered closed, the lids too heavy to lift. Heat crackled over her skin. Vaguely, she realized she could fall into a ditch. She didn't care. She would shed her skin, like a snake, and come out clean.

The mango scent intensified, waking yellow and gold sparks in her brain. No. The lights were outside; she could see them through the papery skin of her eyelids. That was wrong. She opened her eyes. Shrieked.

Lamplight sparkled in a snake's diamond eyes.

CHAPTER TWENTY-FIVE

Diribani

TWO days before Prince Zahid's twentieth birthday, the oxcarts arrived in Fanjandibad. From her window, Diribani had seen a caravan's plume of dust billow into the hot, still air above the plateau, but she hadn't understood its significance until Nissa clapped her hands. "It's Second Camp."

"The prince?" Diribani asked through dry lips.

"Tomorrow, my lady."

As the dust cloud approached the fort, a flock of veiled women swooped from the palace doors and down the four hundred steps to the gate. The noble ladies' husbands and sons and brothers would arrive the next day with the prince's army. Many of the servants, however, had relatives in Second Camp, and everyone was anxious for news.

Before she let herself join them, Diribani wiped pigment from her brush with a soft cloth. She put away her painting materials and considered changing out of her crimson dress wrap, which was creased from a long morning spent sitting at the table. Her hands felt sweaty, her neck hot. The idea of covering her head, even with the light silk end of her dress wrap, held no appeal, but Diribani sighed and did it anyway. "Lead on," she told Nissa.

The maid almost danced down the stairs. "My cousin's a porter in Second Camp," she confided. "Once he's helped stow the tents, he'll tell us the latest."

Victory.

Word spread throughout the fort with a gazelle's burst of speed. Jubilation overflowed from the ladies' quarter. The gaiety rolled over Diribani's head like a spring storm, all wind and heat lightning, without the relief of a good soaking rain. In the midst of the celebration, Diribani felt more alone than ever, a defenseless child of the twelve trapped in a wasps' nest of ferocious Believers.

The next day, Zahid led the army's triumphant entry into Fanjandibad. Under the brazen sun, steel helmets flashed and war elephants trumpeted. Drums pounded with the beat of marching soldiers.

Her face concealed behind the dress wrap's free end, Diribani blinked back tears of relief mixed with sadness. Zahid was safe. His forces had defeated the rebels, but those "dirt-eaters" were her people, too. She couldn't enjoy hearing the white-coats boast about the carnage. Not that the prince did so, to her knowledge, but some of the ladies were downright bloodthirsty. Finally, battle talk gave way to a fresh topic: the Mina Bazaar.

The prince's birthday dawned hot and clear. Even before the sun rose, Diribani heard the thrum of activity. The fort was packed with people, for white-coats had gathered from the entire province to celebrate.

Despite the heat, Princess Ruqayya prowled the grounds to assure that all would be ready in time. Sweating servants toiled to please her. In the garden, they hung silk lanterns in trees, removed dead flowers, and erected booths for the Mina Bazaar. Inside the Hall of Public Audience, the largest covered space in the fort, carpets were spread on the floor. Brocaded cloths draped bolsters and low tables for the feast. The screened balcony overlooking three sides of the hall was arranged for the noble ladies, so they could eat without the encumbrance of their veils. On the dais where the prince usually heard petitioners, Steward Ghiyas supervised the installation of a giant scale from a grain vendor in the marketplace.

Diribani spent the day in her room, weaving flowers into garlands as Nissa dashed in and out to report on the preparations and share the latest gossip.

"Lady Ladli has the Mina Bazaar's best stall," the maid said. "A riding theme, with beautiful saddlecloths and blankets, plumed headstalls, and steel daggers with jade handles carved like horse heads."

Diribani imagined Zahid bargaining with Ladli, she of the eloquent dark eyes and witty remarks. The thought failed to please. "I'm sure the prince and his friends will enjoy the display," Diribani said politely. She added a rose to the garland.

Nissa giggled. "And some of the younger ladies are so excited, they're eating their own wares. I heard two already sending back to the kitchen for more milk fudge."

Diribani wove in a spray of orange blossoms, their fragrance sticky-sweet. "That'll put the cooks out of temper," she observed. "Aren't they busy with feast dishes? Milk fudge takes hours of stirring, and the stuff scorches the moment you turn your back."

"True." Nissa cocked her head. "Most noble ladies don't know, or don't care."

"I'm not most noble ladies." Diribani tasted the astringent flavor of a pale-blue flower with spikes instead of leaves. It pricked her fingers as she wove it into the garland. With equal sternness, she tamped down the desire to jump up and follow Nissa outside, to share in the preparations, the chatter and laughter. The other girls would be talking about how to draw the prince to their stalls.

None of them could be as eager as Diribani. She hadn't spoken with Zahid in months, but he had never strayed far from her thoughts. That was the problem. Hope and longing gripped her so tightly, she was afraid one of the courtiers would read her feelings in her face. With one unguarded remark, her secret might be discovered. The stakes were too high. Better she stay in her room and rely on Nissa for information.

"The steward gave me a small booth, like you asked," Nissa said. "It's under a tree by the east fountain."

"Good." Diribani jabbed a marigold stem in with the prickly one.

"I'm only to set out the garlands?" The maid sounded doubtful. "My father has some inlaid boxes you could have."

"Just the garlands, thank you."

"Well, save out some jasmine, if you would, my lady." Nissa didn't say that she was disappointed by her mistress's floral offerings, but she took extra care arranging Diribani's hair. She wove the dark strands into a confection of braids and loops, secured with jeweled pins and ornamented with fragrant jasmine. Like the hairstyle, the clothes she brought were also unusual. "From Princess Ruqayya," she said, to keep Diribani from insisting on a dress wrap. Unlike Diribani's practical riding outfits, the coat and trousers were made of the finest silk, with pearls trimming the coat's long sleeves. "Pale pink is exactly right for you," Nissa coaxed, "and, look, the shawl matches."

Diribani hardly recognized the elegant picture reflected in the mirrored wall of her dressing area. Silk whispered against her skin. Nissa sighed with satisfaction.

"Your coat is pretty, too," Diribani noticed belatedly.

The maid smoothed the white cotton over her hips. "Her Highness gave us all new clothes, in honor of the prince's birthday. Gardeners, cooks, maids, porters, grooms, everybody."

"Very generous," Diribani said.

After staining the sky the color of saffron, the sun had already dipped below the fort wall when Diribani, Nissa, and Mahan joined the veiled ladies crossing the garden to climb the steps to the upper level of the Hall of Public Audience. A carved screen sheltered the women from the view of the soldiers, courtiers, and favored guests, while allowing them to watch the activity below.

Up on the balcony, the head scarves came off, revealing hair dressed even more elaborately than Diribani's, threaded with strings of pearls and other gems. None of the women were so indiscreet as to push or shove for the best places at the railing. Amid covert eyeing of the gifts their maids carried, compliments were exchanged and rank was silently asserted. Despite Nissa's efforts, Diribani found herself at the opposite end from Princess Ruqayya, who commanded the best view of the dais and scales. Diribani could barely make out the distant figure of the prince as, with a flourish of drums, Zahid stepped into one of the scale's large round pans and sat down.

Steward Ghiyas appeared to have matters well in hand. Within moments, well-wishers were filing past the dais to lay their gifts in the opposite pan. Jokes and laughter rose from the men as the gifts piled up.

Diribani felt a tug on her silk sleeve. She turned to find Ladli standing behind her.

The young woman's face was flushed with suppressed mirth. "Can you guess what Lady Yisha's giving?" she whispered in Diribani's ear.

Diribani shook her head.

"A bag of fennel seeds!" Ladli hiccupped with the effort to contain her laughter. "Can't you see the face of the lucky soul who gets it?"

"I thought the gifts went to the poor."

"Oh, yes. There's a big crowd outside the main gate." Ladli had caught the rose and iris that fell with Diribani's words. Playfully, she tapped the blossoms against Diribani's pink silk sleeve. "Lady Yisha must think they suffer from bad breath. My maid said her daughters were so humiliated, they each added a silver coin to their gifts."

Having been poor not so long ago, Diribani didn't find Lady Yisha's snobbery very funny. "What did you give?"

"My second-best horse blanket," the other girl said proudly. "Our weavers are the most skilled in all of Fifth Province, and my aunt sent me the pick of this season's work. I'm bringing the rest to the Mina Bazaar." She blushed, for no reason Diribani could see, and flitted off to share her tidbit of gossip with another friend, closer to the prime viewing area.

"Clever," Nissa murmured from Diribani's other side. "If someone admires the blanket, the steward will say where it came from.

So His Highness and his friends will know whose stall to patronize at the bazaar tonight."

Diribani had wondered about this. No doubt Tana would have immediately understood and approved the mercantile tactic. "Is that why so many young ladies are giving away sweets, and horse gear, and things from their stalls?" She caught a sapphire, two diamonds, and an orchid in her palm.

"Mm." Nissa neither confirmed nor denied it, but her eyes sparkled with the same humor as Ladli's.

Diribani thought of the poor people waiting for the birthday weighing gifts to be distributed. Besides the usual hunger, a sense of hope, too, must be plucking at their bellies. Hope for an ornament that could be traded for food, or a coin to buy a working share in the mines and a chance at a better future. Whereas they endured heat, dust, and flies, she breathed in the scents of attar of roses, orange water, and ashoka flower. The perfumes made her dizzy. She realized anew how four hundred steps—and Naghali-ji's blessing—separated her from the beggars at the gate.

One of them would get a silver coin, another Ladli's second-best horse blanket, a third Lady Yisha's bag of fennel seeds. The courtiers setting their offerings in the scales didn't consider what people actually needed; the most generous gifts were only given to impress the prince.

A wash of shame cooled Diribani's rising temper. How was she different? Preoccupied with the Mina Bazaar, she hadn't thought much about the gift ceremony, planning to send Nissa down with a handful of whatever jewels she spoke before the pans balanced. She uncurled her fingers and counted. A sapphire, two diamonds, a nice chunk of jade, and a topaz. A small fortune by the world's usual reckoning. A few words to her. She'd grown complacent. The flower girl, the jewel girl. She hardly noticed anymore. Who was this person wearing a silk coat and slippers, her hair piled high, her face covered? Aside from the two gold bangles Diribani never took off, and the fabric's pink hue, she might as well be a white-coat. Would Ma Hiral or Tana recognize her in these clothes? What would her father have said?

She closed her sweaty palms over the rough gems and leaned forward until her forehead touched the carved stone screen. She could make a few friends in Fanjandibad, wear the Believers' costume, observe their customs. She could pay for good works with the goddess's diamonds and improve her painting. She could find peace in a prayer hall. She could love a prince, Diribani admitted to herself. Silently, and from afar, since he must never know.

How foolish, to forget that she could never truly belong here while her gift set her apart. Was Naghali-ji testing her still? Or was this a flaw Diribani hadn't suspected in her own character, that after she had been given so much she only wanted the thing she couldn't have?

Down by the scales, servers were filing in with platters of food. Most of the men had gathered around the low tables, with only a few people left to offer their gifts. The prince's pan rested on the floor, although the other pan was piled high. It was clear, from the comments, that this, too, was part of the entertainment.

Zahid's head lifted. He faced Diribani's direction, his expression full of amused resignation. She remembered that she had promised he wouldn't be left sitting there, the one day of the year when the rest of the court could start eating without him. The weight of these small stones wouldn't count so much. She should have brought something heavier. Ladli's earlier words echoed in her head. "All talk, you people."

Diribani turned to her maid. "Will you take my contribution down to the scales?" Self-disgust made her voice sound angry, which Nissa didn't deserve. "Please," she added.

"Certainly, my lady." Nissa wrapped her head scarf around her face.

With Mahan looking on, Diribani counted the jewels into Nissa's cupped palms. The younger girl's eyes widened when Diribani took an emerald of almost ten ratis from her waistband and added it to the others. Lastly, she stripped the gold bangles from her wrist and dropped them atop the pile. Until the weight was gone, she hadn't noticed how heavy they were.

"But, my lady—"

"Go" was all Diribani trusted herself to say. A yellow lily dropped from her lips.

Nissa bowed over her joined hands in a gesture that combined two modes of respect, and started down the stairs.

Diribani watched her maid find a place at the end of the line. Not staying to see which of the last few gifts balanced the prince's weight, Diribani pulled the shawl over her head and slipped away from the balcony, down the opposite stairs to the garden. Mahan followed, as close as her shadow and as impossible to shake.

They walked down the gravel paths between the flower beds, canals, and trees. In Moonbird Month, the day's heat lingered into the night. Fountains played to cool the air, jets of water rising and falling in pretty patterns. From inside the audience hall, a roar of acclaim signaled that the weighing had finished. Diribani's nose told her that the main courses were being served. The smell of roasted meat turned her stomach, and even the more appealing aromas of buttered rice, curry, and hot bread failed to wake her appetite. She hoped for a quiet stroll to compose herself, but had to dodge the teams of men with ladders who were lighting the tree-hung lanterns.

The moon rose. Its round eye surveyed the last-minute preparations for the Mina Bazaar. Maids bustled around the stalls, making sure trays of sweets were covered against flying insects, and adding final touches to the displays.

Diribani found hers where Nissa had said it would be, tucked under a flowering tree by the east fountain. Mahan waited at her usual discreet distance while Diribani examined her booth. Cloth-of-gold covered a chest-high table, as wide as Diribani's forearm and twice as long. Hers was the only one garlanded with blossoms from every season and province in the empire. The flowers were rather wilted, despite the length of damp gauze Nissa had draped over them. When Diribani lifted the fabric, she smelled lily, honeysuckle, rose, carnation, and jasmine. Leaning her elbows on the table, she dropped her chin into her hands. The jeweled pins holding her hair in place poked at her scalp. She was afraid to touch them, lest the complicated structure come undone.

Her thoughts pricked likewise. Without the great emerald, which she had spoken several days earlier and been saving to display at her booth, nothing special remained to her. Well, nothing except for the stubbornness that had so displeased Ma Hiral. It would keep Diribani's head high when the other ladies arrived. After all, she and her sister had once sold their humblest household goods in Gurath's marketplace. Trader Javerikh's daughter could hawk the wilted flowers that decorated her stall, if that was all she had. Yes, and get a good price for them. It didn't really signify, because no family's survival hung in the balance. This bazaar was a game that rich white-coats played to entertain themselves.

Around her, the garden quieted as the servants finished lighting the lamps and incense burners. Maids dashed back to the audience hall to wait on their ladies. Fountains burbled. Owlets emerging from their nests for the night's hunting muttered "What, what?" at the unaccustomed lights. Moonbirds trilled in reply.

If she didn't look up, Diribani could imagine herself in a temple grove. She was surrounded by the sound of rustling leaves. Music, too. The notes of stringed instruments and drums wafted through the audience hall's pillared porches. The traditional scents of flowers, lamp oil, and incense hung in the air. With a few chittering monkeys and the whisper of a naga's scales over packed dirt, a worshiper of the twelve could feel perfectly at home.

Listening to the night's friendly noises, Diribani heard another: the crunch of footsteps on gravel. Someone was walking through the garden. Behind her, Mahan shifted, a reminder that at least three people were present to savor the night's temporary peace. It wouldn't last. The younger ladies, especially, would excuse themselves from the feast as soon as courtesy permitted, and make enough noise for a hundred monkeys.

The footsteps came closer. No hesitation, so it must be Nissa, tracking down her wayward mistress. Diribani rubbed her eyes. Her wrists felt unbalanced without the gold bangles. She straightened to hear how her impulsive gift had been received.

A white-coated figure ducked under a tree branch. Too tall for her maid, Diribani knew, even before the lamplight showed a shock of dark curls and the glitter of diamonds, rubies, and emeralds on the dagger slung at the man's belt.

Zahid bowed. "Good evening, Mina Diribani."

The prince! What was he doing here? Awkward with surprise, she folded her hands and returned his bow. "Peace, Your Highness." Marigolds fell like tiny suns. *Merchant girl.* That was a role Diribani could play in her sleep. She just had to act like Tana. "How may this lowly one serve you, honored sir?"

He stepped up to her table. "You already have. Those bracelets saved me from another hour, at least, of watching people eat."

He mentioned them so casually! He must not understand what the dowry bangles represented, that to lose them meant to be stripped of fortune and honor. And to give them up to a man not one's husband—scandal. In Gurath, bare arms on a girl of fifteen betrayed her utter lack of good sense. Of course, pale-pink sleeves covered Diribani's wrists tonight. She was dressed like one of his people. She, too, could pretend the bangles were just jewelry. She tried to match his merry tone. "What of the bolts of fabric and sacks of grain Steward Ghiyas was supposed to put by?"

"Vanished." The prince leaned on the table and toyed with the petals of a dark-red peony. "I suspect Ruqayya, but I'll never prove it. My sister's handmaids are known for their ruthless obedience to her commands."

"Or discretion, perhaps?" Diribani suggested. Several small stones plinked onto the table.

"No, thank goodness." Zahid grinned at her. "Or how would I have known where to find the diamond girl's stall? I wanted to tell you that I rode out this morning to see the well. It's finished, and work has begun on two more."

"Oh. Thank you." Pleasure warmed Diribani's cheeks before she remembered Ruqayya's warning. Encouraging the prince's attention put him at risk, she had said. But no one would know about this conversation. Except Mahan. Which might be good. The guard's presence would keep Diribani from saying anything she shouldn't. Unless Mahan was a spy, and Diribani should send Zahid away at once. *Merchant girl.* That was safest. She spread her empty hands over the wilted flowers. "Alas, nothing here merits a prince's consideration."

As if Naghali-ji mocked her, tiny diamonds sparkled in the lamplight as they pattered onto the table.

Zahid's face sobered. "I disagree. You are the one person who can help me."

She rearranged a garland. "How?" she asked, then squeaked with surprise to find her hands captured between the prince's.

"Trader-talk," he said. "I fear my understanding is incomplete, and the merchants at the mine are taking stunning advantage of my ignorance."

"Um." Diribani heard what he said, but how could she pay attention when her entire being was focused at the end of her wrists?

Prince Zahid had nice hands. Callused palms and smooth dark skin, except for a nasty cut, half-healed, that sliced the side of his hand and disappeared under his sleeve. With the narrow table separating them, she stood close enough to observe other signs of the campaign: His collar didn't quite hide a purple bruise; scratches striped his neck. She frowned in concern.

"You don't want me to bankrupt the empire's treasury, do you?" Zahid sounded as earnest as little Indu. "Paying fifty thousand gold pieces for a diamond worth five thousand?"

"You didn't!" Poppies flipped their orange-red skirts over a chunk of amethyst.

He laughed at her scandalized air. "How do I know? We do the bargaining with our hands under the table, or one of those embroidered cloths, and I can't remember which finger is ten and which is a hundred."

Diribani bit her lip to keep from laughing at this nonsense. "Very well. No peeking." She freed one hand to flick off her head covering. *Her* religion didn't prohibit Zahid from seeing her face. She snapped the shawl over their still-linked hands, where they rested on the table. "First lesson. It's not which finger, it's *where* on the finger the other person squeezes that gives you the value."

"Ah," he said.

Diribani counted, touching his finger to illustrate each stage. "Fingertip is one, first joint ten, second joint one hundred, palm line one thousand, half-palm ten thousand, wrist one hundred thousand. Denomination, then quantity. Thumb for one, whole hand for five, both hands for ten." Roses and gems punctuated the lecture, but Zahid kept his eyes on her face. Under the cloth, she touched his hands in a quick sequence. "How much did I just offer?"

"Two hundred three," he guessed.

Correctly. In fact, he missed only one of Diribani's tests. "You do so know this," she accused.

The prince kept hold of her hands. "I've heard you can use it for more than numbers."

"There are other terms," Diribani admitted. As a child, she had exchanged trader-talk for hours with Tana, Hima, even Kalyan. All the traders' children practiced with one another to gain the necessary fluency. But in the garden's warm, flower-scented darkness, in Zahid's company, the ordinary activity seemed charged with danger. Ruqayya would most certainly not approve. And yet Diribani couldn't pull away. "If you're not going to trade directly for coin, you also need the names of the stones: diamond, sapphire, ruby, emerald." She traced the signs on the back of his hand.

"Like this?" Zahid repeated them. Under the flower-weighted cloth, his fingers danced over her skin. His eyes met hers.

Diribani's lips went dry. She wanted to snatch the scarf and pull it over her head. She wanted to lean closer, wanted the table between them to melt like mist. "More study required," she said and signed, helpless to end the delicious stolen moment. "Exchange in kind, delayed payment, agreed, best offer."

Her fingers brushed the healing cut on the side of his hand. Abruptly, she remembered the danger. He had too many enemies for her to add his elder brother to the list. At any moment, the noble ladies would be leaving the audience hall. They mustn't see Zahid alone—almost alone—with her. "Transaction completed," she finished.

"But we haven't agreed on your payment."

Diribani slipped her hands out from under the scarf. She brought the corners together and spilled the collected gems and flowers onto the table, then draped the fabric over her hair. "You already knew most of them. No charge for practicing."

"But this is the Mina Bazaar." Zahid left his hands in plain view on the table. "You're supposed to haggle."

"Fine." She could hear voices in the distance. She touched his first finger joint, tugged lightly on his thumb. *Ten.* "Standard copper weights," she said aloud.

"For that most excellent lesson?" He clicked his tongue in disapproval and squeezed her knuckle. *One hundred.* "Gold."

"Definitely not," she said, amused against her will by their backward bargaining. "I'll settle for silver, though the outrageous price grieves me."

Zahid's head turned. He, too, heard the others coming. "Ah, but I haven't thanked you for the beautiful flower panel in my room." *Diamonds,* he tapped out, then stroked a quick line across the base of her palm.

A thousand diamonds went beyond teasing. Diribani stiffened. "Birthday gifts are excluded from the transaction." She folded his hand into a fist and squeezed it, then rested her hands on her side of the table.

The prince drew himself up, staring down his hawk nose at her. "Offer unsatisfactory?" he said aloud.

She hadn't taught him that one. More than ever, Diribani was convinced that this whole exchange had been a pretext for a private conversation with her. And yet he looked so insulted that she wavered. His next words made her even more confused.

"Of course mere riches wouldn't sway you, diamond girl," he said, too softly for Mahan to hear. "Be advised. Our business is not concluded." His fingers caressed her right hand before he bowed and left her.

With a shaking finger, Diribani traced in the flowers the sign he'd written on her skin. *More study required.*

CHAPTER TWENTY-SIX

Tana

S HE had found a well pavilion. As Tana stumbled through the dusty trees toward the serpent-crowned doorway, she imagined that she could smell the water the great stone naga promised. Her skin burned. The birds' raucous nighttime noises made it hard for her to think.

Too-ill, too-ill, too-ill, the cuckoo complained.

What? What? owlets demanded.

Tana's cracked lips couldn't shape an answer. Clouds covered the moon, and a fitful breeze tossed the leaves. Her teeth chattered; her legs trembled. Her vision was fading at the edges, and she feared she would topple through a dark hole in the earth.

Then she passed under the carved snake and did fall, tripping over the foot-washing basin just inside the doorway. Stone pavement bruised her knees. A trickle of water touched her bloody, thorn-pricked feet. Dry sobs racked Tana's body. She'd come so far, and knocked over the precious water. She scrabbled around the empty basin. The puddle she'd made was already drying on stone that still held the day's heat. Tana sucked her damp fingers. Too exhausted and feverish to stand, she struggled forward on hands and knees.

The lamplight didn't reach far from the door niches. Loud in the dark, the birds' chatter filled her head. Tana crawled on blindly. After she bashed her shoulder against a wall, she kept one hand extended in front of her.

A long ramp ended in stairs. Ahead, or below, she heard a frog peeping. She followed the hopeful sound. One battered knee gave way; she tumbled down several steps and cracked the back of her head so hard against the stone that colored lights shivered across her vision. She would have lain there until morning brightened the world, but thirst drove her harder than an overseer's whip. Wearily, Tana dragged herself into a sitting position. She extended her legs and half slid, half fell to the next step. *Bump.*

Down, and down, and down. The stairs had no end. She would finish in the white-coats' hell, with the demons and the flames. Her head pounded. Her skin burned. The injured shoulder and knee shrieked with every movement. Perhaps she was there already? The thought made her cry out. The only noise her parched throat produced was a harsh rasp.

It was enough to frighten her guide frog. The peeping sound stopped. Before Tana could despair completely, a soft splash renewed her will. The water was down there. Somewhere. Stretch. Slide. Bump. Her spine ached with the force of each landing. The stone steps scraped her skin. She kept on. Stretch. Slide. Bump.

Water lapped her feet. Tana straightened in shock and slid into the blessed, blessed coolness. Weeping, she sat waist-deep in the well to splash her face and arms and chest. She sucked up the water in great gulps and soaked the rags of her clothing, welcoming the clammy feel of wet cloth. She couldn't get enough of it. When her arms were too tired to splash, she wiggled her toes, just to feel the water moving over thirsty skin.

But the fever inside her, briefly quieted by her bath, came back. This time it burned cold, chattering her teeth and waking goose-flesh along her exposed skin. Tana heaved her legs out of the water and curled into a ball on the step.

With nightmare clarity, visions assaulted her: chained villagers driven from their smoking houses, fly-covered corpses rotting where they lay. Worse, she knew they weren't nightmares, but memories. Rats chewed and chewed and chewed. Obscene pieces of snake were strewn among shattered clay pots. Then the scene shifted. Wreathed in dead flowers, Diribani kept asking Tana what her soul desired. Every answer was the wrong one. Slime coated Tana's lips; diamonds cracked her teeth and turned her words into splinters. She tasted blood. She shivered. She burned. The voices shrieked in her ears, owlets and cuckoos trying to outscreech one another.

What?

Too-ill, too-ill.

"Sh, now. Sh, now."

Which bird was that? Hugging her knees, Tana swallowed pain like a handful of hot sand. A soggy, lumpish toad of a girl, she croaked in alarm at the hands that wanted to pull her apart.

"Sh, you're safe with us, Mina. Let go now, eh, so we can move you out of this damp spot?" Callused hands, but a sweet voice.

Light filtered through tree leaves far overhead. Day had come.

Tana relaxed so suddenly that her head thumped the stone. The bolt of pain made her groan. Her eyes squeezed shut. Her limbs flailed, and were steadied.

"She's burning," the sweet voice said.

"Wet clothes weigh more'n she does," a man's deeper voice answered.

"Up we go. Let's get a look at you."

Tana didn't recognize either of the speakers' voices. She squinted through crusty lashes and saw dark forms spattered with drops of sunlight. One held her ankles, the other her wrists. Between them, the man and woman hoisted her up the steps she had slid down. She swung from side to side like a net of coconuts strung under the rafters. Her stomach sloshed. Could a person be seasick from the waves crashing inside her?

Tana waged a fierce struggle not to retch. She understood they'd reached the top because her guts stopped trying to turn themselves inside out. She focused on breathing without sobbing.

"Not so young as I once was," the man said. "Hoo! Well's down another flight since yesterday, you reckon?"

"Mm," the sweet voice murmured. A woman's work-worn hands moved over Tana with gentle authority. When they found the knot on the back of Tana's head, they woke a pain so intense that Tana fainted.

Afterward, she didn't remember much about her illness. Light and dark, heat and coolness alternated unpredictably. She did remember people trying to carry her out of the well to the village. She resisted so strongly at passing under the snake portal, actually rolling off a litter and crawling back to the well, that they decided Naghali-ji wanted her there. So the villagers screened off an area for her in the entry room and took turns sitting with her.

Hands bathed her hot face with water and spooned broth or sharp-tasting herbal tea into her mouth. They wrapped her with shawls when she shivered, and bathed her again when she kicked off the coverings. Through it all, the frogs in the well inside, and the birds in the grove outside, kept up a noisy commentary. During the day, orioles whistled, parakeets chattered, and quail clucked wordlessly. At night the owlets inquired about her progress: *What? What?*

Too-ill, too-ill, the cuckoos insisted, and for a long time, it was true. Then, one evening, Tana woke with a clear mind. She was lying on a pallet, a light cotton sheet drawn over her naked body. Above the screens, the sky had turned palest pink beyond the entry pavilion's overhanging eaves. Moonbird Month had fled; in the sultry air, Tana tasted the sticky heat of Elephant Month. Tamarind season, mango season, when the only relief from the oppressive stillness was a windstorm that scoured grit into exposed skin and left a veil of dust to stick to eyelids and lips. Tana coughed and sat up, wrapping the sheet across her breasts and under her arms. Twig arms, she noticed. How long since she had eaten more than broth?

"Ah, you're with us. All praise to Payoja-ji," a sweet, familiar voice said. A large woman in a rust-colored dress wrap bent over Tana's pallet. She held out a fruit with greenish-orange skin. "Mango?"

Tana folded her hands in thanks, then took the mango and bit into it greedily. The pulpy flesh stuck in her teeth; juice ran down her chin. It was the most delicious thing she had ever tasted.

The woman laughed in a kindly fashion. She returned to her seat in the corner of the pavilion and selected another mango from her basket. Slicing the mango, she laid the strips across a drying screen. "A messy business," she said. "Good to do at a well."

Nodding, Tana sucked the last of the fruit off the pit. She licked her fingers and swiped at her chin.

"How about a wash?" the woman asked.

Tana needed help to stand. Slowly, the two of them descended to the well's bathing pool.

"Water hasn't been this low since my grandmother's day," Tana's companion remarked. "Those three little carved frogs against the step? My mother said *her* mother painted the lucky spots on them. Hadn't been seen from that day to this."

Tana brushed the stone frogs with her fingers, stroking the rounded bodies and powerful legs.

"Lucky for you, too." The woman chuckled. "If my husband hadn't been so curious to see them before he went off to the fields that day, it would have been hours more before anyone found you." She, too, patted the frogs. "A little good fortune wouldn't come amiss for the rest of us. Crops withering in the heat, plague in the villages roundabout, not a house naga to be had in Tenth Province for charity or coin. We're hoping the well doesn't dry up before the rains." She settled herself on a ledge above Tana. "But we'll get by somehow. Everyone has his own troubles, isn't that the way of the world?"

Tana sank into the water until only her eyes were showing. She surfaced, snorting and blowing, and shook her head like a dog. Drops flew from her shaggy hair and pattered into the water around her. She grinned with the joy of being alive, and clean.

"You're a quiet one, eh, Mina?" Tana's benefactor helped dry her shaky limbs. Tana tried not to lean too heavily on the older woman's arm as they climbed back up the stairs. They were both puffing hard by the time they reached the well's entry. Tana sank onto the pallet.

"Will you sleep in the village tonight?" The woman sheathed her knife and set her drying tray across the mango basket. "You're welcome to stay with my family."

Patting her pallet, Tana smiled at the woman.

"Happy here, are you? I suppose. There's a lantern, and some broth in this jar. Care for another mango?"

Tana folded her hands in thanks.

The woman paused at the door. "I'll bring you a dress wrap tomorrow. Good night," she said, and left Tana alone.

Other faces, men and women both, peeked around the screen from time to time to check on her. None spoke, and the visits dwindled as the night deepened. Tana lay on her pallet, watching the shadows from the door lanterns play across the walls. She felt empty, clean, and peaceful. Her thoughts touched lightly on her mother, her sister, Kalyan, and the villagers. She hoped they were well, and not too worried by her disappearance. Even those concerns slid away, unable to penetrate her sense of quiet ease. The moon rose, silvering the leaves overhead and waking the night birds' voices.

What? an owlet asked.

Tana got up and draped the sheet around herself. She prayed silently at the goddess's shrine, then sat against the door frame, under the diamond-eyed snake, and waited.

Too-ill, the cuckoo said.

"No," Tana contradicted softly, a test. Oh, she had missed this, tiny miracles popping into life a breath away from her skin. With the word, a toad dropped. Mottled and moist-looking, it hopped into the night. Perhaps a snake would follow, and be welcome. House nagas weren't to be had here *for charity or coin*, the woman had said.

But through sorrow and suffering? In love and humility? The fever that had shrunk the flesh on her bones had also burned rebellion and distrust from Tana's heart. She felt older than the anguished girl who had shaken her fist at the goddess, not wanting her strange gift. The desire of her soul had been to protect her family, and Naghali-ji had given Tana the means. She just hadn't been paying attention.

Finally, the fever dreams had shown her. The pattern was obvious when you strung the threads together properly. Rats. Plague. Snakes.

Out of superstition, Alwar and his officials had tried to destroy Tenth Province's snakes. But snakes ate rats and other pests. Without the snakes to keep their numbers down, a few diseased rats could multiply into a widespread threat.

Snakes ate rats. What could be simpler? Tana had even noticed that house nagas came the most frequently of all "her" creatures. She had been irritated that people seemed to prefer the ratters to her. How silly that seemed now. Naghali-ji had made Diribani a jewel mine, Tana a snake girl, and sent them both into the world. That was the point—wherever they traveled, they could share the goddess's blessing.

Starting here.

In thinking about Diribani, Tana remembered her sister's

favorite song. The width of an empire and the nature of their tasks might have separated them, but Tana could be with her sister in spirit. Taking a deep breath, she added her low, disused voice to the birds' chorus.

"Tonight, beloved,
I light the lamp
to guide my moonbird home."

Diamond eyes twinkled above her head as the serpents—ratters and boas, tree snakes and vipers and whip snakes and even a majestic cobra—flowed into the night. Lean and hungry, they hunted.

CHAPTER TWENTY-SEVEN

Diribani

ARRIVING on the heels of the Mina Bazaar, the dry season's final caravan brought more than trade goods from Tenth Province to Fanjandibad, though neither party profited from the exchange.

Within days, the putrid fever had spread through the fort. In the female guards' barracks, the few servants still able to carry a bucket were kept busy cleaning the spaces between the rows of pallets. Diribani tried to keep out of their way; in return, they ignored her. The sick didn't notice what she wore, or ask whom she worshiped, if she could bring them some relief. During the heat of midday, the stench of illness was unbearable. Diribani could only come in the flush of dawn or the barely cooler hours of twilight, to help tend the ailing. When a woman died, she was buried in her bedding. The empty slots filled quickly. In the fort's close quarters, disease spread with an arrow's speed and the same deadly results.

Nissa had protested Diribani's efforts, but then the maid had gotten sick. She lay listlessly on her pallet under Diribani's window, where a breeze might find her. They had lost Mahan; Zeen was weak, but expected to recover. The minute she could walk, she had staggered to her post at Diribani's door.

Their concern for her touched Diribani in the small part of her heart she could spare from silent prayer. She gave endless thanks to the twelve that Ma Hiral and Tana hadn't accompanied her to Fanjandibad. Thoughts of her family, who should be comfortably housed next to the sacred well by now, were all that kept her from despair.

For Zahid, too, was ill. Ruqayya and her ladies tended him in the princess's rooms.

Every face Diribani bathed with cool water wore his features; every small act of kindness, she did for his sake. He would never know, but that wasn't important, as long as Sister Payoja accepted Diribani's service.

As the days passed, each hotter and more stifling than the one before, Zeen ate more heartily, and her skeletal face resumed its familiar dour contours. Nissa began to complain about her enforced inactivity. Diribani took both for good signs. On her twice-daily barracks visits, she found fewer patients filling the spaces vacated by the dead and, now, the recovering.

The prince did not improve.

Diribani stopped sleeping at night. As if her lonely vigils could prevent death from slipping past her and into the prince's quarters, she paced the rooftop terrace, singing quietly into her hands. Emeralds and poppies, lilies and diamonds—at dawn, Diribani filled the iron box with jewels and annotated the ledger as scrupulously as Mahan had done. It comforted her to see the lights in distant valleys and know the builders were working on the wells. In all but the furnace heat of midday, teams of laborers were erecting dams to hold the rainwater to come.

Then, one night, Diribani encountered a woman huddled against the baluster, weeping. Moonlight betrayed her, outlining a riot of dark curls over the white coat.

Zahid! Was he—no.

At the woman's sobs, the question died in Diribani's throat. Love broke her, where loneliness had not. She felt it like a bodily separation, a desolate wind blowing faith from her heart. What good were Naghali's gems when they couldn't buy one man's health? Diribani had gone through the days convincing herself she cared whether some mine workers she didn't know would have water conveniently at hand. She painted flowers as if a lifeless record could preserve their scented loveliness. All along, her pulse had beat to one name only. If Zahid was gone, how could her eyes continue to see beauty in the world? Clearly, the goddess had mocked her with riches, since Diribani hadn't had the wisdom to wish for protection for her dear ones.

What had Tana asked for? Something worthy, no doubt. For the first time in her life, Diribani felt a bone-deep envy of her sister. The smell of lilies filled her with disgust. She stepped to the railing and opened her hands, casting jewels and flowers into the sultry air.

Ruqayya sprang to her feet. "Flower girl, is that you?"

"My lady." Diribani bowed her head.

"Then you shall be the first to hear the news. Praise to Almighty God, my brother is getting better!"

"What?" Diribani squawked like a crow. Marigolds dotted the terrace, their peppery scent as distinctive as a voice.

"Is it not marvelous?" The usually self-contained princess embraced her, tears glinting on her cheeks. "We hoped, yesterday, but dared not say anything, in case it was a false recovery. But he knew me just now. He told me I was all eyes and teeth, like a fruit bat, and that I should rest before I frightened the court." Ruqayya almost danced to the stairwell. "I can sleep, finally. I just needed a moment to myself first."

Diribani sat down where she was, leaning against a tall flower urn for support. "I am so pleased to hear it," she said. Small stones plinked around her.

The princess paused at the door. "Yes, I thought you might be," she said with a touch of her usual asperity. "Get some sleep yourself, eh?"

Diribani didn't know how to answer Ruqayya's retreating back. She was more relieved than she could express. At the same time, she felt cheated by her own weakness. Her faith must have been a fragile bloom indeed, to wither in one arid moment.

Naghali's bounty continued to flow; the marigolds and jewels told her that. But how could Diribani rejoice in the gift, having rejected the giver?

Zahid lived. The cup of joy had been filled, and Diribani would never drink from it. The difficult truth must be faced. He would never belong to her. It didn't matter what connection she had felt between them the night of the Mina Bazaar. The prince had never offered her more than respect, friendship, and a shared purpose in the construction project. Her dreams were a costly illusion.

From a distance, she would watch him build a new wing on the palace for his own family. They might exchange pleasantries, discuss commerce or construction, but nothing more personal. He would marry a noblewoman his sister approved. They'd have children and weigh them on their birthdays, and Diribani would add a handful of jewels to the scales, to be distributed to the poor at the feast.

And it would all be hollow, her efforts at modesty and goodness and charity, because she no longer believed. Not in her gift, but in her wisdom to use it. She had been so mistaken about Ruqayya's weeping—what else had she misapprehended? The well project? Had that, too, been a prideful gesture? Perhaps Diribani had imagined that she held the answer to those women's prayers because *she* wasn't so good at carrying big jars of water on her head. Maybe they would rather have had new clothing or better houses or their own mine leases. Diribani hadn't asked; she'd assumed she knew best.

Sunk in self-recrimination, she didn't look up at the approaching tread.

Too heavy for a woman; too slow for the prince. The significance escaped her, until a hand jerked her chin up. Fingers pinched her nose closed and her mouth open, and poured the liquid down her throat. Diribani struggled, but she had already swallowed too much.

Poppy juice, her mouth told her, before her attacker gagged her with a sour-tasting cloth. *Governor Alwar,* her astonished eyes reported, and then the bag descended over her head. Her arms and legs were tied; a heavy carpet was wound around her body. With a grunt of effort, Alwar hoisted her over his shoulder.

She screamed against the gag. If he made it down the stairs without being stopped, no one would know what had happened to her.

Dizzy and sick, Diribani opened her eyes into darkness. She fought to collect her scattered senses. Sweat beads rolled across her forehead and into her hair. She couldn't move her hand to brush them away. Mustard oil burned her lips, on a twisted cloth that tasted of burned onions and rancid curry. The world heaved with a rocking motion that wasn't the gait of horse or elephant. Camel.

Alwar had gagged, bound, and carried her away from the palace. He'd unrolled the carpet and bundled her into a desert nomad's hooded robe, then tied her feet to a camel's saddle. She'd lost consciousness, the first of many times. That was why her spine was arched in such an uncomfortable position. When she straightened, that pain eased. By wriggling her neck and shoulders, she succeeded in shifting the hood so she could see out the bottom. The narrow slice of world between the edge of the hood and her wool-covered chest was nearly as dark as the inside of the hood. Night. How many had passed since the last time she woke?

Diribani clenched her teeth on the gag, closed her eyes, and listened. The camel's feet struck the ground, spongy thumps that ended in the hiss of sliding sand. As she did in each moment she surfaced from a poppy-juice stupor, Diribani tried to calculate where they might be. Far from Fanjandibad, but not on the same route she had taken with Ruqayya and Zahid. She couldn't smell the medicinal scent of the plants that grew at the desert's edge.

Not east, past the mines. Diribani would have bloodied her nose against the camel's side, descending those steep tracks. She couldn't smell village dung fires, or the freshly turned earth of the plateau's cropland. She heard nothing but the beat of two camels' hooves and hissing sand.

Deep desert.

No one but the desperate or the mad crossed the desert in the blazing-hot days before the rains.

Was her captor desperate, or mad? Or both? Was the white-coats' god so powerful that Alwar could threaten Naghali's worshiper without fear of retribution? Except, Diribani remembered, she had rejected the goddess when she thought Zahid dead.

As if he sensed the apprehension that colored Diribani's thoughts, Alwar yanked her camel to a halt.

The rope around her hands pulled tight, then loosened. The older man grunted as he dismounted, slung Diribani off her camel, and dropped her onto the sand. Diribani's bones protested the hard landing, but it did knock the hood away from her face. She lay still, grateful to breathe air untainted by the stink of sweat and musty wool. A line of apricot-colored light outlined distant hills. Dusk? Between here and there, nothing but sand.

"You awake, girl?" Alwar's voice, harsh.

Diribani flinched from the fingers untying her gag. Without speaking, she wiped her mouth on her filthy shoulder. The rough wool scratched her skin.

"A drink of water, what do you say?"

Sand coated her throat. She stared at the sky. Stars twinkled, bright as diamonds spoken in Sister Manali's celestial voice. Liquid gurgled into a clay cup. Diribani imagined fresh, clean water washing away the drug taste. She remained silent.

"One word." Alwar strained for a coaxing tone. "One little word, and you may drink as much as you like."

Diribani listened to him slurping from the cup. Each time he smacked his lips and swallowed, her thirst increased. She said nothing.

"A pity to waste it."

Hearing the last few drops trickle onto the sand, Diribani ground her teeth against a whimper.

Already, the white-coat had tried wooing her with bribes and promises, the oh-so-reasonable words. She wasn't fooled. The very first time they had stopped, he had pinched her nose closed and slapped her cheeks until she sobbed for breath, but neither flowers nor jewels had emerged. Diribani had screamed when the flat of his sword battered her sore arms. The wordless shrieks had also failed to produce the riches he demanded. The goddess's gift could not be compelled.

Alwar spat on the ground by her face. "Defy me at your peril, witch. When we reach Lomkha, we'll see who is the stronger." With a final curse, he stamped away.

Diribani stared at the sky, confused that it was getting lighter, the stars fading. With a mental wrench, she realized the orange line in the distance marked the sun's rising, not setting. She'd lost a whole night.

Behind her, she heard Alwar feeding the camels and staking out the canvas shelter. Twigs crackled. The familiar smell of burning dung reached her nose, followed by the odor of curry leaves and the reek of drug-laced tea he'd pour down her throat, to make her sleep through the scorching daylight hours.

For the hundredth time, Diribani wondered whom he had bribed to reach the rooftop terrace. Had illness thinned the palace guard and left a door unwatched? Alwar must have been at the fort for some days to know exactly where to find her at that late hour. Diribani thought she had kept her nightly vigils quiet. But in the ladies' court there were no secrets. And Ruqayya had warned her about ambitious men.

What did he intend? Clouded by poppy juice, Diribani's mind moved sluggishly. Alwar spoke of Lomkha. Was he taking her to the emperor, or to Crown Prince Jauhar? Or to some other nobleman, whom Diribani hadn't known to fear?

Zahid couldn't come to her rescue; he'd have no idea where she was.

Diribani twisted inside the thick wool robe. Underneath, the silk dress wrap was so encrusted with sand and sweat, it could probably hold its shape without her. In a haze of misery, she remembered the palace's warm bathing pool. Even better would be the cool depths of Gurath's stepwell. Diribani squeezed her eyes shut. She imagined herself at home, splashing about with Parul and Geetika and Tana.

Tana!

Her eyes popped open. Would Alwar threaten her sister in order to make Diribani say jewels for him? She could be silent on her own behalf; he was unlikely to kill the diamond girl while there was any hope of her cooperation. But Tana wouldn't have the same protection. Alwar hated snakes.

The sun's big red eye peered over the hills. At once, the temperature leaped from uncomfortably hot to roasting. Inside the wool robe, Diribani couldn't stop shivering.

CHAPTER TWENTY-EIGHT

Tana

TANA traveled by night, for the days were too hot to walk through. The blazing sun seemed to enliven the nest-building birds. They crowed and cackled and whistled from the fragrant branches of flowering trees. Tana, like most other creatures not gifted with wings, sought a sheltered spot to endure the oppressive daylight hours. With mangoes and other fruit hanging ripe in the groves, wells were ideal, though Tana's insides rebelled against a steady diet of fruit and water. When she could, she stopped in a temple grove, sharing a meal of soup or rice with the priests and priestesses. She didn't speak to them.

Loneliness was her only companion. Tana didn't mind. After months of confusion, she finally grasped the purpose of her gift. For the moment, it was enough.

When the sweet-voiced woman who had taken care of her understood that Tana was determined to leave, she had pointed out the various directions: north to the capital, south to Gurath, west to the sea, east to the desert. She might have insisted Tana wait and travel with a party leaving the village, but she was distracted: A multitude of ratters had been discovered inhabiting the well's mango grove. All the villagers were eager to invite a house naga to share their homes.

Of the directions, each had its attractions. Across the desert and south from there lay Fanjandibad. But as much as Tana would have loved to visit Diribani and share her discovery, she dismissed that plan as impractical. She had no pack animals to carry water, or money to hire a guide. Kalyan wouldn't stay in Lomkha after bearing witness to the emperor; she might miss him on that road. And how could dropping snakes into the ocean help people? So she took the path that led to the emperor's road, and followed it south, toward Gurath.

Every night she grew stronger and could walk farther. Engaged on Naghali-ji's behalf, Tana didn't fear attacks by wild animals, like jackals or leopards. As she walked, she sang. Snakes and the occasional frog streamed past her lips to land with soft thumps and hisses on the ground. By the goddess's grace, Tana never stepped on one, and the poisonous serpents didn't threaten her. When Tana heard the creak of oxcarts or the tramp of marching feet, she slipped off the road and waited for the other travelers to pass. Naghali-ji held a protective hand over Tana's head; the worst that befell her was stepping on a thorny plant in the dark.

At another time of year, she might not have passed with such ease from village to town, temple to well. But in the last gasping days before the rains, Tenth Province's inhabitants spent every possible hour preparing their fields to plant rice and millet, the rainy-season crops. Sunburned and exhausted from their labors, they had no interest in a lone girl's comings and goings. If healthy people didn't question her, ill people had even less concern. There were all too many of those.

Tana was sure that what she was doing would help, eventually, or she would have been tempted to stop somewhere and tend to the sick, as the villagers had cared for her. In some of the towns she saw evidence of so many rats that she would spend a couple of days in the closest temple grove. Before any of the priests could connect her arrival with the appearance of sorely needed ratters, Tana would slip away as quietly as she had come.

The last few days, Tana had watched with hope as gray clouds boiled up on the horizon, only to dissipate before night fell. Darkness brought less relief than ever. The heat pressed against her. With every labored step, she dragged in a lungful of thick air and sang through a throat gritty with road dust. Powdery dirt coated her bare feet and legs, mixed with sweat, and stuck to her in a disgusting film. Even the heady smell of night-flowering trees was muffled by dust.

When, a few hours before dawn, Tana reached the outskirts of a large mango grove, she pushed on in the hope she would find a well nearby. Birds made their usual racket, and bats squeaked overhead, swooping through the trees to feed on insects and dropped fruit. Tana lifted the free end of her dress wrap over her hair. Immediately sweat prickled behind her ears and along the back of her neck. She kept singing, encouraged by the sound of snakes falling to the ground beside her. *Thump-thump, thump,* like the goddess's heart drum. *Thump, thump-thump.*

Weary as she was, Tana's feet responded. Almost dancing, she made her way along the road. She searched the darkness for a pair of lanterns that were always lit.

There!

Very grand indeed, this well. The entry pavilion boasted nine arches and a domed cupola. Tana must have reached the outskirts of a large town, with a patron as wealthy and artistic as she was pious.

When Tana stepped inside, she discovered that, in spite of the burning lamps, the interior showed signs of neglect, beginning with the empty foot-washing basin. Tana saluted the shrine, and found a bucket to fill the basin. She almost slipped on the well's slimy lower steps. Although she had to descend a long way to reach the water, there was still plenty of it. Moonlight revealed a large open tank. When full, it would be almost as big as a lake. As with Gurath's stepwell, pavilions were staged at intervals around the edge, and flights of steps divided areas for people and animals to use. When Tana walked along, she found more slippery steps. Leaves choked the livestock basins and outflow channels. Perhaps some calamity had befallen the district. More sickness? If the local people had been ill, they wouldn't have been able to clean the well properly as the water level dropped to its lowest point of the year. Soon, however, the rains would return. Those gray-bellied thunderclouds wouldn't tease forever.

If not tonight, as Tana hoped, rinsing the sticky sweat and dirt from her skin, then soon.

The cool water roused her. Like grit under her nails, the plant-scummed steps called out for scrubbing. A few hours of darkness remained. But rather than continue, why not sing here? Then she would have a cool place to sleep during the day. The snakes could slither up to the grove, and the frogs would be quite content near water and shade.

In an upper alcove, Tana found cleaning supplies: rakes, another bucket, a lantern, a bag of sand, rags. She carried them down flight after flight of steps. The load was heavy on her shoulder, and she began to regret her idea—she could have sung more comfortably sitting under a mango tree. But when she tied the rags around her feet, scattered sand near the first slippery step, and shuffled along, scrub-scrub, her mood brightened.

Heard from deep down in the tank, the birds' night noises made a pleasant accompaniment rather than an ear-numbing din. As if by the same magic, Tana's voice, too, echoed sweetly over the water.

Her heart pumped blood through her body. Musical plips and plops added the spirit rhythm as frogs leaped into the water, contributing their peeping notes. All the snakes came: gold, tan, gray, black, pale, and green, rough-scaled and smooth-scaled, solid, banded, and striped, venomous and gentle; an entire kingdom of snakes honored her lamplight's circle. Tana scrubbed and sluiced, raked and polished, dancing and singing all the while. She sang temple hymns, childhood rhymes, the ballads of love and longing she had heard during her travels.

She sang for her mother and Diribani, Gulrang the white-coat girl, Kalyan and his family. She danced for the sick gem-cutters, and the people who had given her food, shelter, and selfless care. As she saluted the twelve directions, Tana saw the parade of beloved faces so clearly in her mind's eye that her loneliness was eased. Surely the goddess wouldn't require her to wander forever, speaking snakes?

One hissed at her, bands of black and white flashing in warning. Venomous krait or harmless wolf snake? Tana's voice faltered. The snake darted away before she could decide. Stillness rippled out from her, shushing the night noises, until the air was as quiet as the tank's still water. The moon hung low, peeking under a rim of cloud as if the heavens waited for her to go on. A toad made a loud, rude noise.

Tana laughed at the reminder. Not everybody had the privilege of serving as Naghali-ji's emissary. If that was Tana's fate, she would do her best. At present, she had a simple task, the goddess's creatures to keep her company, and her sister's favorite song to sing. She would content herself with that. Tana lifted her voice once more, changing the usual words to fit the night:

> *"Come, brave rains,*
> *swift-stooping as falcons,*
> *come, rains.*
> *Come."*

CHAPTER TWENTY-NINE

Diribani

"Fragrant as the lotus,
dancing on the water."

Strapped to the camel's saddle, Diribani yearned toward the distant singing. The sound parted the poppy juice that veiled her thoughts like a howdah's filmy canopy. With unusual clarity, Diribani imagined a woman unable to sleep in the smothering heat. She'd risen from her bed, perhaps hearing a fretful child and seeking to soothe it. The voice caressed the night with a tenderness that brought tears to Diribani's closed eyes.

Under the robe, her hands were bound, as usual. The hood drooped over her face, hiding the moisture that wetted her cheeks and stung her cracked lips. Every day, she grew more weak, her awareness more fragmented. The one truth she clung to with both swollen hands was that she must not speak.

Once the camels had reached the imperial road to Lomkha,

Alwar had kept Diribani drugged while he pushed their mounts to exhaustion. He wanted to reach the capital before the rains. Or kill her trying. Or something. She wasn't sure. But whatever happened, she must not speak. She held to the knowledge with a stubbornness worthy of her sister, Tana.

Tana. The name woke an echo in her body. *Tah-na. Tah-na.* Heart drum.

"Come, rains, come." The singing voice trailed away.

Airy as a spirit drum, the song repeated in Diribani's mind. *Fragrant as the lotus.* She knew exactly how fragrant a lotus was. Lotuses had rained from her lips, once. Lotuses and peonies and jasmine. And diamonds. The hardest stone. The most precious, the most coveted. Men sweated for diamonds. Men killed for diamonds. *Come, rains, come.* Tana.

Her sister's name drove out the drug trance, awakening Diribani's listless pulse at throat and wrists and ankles. Under the hood, she opened her eyes. Knowledge tingled along her veins. *Swift-stooping as falcons, come, rains, come.*

Diribani swayed back and forth with the camel's lurching gait. She knew this was her chance. The singing woman or Tana's memory—some elixir had cleared Diribani's brain. She would have to take advantage of this clear interlude and think.

If Governor Alwar had sent Tana to Lomkha, if he threatened her to ensure Diribani's obedience, how could she refuse to speak? The idea of her captor's getting richer and richer with her every word made her ill. What would a man like that do with unlimited personal wealth? Buy a puppet emperor? Hire an army to burn temple groves and poison sacred wells? Kill snakes throughout the empire, as he'd done in Tenth Province? Punish Zahid and Ruqayya for yielding to Diribani's wishes and spending her diamonds on projects outside his influence?

Naghali had blessed Diribani. After Diribani's rejection, why should the goddess care for a wayward daughter? Where else could Diribani turn?

To beauty. Her soul's desire.

Beauty wasn't in this body, crusted with filth and sores. It wasn't even in the paintings Diribani had created, dry pigments arranged on flat paper. It was in life itself: the boldness of daffodils, the sweetness of violets, the resolution of diamond. Like Tana's resolution, Tana's priceless mix of cleverness, loyalty, and strength. Diribani had lost her way, so she would be guided by her sister's example.

When the camel stopped, Diribani gave no sign that she had noticed. Eyes closed, she let herself be hoisted off the saddle and dumped on the ground. Heart drum and spirit drum beat steadily within her. She saluted the twelve directions silently and stretched her limited senses, waiting for her chance to act.

Not here, leaves murmured in warning. She opened her eyes to a grayish light. Dust puffed under her cheek. *Not yet.* Diribani listened to Alwar muttering about cursed idols as he secured the sullen camels' reins. A roadside shrine, maybe? And then she heard the most astonishing sound: *Peep. Rrrrr-eep!*

Frogs. A multitude of them, to judge by the joyful noise they made.

Alwar pulled Diribani to her feet. He slapped a pair of empty water skins over her shoulder and dragged her by the arms. She shambled after him. Inside, she tensed her legs to run. Leafy trees. Water skins. Frogs. A well. People? Help?

"Down," her captor grunted.

She tottered from step to step, testing the limits of Alwar's grip. He shook her in exasperation. The long scabbard at his belt smacked her in the leg. At her strangled sound, he flipped back her hood to expose her face.

Diribani blinked in the ruddy glow. Around them, dawn lit the stepped walls of a large tank.

"*Now* you decide to talk?" Alwar jerked the grimy cloth from her mouth as if he couldn't wait to take possession of whatever she said.

"Thirthty," she mumbled. The miracle happened. Over the reek of her unwashed body, Diribani smelled jasmine. Two good-sized gems also fell. A sapphire landed by Alwar's foot. He snatched it up. The other stone, bigger and brighter and pale yellow in color, rolled off the edge of the step, *tink tink tink*. It landed a flight down and winked. Insolently.

Through lowered eyelids, Diribani saw emotion twist Alwar's face. The orange light wasn't kind, illuminating the anger that tightened the corners of his eyes, the greed that moistened his lips. He would have liked to strike her. His hand twitched, then clenched with calculation against his filthy robe. He thought her defeated, she saw. And in any case, his desire for the stone—topaz? diamond? five ratis, maybe more—outweighed his caution. The well was empty, her hands were tied; what could she do? He pushed Diribani's shoulder.

She collapsed obediently, legs sprawled on the steps. While he descended the stairs, she gathered courage like a bouquet of flowers: stem by stem, muscle by muscle. When he turned his back to pick up the rough gem, Diribani acted.

In a single desperate motion, she pulled her ankles together and stood. Her bound hands couldn't help balance her, but her dirty bare toes gripped the stone. Hop, hop, a toad girl, she maneuvered herself to the edge of the step.

The water was very, very far down. If she missed, her head would smash like a melon against the stone stairs.

"Stop!" The shout echoed across the well. Alwar had seen her.

Diribani thought of her dear ones: Zahid, who always found a way to turn shame into honor. Ruqayya, throwing her knife in a deadly arc. Tana, speaking snakes and toads, gliders and leapers. Precious as jewels, she held them all in her heart, and jumped.

Headfirst, Diribani plunged into the water, down and down. Wet, the heavy, tentlike robe wanted to strangle her. But though Diribani's arms were tied, her legs were free. She held her breath, kicking and wriggling, a frog girl determined to reach the surface. Her long hair swirled around her face. She pushed up, toward the glorious sky, and broke through, gasping with relief.

As she gulped air, the sun cleared the edge of the tank. A deep, ominous red, it trailed gray storm clouds. In the flood of ruby light, Diribani realized that she and Alwar weren't alone here, as she had thought.

Her abductor was climbing down the stairs as fast as he could go without tripping over his long sword. He had abandoned the water skins, which lay as flat as empty promises on the steps above. He cursed with rage, his face a grimace of hate.

Strolling toward him at the water's edge was a curious figure carrying a bucket and rake. A young woman, by her pale dress wrap. Short dark locks stuck out from her head like a lion's mane. She was speaking in a low, reassuring tone. When Diribani heard her voice, disbelief shook her.

And then she saw the sinuous shapes that followed the girl's speech and knew for sure. Tana!

Had they returned to Gurath? Diribani kicked hard to keep her head above water, and twisted her neck to look around. Unless masons had rebuilt the well entirely, this one was different. Deserted, for one thing, which Gurath's well would never be at dawn during the hottest part of the year. And the sun was in the wrong place, relative to the main pavilion. And . . .

"Please, sir, you mustn't threaten people here," Tana was saying. "Violence at the sacred wells is forbidden in the goddess's name."

"I spit on your goddess." Alwar tore off the enveloping nomad's robe. The white coat underneath looked as bad as Diribani's silk dress wrap felt. Had felt. Now it stuck to her like strands of water weed.

"That's between you and Naghali-ji, sir," Tana answered cheerfully. In the eerie light, a snake's tan scales shone like burnished copper.

"No, Tana," Diribani called. "Don't go near him."

"Diribani?" Tana's voice cracked. *Plop-plop.* Two frogs leaped in different directions. "Is that you?"

"Stay back, Tana. It's Alwar; he kidnapped me from Fanjandibad." Like colored pebbles, jewels dropped into the water.

Alwar's groan at seeing the gemstones sink beyond his reach was instantly transmuted to fury as he recognized Diribani's stepsister. "Witch!" he shouted. Drawing his sword, he slashed at Tana.

She darted out of the way and ran up the stairs. A flight above him, she set down the cleaning implements. "Shall we play snake and mouse?" she asked. A bright-green tree snake arced from her lips.

With another shout, Alwar leaped up the stairs and lunged at her. He missed.

Diribani kicked her feet and swam awkwardly to the steps. It had seemed a grand and tragic gesture, jumping into the well to escape the fate Alwar had planned for her. Then Utsav the crow god had intervened, twisting events into a ridiculous tangle. Diribani didn't know what to do, but she couldn't let an armed man chase her sister around the well while she floated in the middle and waited for her turn to be skewered.

Her toe stubbed against stone. She struggled up the slippery stairs, managing to shed the hooded robe along the way. The wet rope had tightened around her wrists, but she could raise both hands to push the hair out of her eyes.

"Oh, no," Tana said urgently. "Hold very still, please."

Alwar's rough breathing filled the sudden hush. Diribani looked up. Several flights above her head, Tana and the white-coat stood as motionless as painted figures. Tana held her arms flat against her sides. Alwar's sword was poised above her shaggy head.

Between them coiled a black-and-white-banded snake. "Did you know," Tana said faintly, "that a krait's venom is many, many times more powerful than a cobra's?" A frog jumped over the snake's head. The naga hissed.

Slowly, Tana backed away and upward. Alwar did likewise, matching her step for step. When they had climbed several flights, mirroring each other, the snake moved in the opposite direction. It slithered down the steps, toward Diribani.

She sank to her knees and waited for the goddess's messenger. Good fortune had done her no good, wisdom came too late. Only death remained. "Wait," she said.

Her sister and her pursuer both turned. Again, they froze where they stood. Alwar's breath rasped in the silence.

With her bound hands, Diribani scooped up the banded snake. She clamped her fingers around its jaw so the venomous fangs couldn't emerge. "Let my sister go, or I release the krait," Diribani said. "Who do you think it will bite first?"

"Oh, Diribani." Tana's voice shook. "You don't have to sacrifice yourself for me, truly." At her words, three more snakes writhed upon the steps.

"Don't do it! The witch can leave, and may devils take her!" Alwar retreated, but kept his sword pointed at the snakes by Tana's bare feet.

Tana didn't move. "Sir," she said.

"Get out!" Alwar shouted. "Demon spawn."

"But, sir . . ." Tana pointed behind him.

Whirling, Alwar brought the sword down in a mighty chopping blow that would have beheaded a cobra. Steel hit wood, then stone; sparks flashed.

"Mind the bucket," Tana added helpfully as the man's ferocious swing carried him farther than he meant to go. He caught his heel on the edge of a step and flailed his arms, fighting for his balance. He might have recovered it, but the long scabbard swung around his waist and tapped him on the leg. He jerked away, as if from a serpent striking, and fell.

Diribani had kicked off the steps with all the strength in her legs. Alwar toppled like a downed tree. With a resounding crack, bone met stone. The harsh sound of his breathing ceased.

Was he dead?

Diribani couldn't look away from the snake that thrashed in her hands. "Help," she said, as Tana ran down the steps. "What do I do?"

"Let it go," Tana said.

"Get back." Diribani risked a glance upward. "I didn't grab hold of a krait so it would bite both of us."

Her sister grinned at her. "If it did, we'd be sore for a couple of days," she said. "That's a wolf snake. Not poisonous."

"But . . ." Diribani stared at the irritated serpent, whose tail flicked mimosa blossoms from side to side. "Black and white bands. You said krait."

"They're often confused," Tana said. "Here. I'll take it." Deftly, she slid her hands behind the snake's head and lifted the wiggling length out of Diribani's grasp. She carried the naga some distance away and set it on a step. "Peace, friend." A ratter dropped at her feet. The wolf snake retreated.

Diribani sagged against the stone as her sister ran back to her. Tana launched herself at Diribani and hugged her so fiercely that the soaked dress wrap left big wet splotches on her own. Diribani buried her face in Tana's shoulder. Shudders racked her body as fear drained away, leaving her limp.

Naghali-ji hadn't abandoned her. Who else could have brought Diribani's sister to her side at the moment when she expected to die? The goddess's hand had surely guided Tana's snakes; the fear and hate that ruled Alwar had completed the man's destruction. As far as Diribani could tell, he hadn't moved or breathed since his fall.

Relief tasted like nectar on her tongue.

Tana pulled back, though she kept hold of Diribani's elbows. "The goddess must have sent you," she exclaimed, echoing Diribani's thought. A boa slithered past her knees. "I've missed you so much. Tell me everything!"

Diribani lifted her bound hands. "Cut me loose?" she suggested. Ashoka flowers and rubies glowed in the dawn light.

As she struggled to untie the wet rope, Tana exclaimed at her sister's bruised and swollen fingers.

"Do you have a knife?" Diribani asked.

"Alwar's sword." Tana fetched the weapon and carefully sawed at the cord. Strand by strand, it parted. Diribani shook her numb hands. With a grimace of distaste, Tana put the sword aside.

Diribani stood and looked down at the governor's still form. "May his next life teach him what he failed to learn from this one," she said soberly. White starflowers drifted into the still air.

Tana squinted up at the sky. "Not to be unfeeling, but we'd better get his body out of the open before the day gets any hotter and the carrion birds come."

Together, the two of them wrapped Alwar's body, sword and all, in the woolen robe and carried it up the stairs to one of the outer pavilions. Diribani's unexpected swim had refreshed her, but she knew that all the poppy juice she'd been forced to drink would make her weak and sick for some time. "Baby steps," she told Tana, and her sister agreed.

Even if she'd been stronger, the heat was punishing. It pressed on them, making every step an effort. Tana helped Diribani wash properly, avoiding the chafed places around her chin and wrists from the gag and the ropes. The sun glared off the tank's surface and all the exposed stone, heating it like a bread oven.

After Tana had watered the camels and foraged for food in the saddlebags, they retreated to the shade of a pavilion. All the while, they shared their stories. Tana collected the gemstones and Diribani the flowers, weaving garlands for their hair. They let the snakes and frogs go their own ways. As the sun approached its highest point, they rested, assaulted by the light that blasted into every shadowed nook.

Tana pointed. "You can see the water drying down there."

"Uh." Diribani fanned her cheeks with the end of her once-grand dress wrap. The yellow silk was ruined. She just wished it would cool more of her face. Then she smiled at herself. She and Tana were together; they were free. What else could she desire? As if in answer, the hot air stirred by her face. "Tana?"

"What?"

Diribani stood up, briefly distracted by the antics of several spotted frogs. "Did you feel that?" She heard it, too. Around the tank, trees were stirring. Leaves danced, shaking off the dust. The wind strengthened, pushing big black thunderclouds across the sky.

"Oh." Tana followed her to the edge of the pavilion.

The sun fought the clouds. One by one, its arrows of blazing light were quenched. As if dusk had fallen early, the sky darkened. The wind, victorious, blew in earnest, scattering twigs and leaves across the surface of the tank. It tugged at Tana's and Diribani's dress wraps. They leaned against the pillar, unwilling to go into the entry pavilion and miss the cosmic drama playing overhead.

At the distant rumbling sound, they drew closer together. Side by side, they let the wind play with their hair, whipping it around their heads. Or ears, in Tana's case. Diribani grinned at her sister. Hot, heavy air shimmered with expectation. Not yet, almost . . .

CRACK!

Lightning split the clouds. Grandfather Chelok's diamond

lances had bested the sun again. Diribani held her breath and Tana's hand. Her hair fanned away from her face. One, two . . . five. Thunder boomed, shaking the well's stone pillars. With a noise like an infinity of tiny frogs hitting the water all at once, the rains came.

Water cascaded over them. It hissed against the well's baked stone and cooled the air instantly. Curtains of rain swept across the tank, hiding the far side. Within moments, Diribani was drenched. Her hair and dress wrap stuck to her, as sodden as if she had jumped into the well's depths again. Reveling in the sensation, she let the blinding rain wash away everything but gratitude. And hope. Having escaped from Alwar, found Tana, and greeted the rains, all in the same day, she felt anything was possible.

"Tonight, beloved, I light the lamp," she sang softly. "Come home to me, my moonbird. Come."

CHAPTER THIRTY

Tana

"YOU saw Naghali-ji?" children would ask Tana in later years. "What does she look like?"

"Sometimes she comes as a beautiful queen, dripping with jewels, and tests your pride. Sometimes a sick old woman tests your compassion. And sometimes she looks like a laborer, and drives a wagon full of corpses."

"Eeew." Her listeners would shiver in fascinated horror. "And tests what?"

"Your sense of humor," Tana had concluded.

It had taken her a while to understand. After a night and another day of torrential rains at the well, the skies above the tank had cleared late in the afternoon. Dark clouds faded to pale gray and then fleecy white, as if they'd been washed and hung out to dry. The sun's late rays swept the sky, showing that there were no hard feelings. Bestowing a parting gift on the clouds, the sun dyed them colors that Diribani sighed over: hyacinth and lotus, tawny rose, lily yellow. Washed of their dust coating, the trees shone dark green, every leaf renewed. Puddles steamed on the wet ground. Awakening from their seasonal slumbers, insects buzzed and shrilled as the temperature climbed again. Into this gorgeous scene, misty with possibility and promise, a broad-shouldered woman in a laborer's short wrap drove a canvas-covered wagon.

Tana and Diribani heard the oxen complaining and came out to see who it was. The driver pulled up and grinned at them. "Two pretty young ladies in reprehensible outfits. That's a picture you don't see every day."

Tana was trying not to gag from the stench. The woman's load had the unmistakably pungent, horrible smell of decay. Her oxen, it appeared, wanted nothing more to do with their load, or the insects that followed.

The driver didn't seem to notice. "I'm bound for the cremation field," she said in a confiding tone. "If you hadn't guessed."

"Excuse me." Carnations fluttered from Diribani's lips. She ran to the other side of the pavilion.

The woman raised her eyebrows at the flowers. She turned to Tana. "Got any ripe ones for me?"

Tana breathed through her mouth. Below the disgust, another sensation tugged at her awareness. As they had just before the clouds opened, the little hairs along her skin were standing up in alarm. She would have looked up for Grandfather Chelok's diamond-lightning lances, but the danger wasn't above her; it was before her. The woman sat on the cart bench, elbows resting on her knees, dark skin and hair radiant with health. Those white teeth, when she smiled—had they been filed to points?

"Peace, Ma-ji." Tana folded her hands. A frog and a toad went separate ways. "We do, yes. Over here, please."

"The toad girl and the flower girl, eh?" The woman jumped off the cart and tied her oxen to a tree a good distance from the restive camels.

All of Tana's sense screamed at her. Fall down and beg forgiveness. Be still. Run away! She bit her lip and walked to the pavilion where she and Diribani had left Alwar's body.

Her head lifted with a cobra's regal assurance, the corpse collector strode beside her. "Eh, he's a big one." She picked up a corner of the robe they had wrapped him in. "Give us a hand, toad girl?"

Glad she didn't have to see the dead face again, Tana picked up the other side. The corpse's weight pulled at her arms, but together the two women managed to carry Alwar's body out to the cart. The stranger flipped up a corner of the canvas. "In we go," she said, ignoring the flies that whirled out in blinding numbers.

Tana held her breath, shut her eyes, and pushed the body over the cart sides. It landed with a thump. The smell got worse, if that was possible. While the woman fastened the canvas, Tana went to lean against the front of the cart. She panted, sure she would never get the horrible smell out of her nose. The spectacular colors had fled the sky. Twilight descended softly.

Diribani held a bucket under an ox's muzzle. She waited while it slurped and slobbered. The other beast had finished drinking and wiped its face on Diribani, leaving dribbles to run down the front of her dress wrap.

When Diribani saw Tana looking at her, she shrugged. Our

clothes are ruined already, she seemed to be saying. "I brought another bucket," she did say aloud, and pointed with her chin.

The ox snorted at the branch of jasmine and small stone that dropped into its water. When the creature lipped Diribani's fingers, she freed one hand to rub its forehead.

Tana hoisted the full bucket. "May I pour for you?" she asked as the corpse collector came around the back of the cart to join them. A whip snake streaked past her, making for the shelter of the mango trees.

"Very kind," the death woman said. She rinsed her fingers under the stream of clear water, then held out her wet hands for the bucket. "Your turn."

Tana stretched out her palms. She had refused to be served the last time. She knew better now. Awareness, and awe, made her shiver.

"And you, Mina." The woman crooked her finger at Diribani.

"Thank you, Ma-ji." Tana's sister approached to hold out her own empty hands. Her face was quiet with the same reverence Tana felt, and the same fear.

They had borne the goddess's gifts for months. How would she judge their service?

The woman put down the bucket and rested her hands on her broad hips. The last remaining light gathered in her features. Surrounding darkness concealed all but that strong nose and chin, the high forehead and unfathomable eyes. She stretched out her arms to lay one hand on the side of Tana's head and the other against Diribani's ear. Lightly, she knocked their heads together, a she-bear cuffing her cubs. "Be good to each other." Her voice was as sweet and strong as incense. "Everyone rides with me, in the end."

Tana and Diribani folded their hands.

Naghali-ji loosened the reins from the tree and vaulted into the driver's seat. "Almost forgot. This is for you." She tossed a large bag off the bench.

Tana was so afraid of what might be inside that reaching for it required an effort of will. But Diribani had already stretched out her arms. Tana knew that, whatever the bag held, she couldn't let her sister take its weight alone. Together, they would endure it.

The bag yielded with the soft heft of fabric. It smelled of sandalwood and rose petals.

The goddess twitched the reins. "A couple of good-looking young men are wandering the road," she called over her shoulder. The protesting oxen pulled their burden away from the well. "Separated from their parties by bad luck or bad weather. You might want to be dressed a little better when they arrive."

Tana could no longer see her face, but the unforgettable voice was rich with amusement and tenderness. And power. Bad luck or bad weather? Maybe.

"Thank you," Tana said softly. Inside, her heart was singing. Truly, the goddess had read what Tana desired. She had no doubt that one of those lost young men rode a white horse. *Kalyan.* She would have to ask Diribani if Zahid still rode the bay.

"Tana!" Her sister tugged her to the doorway, where the lamps burned day and night in their niche. "What did you say?"

"Thank you," Tana repeated. "She gave us new dress wraps, don't you think? In the bag?" And then she heard what Diribani had heard. Silence.

She set down the bag. No snakes had slithered away from her. Frogs sang in the tank, but no toads hopped on the wet earth at her feet. She touched her fingers to her lips. They felt the same as always, but the miracle had gone. A tinge of regret touched her. Swelling relief replaced it.

"She took it away!" Diribani swept her empty hands wide. "We're ourselves again!"

"But different," Tana suggested.

"Better, I hope," Diribani said. "Stronger." She giggled. "Except for your hair. What will Ma Hiral say?"

"'Why can't you be more like your sister?'" Tana suggested. A smile pulled at her mouth. "Some things will never change. I hope." She seized Diribani's hands and whirled her in a circle.

Ragged, barefoot, joyful, with the music of frogs and the beat of their own hearts for accompaniment, they danced.

AUTHOR'S NOTE

I would like to acknowledge a great debt to Charles Perrault's story "*Les Fées*" ("The Fairies") and Morna Livingston's wonderful book *Steps to Water: The Ancient Stepwells of India*, which together supplied the premise and setting for this novel.

Astute readers will notice a resemblance between my fictional Hundred Kingdoms and the factual Mughal Empire. During that period, between 1526 and 1858, the Indian subcontinent witnessed a great flourishing of the arts. The ruling Muslim class especially loved fine textiles, paintings, jewelry, and architecture. Thanks to skilled local Hindu and foreign-born artisans who implemented the Mughal emperors' grand projects, the Taj Mahal, Shalimar Gardens, and other sites continue to delight us today. Tana and Diribani's hometown of Gurath was modeled on Surat, a lively seventeenth-century port. Fanjandibad is what the historical fortress of Golconda might have looked like, if Agra's exquisite palaces had been magically transplanted within its walls. Trader-talk was an actual phenomenon (if not exactly as described here); diamond merchants bargained with hand signals under a cloth so that rival traders couldn't overhear the prices being offered and accepted for the choicest gems.

While these and other details were inspired by the period, I took significant liberties with the region's geography and culture to spin my tale. The two religions, in particular, are invented. Neither the vegetarian followers of the twelve gods and goddesses nor the monotheistic, white-coated Believers represent a particular faith. However, the guiding principles of nonviolence, the equality of all souls, quiet contemplation, and selfless service to others may be found across the wide spectrum of India's religious traditions, including Jainism, Buddhism, Hinduism, Sikhism, and Islam.

For readers curious about the true-life adventures of some remarkable young women of the era, here are a few names to pursue:

Jahanara (Mughal princess and architectural patron);
Mirabai (Hindu mystic and poet);
Rani Durgavati (Rajput warrior queen);
Zeb-un-Nissa (Mughal princess and poet).